ALEXEY

OLEG SAPPHIRE

THE HEALER'S WAY

With our best wishes,
A. Kovtunov

Enjoy the adventure!

BOOK TWO

PUBLISHED BY MAGIC DOME BOOKS

The Healer's Way
Book # 2

Cover Design: Vladimir Manyukhin

Published by Magic Dome Books, 2024

ISBN: 978-80-7693-323-1

ALSO BY OLEG SAPPHIRE:

The Hunter's Code
by Oleg Sapphire and Yuri Vinokuroff

An Ideal World for a Sociopath
a LitRPG series by Oleg Sapphire

TABLE OF CONTENTS:

CHAPTER 1

IT'S INTERESTING, THIS LIFE. Really. There are times when you find yourself planning something big, and working out the details, considering what could go wrong, and how to make sure nothing does. And then, right when the time comes to make your big move, it turns out to be no big deal, really, because what seemed like such a major undertaking is, well, not hard at all.

Like capturing the castle. I mean, here I am, hundreds of years old already, and yet I failed to see that it was a simple matter.

I thought I'd be testing my limits when it came to wresting the castle back from the enemy, and that I might even have to pull back and regroup. But here I am now, ensconced in the former count's armchair watching the fire crackle.

Did I greatly overestimate these mercenaries?

Or could it be that the Family's enemies actually weren't all that powerful? That was probably it. In my previous world, I'd battled some truly formidable foes, and yet, when it came down to it, some of them turned out to be underwhelming. The exception to that would be my brother.

Anyway, here I was sitting in front of the fireplace, and like always, it calmed me down. True, back in the day I could enhance the calm by tossing some medicinal herbs into the fire, but there were none here. Just some dust bunnies, and general filth around the place. The filth, by the way, was brought in by the mercenaries who'd been occupying the castle. Ah, well. I was here now

I sat there thinking, but just couldn't relax. I couldn't escape the thought that if I'd only shown up sooner, I could've made this all a lot easier on myself.

The process of seizing the castle was interesting enough, even though my forces weren't in the best of shape and half of them could have died. Lucky for us, they only sustained some wounds, but, of course, that wasn't on me.

Thinking back on how our attack had gone, I can say that two things in particular struck me. The first was the shocking carelessness with which the mercenaries approached their duties, and the second was the powerful dedication displayed by my men. They attacked the enemy as if this was the last battle of their lives. They spared themselves nothing, and went at it as if they were ready to rip to pieces with their bare hands whoever stood in their way. I was impressed — this raised their stature in my eyes. I had nothing but respect for anyone who was loyal, and who also knew how to exact vengeance.

Of course, were I not there, things wouldn't have gone quite so smoothly. Naturally, I went first, and was so stealthy in my approach that I managed to walk right up to two guards stationed by armored cars at the gate to prevent any uninvited guests from showing up. With a touch, I put the guards to sleep, and then, I entered and dispensed with several other mercenaries inside, and then I grappled with others in close combat. That created the noise required to signal to my forces to join the fray.

"Sir!" Valery, the captain of my guard entered just then. "The Imperial interrogators have arrived. What are your orders?"

"Good news," I nodded. "They showed up sooner than I expected."

"When it comes to this kind of thing, they always act with lightning speed," chuckled the captain. "Shall I show them in?"

"Make it so."

I'd had a table and chairs brought in just for this. I'd turned my attention to the Imperials as soon as I finished off the last of the mercenaries. I figured I'd best not wait before informing the Empire as soon as possible that I, the head of the Bulatov Family, was the one who'd set about taking back his property. Otherwise, they might think it was some despicable impostor who'd randomly decided to decimate Snegirev's mercenaries.

Thus far, I didn't yet exist as far as the Empire was concerned because it wasn't like the former count could officially register the transfer of his Family's estate to me. This wasn't a problem, though, since I had the ring, which was impossible to counterfeit.

"Greetings!" Three middle-aged men entered the main hall. The hour was late, but they all looked cheerful and neatly dressed.

"So then," began the head of the trio, who'd preceded the other two. "You're Mikhail Bulatov, the new head of the Bulatov Family?"

"That's right!" I responded, showing him the ring.

"Just for the record, I have to ask you what happened to Gregory Bulatov? It seems he's been missing."

"He's dead!" I shrugged.

"I see," he nodded to himself and began taking notes on his tablet. "In that case, if you don't mind, we will begin the verification procedure immediately."

"Go right ahead."

I indicated the empty chairs. Then all three of them sat down at the table, took out papers, a tablet, and documents, and asked me some simple questions. Like, how, when, and under what circumstances was the Family transferred to me. Also, one of them checked the authenticity of the ring, and nodding, gave me a paper to sign. Easy peasy. That was done. All it had taken was half an hour.

Roughly speaking, that's what transpired in that time. Now, I was officially registered as the head of this Family. I'd spent a lot of time researching how to make that happen, because not everything was simple in this world. The way the old count transferred power to me was legal, but the problem is that these are very ancient laws, and nowadays they rarely applied to real-world events. Before the world was wired up with all this technology, such laws were more widely employed, but now, these family signets were sort of like living artifacts that fed on the power of the owner, and were part and parcel of their being. Unless I voluntarily gave the ring away, nobody, nor anything could get if off my finger. From time to time, though, shysters would show up in the Empire trying to deceive the authorities. Thus, there was a case where, in a war between Families the victor slaughtered everybody in one Family, forged their ring, and then announced that the Family head had bequeathed his holdings to him. Then, he was able to dispose of the assets and sell off all of the Family's lands. This all happened around a century ago. Only 30 years after the events, the deception was discovered, but by then, so much time had passed, that nothing could be done about it.

Interestingly, the system here was such that one Family could literally own several other Families at once, but not like feudal lords, rather, more like managers of their estates. It wasn't uncommon to see several patriarchal rings on one man's fingers. Anyway, now my paperwork was in order, so nobody could set me up, kill me on the sly, or allege that they thought I was an impostor. I'd put the game on a whole new level.

Once the Imperial agents were gone I breathed a sigh of relief, and got down to examining the wounded. Everybody was doing well, and would be on the mend in a couple of days. Maybe even sooner, of course. As long as we weren't under attack, I wanted to heal them properly.

What was interesting was that, since I was now registered with the Imperial Service for Aristocratic Affairs, I could access via my phone the Family email account, and also the office where all the documents were kept.

It was only then that I fully understood what deep sh*t we were in. Yes... I meant not just I, but “we”! Because half these debts were held by Victoria. Incidentally, that name — beautiful. I was often impressed, even amazed by the names in this world. Could it just be that it was because all this was new for me?

But the debts... Seized lands that had already been sold, laborers and others who'd disappeared, and that wasn't all. I saw that an invitation to a ball had been sent quite recently. It was to be held at a house belonging to a Family by the name of Vlasov, and, apparently, Victoria planned on being there. No big deal, except that the viscount was the one who'd sent the invitation in a message via this very official email account. I was able to read all of their correspondence and realized that he was a heinous specimen of a man. So many nasty things... Was he really so strong that he could allow himself such latitude? What really infuriated me was that in every email he threatened to force her into marriage, although she clearly was opposed. Of course, unbeknownst to him, even if he did take her as his wife, he was no longer eligible for the title, nor the Family holdings. I was now entitled to either give permission or not to any union, as I was now the head of the Family.

That was another interesting thing about the how these Families operated. For example, should my daughter get married, I could make her husband the count, but if I then found out that the wedding was fictitious, then we'd all have problems.

I could see why he'd summoned her to the ball. It was scheduled for tonight, and I decided I'd attend. But first I needed to do a few more things. I still had time, after all, but was short on money and resources.

The email account was full of all sorts of interesting matters. There was so much that I couldn't read everything. But another notice from the viscount caught my eye in which he promised the countess he'd release her wounded soldiers. He even hinted at where he was holding them. It was a hospital of sorts, only prison-like. It wasn't hard for me to find it, as it was located in a village that once belonged to my Family, so it wasn't terribly far away.

This was a case where fate intervened, as if screaming at me to" set my people free," that sort of thing. On top of that, Snegirev's sneering tone disgusted me. Seriously, someone needed to teach him a lesson, no doubt about it. He'd kept these wounded soldiers alive only to put pressure on the countess, knowing how much she cared about her people.

"Valery, come here, please," I called the guard commander, and within five minutes he entered the hall. "How are the wounded?"

"Almost everyone is recovering, I would even say it's a miracle, but knowing your capabilities..." he hesitated.

"Almost?" I was surprised. I'd treated all of them, after all.

"Yes. There's one who's not doing well."

Looks like I had to spend more energy. On the way to the room holding our wounded I told Valery about my plan to free the captured guardsmen.

I figured we had time to get it done before I went to the ball. That was a must-do event, actually. I'd finally get to meet Victoria, and yes, time to let the viscount know about my existence. I, too, wanted to size the viscount up in person. And I anticipated seeing the fear in his eyes upon beholding me. Okay, that might be too much, but in any event, it was time for me to emerge from the shadows. I didn't like living like a rat, skulking about in dark alleys all the time.

Valery was enthusiastic about my plan. So after we dealt with the wounded soldier, he set off to prepare for our raid. I told him to select seven of the strongest fighters and some kind of transport. “And pick some fighters who can drive.” It turned out, all of them knew how. Alright then. Guess I needed to learn how to drive, too, but I had to do a lot of healing, as well. A whole lot, in fact. In this way I’d grow ever stronger, which was the main beauty of the Gift of Healing.

With any other Gift, the only way to grow stronger was by taking part in mortal battles and pushing yourself to the edge. I, too, could benefit from this, but it was much simpler, really, to heal others who needed it. I no longer needed to suck the life out of others to grow. My source had by now developed to an acceptable level so that I could produce a sufficient amount of energy on my own. In fact, as I further developed my source, other people’s energy would only harm me. This is why healers didn't often employ their abilities to drain people in battle. Only in emergencies, when I had an urgent need to recover, would I be resorting to such measures. Yes, this is why I’d sucked the life out of half of the badasses in the port district. If I hadn’t had to swiftly improve my source I could have instead meditated for six months, but yeah, then I’d have ended up with a pathetically weak source that would absorb strength instead of producing it. In fact, who knows if that would really have worked?

But hey, enough with the musings. Just

when I thought that I no longer needed to absorb other people's energy, I came across this interesting case. The wounded melee fighter was someone with a rather interesting Gift. Right now, his source was hard at work, and it was the excess energy being produced that was burning out the channels in his body.

There was even a term for this: magic allergy. From my studies here in this world I knew that when this happened, death was a certainty in one hundred out of a hundred cases. Statistics like that amused me, because before coming here I'd never heard of anyone dying from this. In my old world, any doctor, even student medics, could cope with excess energy. But this was going to take a lot of time, which I didn't have right then. Thus, I had to employ a creative approach. In a couple of minutes, I stabilized his source, then plumbed his magical channels so that the excess energy was expelled. What was this fighter's Gift?

I soon found out. Due to the energy flowing from his body, mold was starting to form all around us. "Nature" is a very rare Gift. And it seemed to me that this fighter hadn't yet been able to access it, or else thus far it was expressed only weakly. But now, after my manipulations, he'd be able to develop it.

But meanwhile, I had to absorb the excess energy. Then, I had to process it into a vital element. Fortunately, I could use it, as my organism employed something similar. It might be different if this guy had been a necromancer... Yes, even then I could still help, and it would even be productive, but painful. After all, life and death are always around us, and they are far more closely linked than most people realize.

The entire treatment took about forty minutes, and I asked the commander to remind me to check in on this guy later. His energy would all drain, and then his channels needed to be filled again before he could return to normal.

Meanwhile, Valery readied a group of seven guardsmen. One of them was "grandpa," otherwise known as Timothy, who wanted to come along, knowing that little Masha would be safe under the supervision of the other soldiers. There she was now, already knitting bright hats for them.

I was pleasantly surprised when I saw the armored vehicles outside. I'd forgotten that we'd captured them. They were one of the reasons Timothy was so set on going with us. He'd been missing driving a ride like that.

"Real junk, this stuff, at least compared to what we used to use," said the old man as he slid behind the wheel of the first armored car. But yes, he couldn't help but smile as he started it up.

I didn't argue, I just sat in the back, and after waiting for everyone to take their seats, I gave the command to set out. As we made our way to the village, we planned our strategy, which consisted of essentially storming the hospital. We'd proceed as usual. First, I would enter, and then, when it sounded like lots of fun, the others would join me. Now we had lots of technology to work with, which made everything more convenient. This thing even had a cannon on top, although Valery said that it didn't have much firepower. Not that I needed it. I could, after all, do a lot of damage with my bare hands.

The journey took only about thirty minutes, during which time I decided I'd rather take my SUV next time. This thing was shaking like a claptrap, and I disliked being slammed against the metallic interior of the cabin all the time. Great vehicle and all that, but why suffer unnecessarily? We stopped about a mile and a half from the village, and then the driver maneuvered the vehicle into a ditch behind some shrubbery.

I set off toward the village. Nobody was expecting us, so there was almost no security. But I immediately spotted several trucks that could be easily stolen. And two of them were loaded with cargo, hopefully something valuable.

The so-called hospital did, indeed, look more like a prison. It looked like a hangar, or even a big barn, with small barred windows. In the big space on the ground floor, I sensed many heartbeats. They clustered around the iron stoves, and no wonder -- the temperature inside was almost the same as outside.

I took my time checking the perimeter of the hangar, and spotted a few guards. There were four of them, all armed, two of whom were sleeping on the job. Inside were twenty-two wounded individuals. These were all probably my people, which was fortuitous, because they included some seriously wounded men. I'd grow my source even more in the process of healing them.

I saw that there was an attic to this so-called hospital that served as barracks of a sort for the enemy's men. Up there were nine weakly Gifted types all huddled in one warm room. Some of them were sleeping, while the others seemed to be relaxing and chatting, enjoying their down time. What a shame, but I'd have to spoil it. However they were holding my people captive, and, from what I could tell, they weren't treating them well.

Next, I walked around the village, but I couldn't tell right away who the enemy was, and who were simply regular people. I noticed three with average Gifts who no doubt weren't going to sit around if a fight broke out — they'd have to be dealt with right away. But in any case, my men would take care of the village. I didn't want any casualties, as they say, among the regular citizenry. I might want to hire them on as laborers later on. That wasn't the case with the mercenaries who here hired by the viscount.

"Valery," I spoke, after calling him. "I'm done with reconnaissance. So here's the plan..."

Fifteen minutes later
Hangar holding the prisoners

"Syoma-a..." wheezed the man lying on some dirty rags. He was skin and bones, pale, and his whole body was shaking, either from cold or from pain. "Syom..!"

"What?!" responded a guy missing a leg. From the bloody stump, it was evident that it had been lopped off quite recently.

"Syoma..." uttered the pale man in a pained voice. "I won't survive this night... Tell my son that..."

"Yadda-yadda-yah!" muttered another guy who was totally wrapped up in dirty bandages. He'd been burned all over his body, but thanks to his Gift, he'd survived. And now, he was bound to the bed with wire, which is the only thing that kept him down. "For two weeks now you've been dying on us! You look fine to me!"

"I'm getting worse and worse every day!" whined the "dying man". "My entire body is trembling and I'm friggin' cold! It means I'm nearing the end..."

"It means it's friggin' freezing in here, that's what, idiot!" barked the man with the burns.

"T'ain't fair! Them bandages are keeping you warm!" joked the man missing the leg, and quiet chuckles resounded around the stove.

But just then they heard doors creaking open in the distance. That's where the security on duty usually hung out. Only this time they heard the doors open, but they didn't shut. In the darkness, measured steps sounded.

"Dam it, close the door!" barked the man in bandages. He wasn't afraid of any of their "overseers." He'd tried to escape so often over the months, they were tired of beating him. That's why they'd burned him this last time...

To everyone's surprise, somebody did close the door. And steps were heard approaching them. Soon, a figure wrapped in a cloak appeared in the light of the fire. The stranger wore a mask that made their flesh crawl. Not all of them, though. The burned man tried to sit up. Ignoring the pain, he struggled to rise to his feet.

“Who are you? I haven’t seen you here before,” he said calmly looking at the stranger. “A new doctor, is that it? Hah!”

“You could say so,” said the masked man as he quickly looked at them before placing his hand on the sleeping man’s forehead.

“Well, the usual one is a sadist, so you can’t be worse,” said the man through clenched teeth.

“Doc, help, I’m dying!” wailed the pale man again, but the stranger only shook his head.

“You’re not dying, but this one already has one foot in the grave,” he pointed to the peacefully snoring guy.

All this time, the guardsman wrapped in bandages looked carefully at the guest, and could not understand what it was that bugged him about the guy. But then his gaze fell on his hand, and...

“You... You...” he looked at the ring, and hesitated. “Count? No... you are not him... I know the aura of my master... Who are you?”

Mikhail could see how the man’s eyes had lit up with hope, which quickly died.

“Mikhail,” snapped the stranger. “The new head of the Bulatov Family. And I’ve come for you.”

“New? Damn... He’s gone...” the one-legged

man clenched his fist and hit the concrete column. For a second he forgot that he was dying.

"Yes, he is..." said Mikhail, in the guise of a plague doctor. "But the Family lives on! His daughter is alive! Will you still serve the Family?"

"What... us?" the burned man chuckled and looked at the stranger skeptically. "We couldn't even stop them..."

What he said was true. The enemy had offered many of them employment. They'd wanted them to betray the Bulatovs, tell them everything they knew. Then, they'd supposedly be given real medical treatment, food, and... freedom. Some took the bait, and were taken from here.

"But we're the ones who are still here," said the burned man. "We're the ones for whom loyalty is not an empty word. We're the ones who are ready to die for our convictions. That's who we are!"

"I see!" nodded the stranger. "This is why I've come for you," he responded, dead serious. "We have no more than an hour to leave this place."

"Leave it? That's not likely to happen," said Vasily, the burned one, with a rueful smile. "We're a mess... Only two of us can move faster than a dead turtle. No... We can't leave... New count, if you really care about this Family, then leave us and go. There are at least twenty men nearby. And in the village, there's a station with about forty others. As soon as the alarm is raised, they will all give chase."

"Is that all?" chuckled the stranger. "Are you

really afraid of them, Vasily the Burned, commander of the fire locusts? What, no? Well, then listen and heed my instructions," Mikhail raised his voice and added power to it. "Stop whining and prepare to bust out of here!"

And thusly speaking in an imperious tone from his past life, he grabbed Vasily by the neck with a glowing green hand. Not just his hand, but his eyes, too, glowed with a greenish light.

After a rush treatment like that, Valery collapsed to the floor, wheezing. It was rough and hurried, but the process worked. It wasn't just any healer who could pull that kind of healing off, and this included the healers in Mikhail's world.

Without further ado, the stranger began to approach every wounded man in the room, treating them as he went along. Some tried to resist. They didn't understand what he was doing, but in the end, he prevailed.

"And now... I'm off to have some fun! I'll wait for you outside," said Mikhail after most were more or less ready for action. Just before walking out the door, he looked over his shoulder and said, "Arm yourselves... you'll find plenty of weapons lying about."

And he was gone. Soon, rapid-fire shots were heard outside, including from machine guns, and shouting and screams resounded.

"You all know this is our chance, right?"

"Yes sir!" the others chorused.

* * *

"What's your status?" I asked, looking in the truck at one of my men behind the wheel. He responded with a thumbs up sign.

Alright then. Our attack had been swift and bold, and we'd taken the enemy totally by surprise. It was like beating up sleeping kittens, more or less. I had a bit of fun in the barracks when I surprised the guards, but even then, I took them all out in a matter of seconds.

As I took care of the hangar with the prisoners, my men had cleared the village. As agreed, nobody hurt the civilians. But anyone with a weapon was summarily shot by the gun atop the armored car.

After crushing the enemy, we commandeered three trucks and loaded the wounded into them, and off we went back to my castle. We had no reason to linger in the village — we'd already taken all we needed from the viscount. I'm talking about the trucks, of course. There wasn't anything else there of value. No doubt he kept other valuables, including money, elsewhere. As for the vehicles, ironically, the viscount had stolen them from my Family, and so I was only taking back what was mine. Unfortunately, though, one of our armored cars was seriously damaged. Somehow it was still functioning, but a charge of blue plasma had hit it, and now the motor was exposed.

We were all situated in our vehicles while I

tended to the wounded. None were at death's door any longer, but I focused on one man who needed immediate attention — the others just needed time to recover. The trip back was going to take awhile, nothing to do about that. So I took the opportunity to run a full diagnostic on everyone. I even launched the recovery process in some of them. Later, I planned on performing a more detailed examination, but now, I couldn't afford to devote much to it. A new day was dawning, and I had to prepare to make my big entrance in society.

I hadn't forgotten about the ball, and so while on the road I called Georgy and told him to pick up an appropriate outfit for the event. He asked me for my measurements, but I was at a loss. He had to do his own estimate.

I was so busy with treatments and all this other business that I didn't even notice when we made it back. As the others unloaded the wounded, I jumped out and took a look what the other trucks had been carrying.

"Food..." said Valery, looking at the cargo. "In this one, too..."

"What a shame," I said. "But hey, we need to eat, as well."

Really it's not like I expected mountains of gold or artifacts from this raid. I took the trucks because they were mine. To leave them for the scum working for the viscount would be to disrespect myself.

Anyway, food is good. Now I had something to feed the army of disabled soldiers I'd recruited to my cause. Of course, they wouldn't remain disabled for long, and so I was killing two birds with one stone. First, I'd brought back into the fold men who were fiercely loyal to the Family. My Family. Most of them were loyal, anyway... Although among the prisoners there were two mercenaries, and if they didn't want to stay, I'd simply release them after treating them. Secondly, I now powered up my source through treating others, and so these wounded were a boon to that process. Really, this was important, at least to me.

And with all these new forces, I needed men to guard the castle. That man wrapped like a mummy in those bandages was pretty strong with his average Gift, and it wouldn't be too long before he'd be ready for action. He'd already coped with much of the burns on his own, so I didn't have to expend much of my own energy to simply accelerate the healing process. Now, he needed to simply take it easy and eat, and time would do the rest.

As I examined my patients, doing this and that and issuing instructions, Georgy arrived.

"Here's what I found with the funds you gave me," he said, handing me a package. "I'm sure it'll do for a ball out here in the provinces."

It turned out that he'd researched what the local aristocrats were wearing these days. Good going. I myself would have been at a loss at selecting what to wear. And yes, looks mattered. Sadly, I'd noticed that about this world. What you were wearing mattered. Unless you were appropriately dressed, you'd never find common ground with other aristocrats. All of this seemed incredibly backward to me, but the fact remained that in this world, dressing expensively and fashionably was important.

This was just the rules of the game here. It wasn't any big deal, really. At least the latest fashion was comfortable. My movements weren't in any way restricted. No doubt that's why the cost was high. The materials were designed to enable the aristocrats to jump into action as needed. Not just duels and other showdowns with each other, they had to be ready for random Interfaces, like at the fair at the port that time. When an Interface opened up, any self-respecting aristocrat was simply obligated to jump into battle with the offworlders. And for some reason, I assumed I'd best be prepared for action at this ball. I'm not talking about dancing, either.

I had an hour before the ball, so I invited Georgy to stay at the castle since he was no longer going to serve me as my driver. That was now grandpa Timothy's job. Of course, he didn't look that much like "grandpa" anymore. Now he looked younger and healthier.

"Timothy!" I called to him as he rummaged around under the hood of the armored car.

Boom!

"Damn!" he swore, rubbing the new lump on the back of his head. "Who designed this heap of junk? What a mess! We had better combat vehicles back in my day..."

“Don’t get dirty; we’re going to a ball...” I shook my head. But then I saw that he looked spotless, in fact. Yet in a movie I’d recently seen, the mechanics were all covered in black gunk.

“I’m almost ready, sir! I’ll get the car. Be back in a flash!” said Timothy, rushing off.

It took him more than a “flash,” even if it wasn't too long. In the meantime, I looked at the guys milling about in the courtyard.

The wounded fighters I’d brought back from the clutches of death to rid the castle of mercenaries were already looking great. Sure, there were a few still on the mend, but most were busy doing what they could to put the castle back together and clean up the mess. I’d have to hire some professional housekeepers, of course, so these guys could all be put to work guarding the castle.

Just then, the SUV flew out of the garage like a bullet and stopped right before me. I didn't even have to take a step. Soon, I was in the back seat, and the roaring monster took off with a squeal. I no longer worried about being late. In fact, we arrived just in time. We even found ourselves in a bottleneck at the entrance to the Vlasov Family’s mansion. I could observe other aristocrats and see how they communicated with each other. Check them out unseen, as it were.

The ball was hosted by the head of the Family, Vladislav. I couldn’t imagine why he invited the countess. I was sure that someone far above the viscount was responsible. But over the past six months, my Family hadn't received a single invitation. I'd checked.

So to me it was obvious this invite was designed to lure the countess out. What they didn't anticipate was that she had others in her Family now. Yes, these invitations extended to the entire Family. They had to let me in. There was just one thing I didn't understand. Why invite the countess to an event with so many other aristocrats? That's all Vlasov needed to spoil his daughter's birthday.

The line of expensive cars stretched for a good hundred yards. All of them were showy vehicles. Some of the aristocrats drove themselves, even. Others brought security with them, although they weren't allowed inside. All of the personal bodyguards were shown into a special courtyard, as entry into the mansion with firearms was prohibited.

Of course, edged weapons were allowed, meaning swords and, say, rapiers. But no knives, daggers, axes, or anything else that could be easily concealed.

How curious, really. But why? I mean, if I wanted to kill someone, I could do it with my bare hands. Who needed a weapon?

Elegant ladies in evening dresses, stately men in formal suits, and even people in full military uniform milled about. They all exited their vehicles, and then flocked to the open doors of the mansion, from which music and a hubbub of voices sounded.

At the entrance they were all greeted by the head doorman. He stealthily checked the guest list. No need to offend the guests by being obvious. In any event, it's not like anyone who wasn't invited would try to enter this way. Just in case, though, he checked everyone's rings, noting them on his tablet.

Finally, it was our turn. Timothy ran out to open my door for me. I could tell he'd formerly served a Family. He knew how to drive, what needed to be done, and I didn't have to tell him anything. Good thing, because I wouldn't have known what to say.

"I won't be long," I told him. "Stay nearby."

"I won't even turn off the engine," he nodded. "If something happens, might I join the fight?"

That's right. Would I need him? Let's say I get attacked, like, from the viscount's people, and my man Timothy then opens fire on them. Would that launch a war with the Vlasov family? In theory, since this event was at his estate, I was supposed to rely solely on his security. Anyway, what could Timothy do all on his own?

"No, you need to focus solely on evacuating the countess and myself. If necessary, that is. Hopefully it won't come to that."

Timothy nodded, slid back behind the wheel, and drove to the parking lot as I headed for the entrance.

"Pardon me," said the doorman behind me. "But..."

"Is there a problem?" I said, pausing as other

guests gathered behind me.

The doorman looked at my ring, then at his tablet, but seemed confused. I just shrugged and walked on by. Yes, I'm not on the list, but the Bulatov family was invited. So I left him to figure it out. It wasn't my problem that I became a Bulatov after the invitation was issued.

I felt like mingling, checking out the local elite, assessing their powers, but I didn't have time to do much of this. Just twenty or so minutes had passed since my entry when I beheld an unpleasant scene. Two people stood apart from everyone: a short, thick, bald man and a stately, beautiful raven-haired girl. Right away, I knew it was Victoria. Of course, there wasn't much information about the Bulatovs on the Internet, but in the castle, yes... There were several portraits of her on the walls. One thing's for sure, and that is that Victoria's beautiful name suited her. She was lovely, although her face bore scars. But if everything went as planned, I'd deal with those. Nothing to it. That is, assuming she wanted to be rid of them. Who knows? Maybe she bore such wounds with pride, like a warrior sporting battle scars. I'd met some who were into that kind of thing.

But I didn't have to spend much time looking at this "darling duo." Before long, their conversation began to heat up, and the chubby chump flared up, and raised his hand, preparing to actually strike the countess.

Really by then I wasn't far off, but I hadn't

been in any hurry to interfere. What for? I felt like I should observe them, see what transpired. But I wasn't allowed to stay in the background for long. The fat fool stood there, his hand raised as he imbued it with force using his Gift. Yes, I could tell there was more to this situation. She apparently had a sharp tongue, judging from how offended he was. And she also was no coward... I could see from where I stood that she wasn't in the best shape, and yet she'd provoked him.

I had to act. I strode forward and intercepted the viscount's hand. Bastard! He'd poured energy into it! All I could do was make minor changes to his body. I weakened the nerve conduction a little; it wouldn't affect him too much. He was, in fact, stronger than me, as sad as I am to admit it, and so I couldn't influence him much.

"I ask that you keep your hands to yourself," I said, and turned on my aura.

The viscount was flabbergasted, to put it mildly. How dare anyone treat him like that, right?

Victoria, too, was shocked, probably because she noticed her father's ring on my hand.

"Who are you?" asked the viscount, rage and contempt on his countenance.

He tried to free his hand, but in vain. I'd poured a lot of energy into it, as much as I'd poured into weakening his grip. And with every second my energy was penetrating his defenses. But still, I lacked the strength to significantly damage him.

"I? What makes you think I need to introduce

myself to such as you?" I enjoyed seeing the expression on his face. It was rapidly changing, actually. Now, the veins in his forehead were swollen, his face was red, and he looked like he was ready to burst.

Meanwhile, the place was packed with aristocrats, all going about their own business, with no one paying us much attention. Apparently, such skirmishes were not uncommon here. And, although was my understanding that aristocrats were all well-educated people, this viscount struck me was an ordinary pig, both in appearance and in manners.

Take right now, for example. He displayed his true nature by yelling at the entire room. It was so easy to piss him off. All I had to do was introduce myself. I surprised Victoria even more, but I'd achieved my goal. Viscount Snegirev challenged me to a duel. And by this time everyone had already gathered around us, so everyone heard his words. And everyone realized that he'd challenged me to a duel only because I was a healer. I was glad that here, everyone assumed healers were weak. Little did they know that healing was a two-edged sword...

CHAPTER 2

THIS WAS NOT SOMETHING Andrei Snegirev expected, and so he was taken off guard. Just a second ago, he'd been feeling like victory was near, and he'd soon be "Count Snegirev," but then, out of nowhere, this stranger with glowing green eyes shows up. That in itself was no big deal, really, except the stranger was wearing the Bulatov Family ring, and that meant he wasn't just some random nut job.

But as soon as the viscount realized the stranger was a healer, he breathed a sigh of relief. In fact, he felt like laughing at the old count's foolishness. How desperate he must have been to give the Family ring to the first person he met! Although, yes, it was depressing that he'd managed to do this. They'd told Snegirev that the Bulatov Family would disappear forever. But in any case, it was short-sighted of old man Bulatov to hand over his Family to a healer. No healer could save them. Everybody knew that healers were, by their nature, not strong. Throughout the world, there were only few who made names for themselves, but that was just as healers, and not through any kind of might. And now that there was a war ongoing between the Families, strength is what was needed. "Might makes right." End of story.

"So this, then, is your defender, Victoria?" sneered Snegirev, looking at the astonished young woman. "Seems to me he's on the weak side. In fact, let me show you," he went on, and then he focused, and transferred a small ball of energy into his open palm, and threw it into the face of the newly-minted head of the Bulatov Family.

The stranger looked steadily at him. He was unnervingly calm, in fact. This was despite the fact that he'd just been challenged to a duel to the death. The viscount was surprised, as he was sure that the young man would be, at the least, alarmed, and would even try to get out of it. However, instead of fear, the stranger simply looked contemptuously at the viscount.

Then he bared his teeth and said "I accept your challenge."

A crowd began to gather around them, and everyone began chattering about what was happening. Such spectacles rarely happened anymore and the aristocrats were loving it.

Andrei Snegirev stood and smiled, already

anticipating an easy victory. What kind of idiot do you have to be to agree to certain death? But that wasn't the main thing. Once this pathetic healer was dead, Snegirev's problems would be solved. The new head of the Bulatov Family was a complete idiot for showing up here. He was doomed!

* * *

Good thing I'd read that book on aristocratic etiquette. It was boring, and yes, it is rare for a book to bore me, making it, I guess, a rare book, but I knew it contained useful knowledge. So I read it from cover to cover. And that's how I knew what it meant when Snegirev threw that concentrated pure energy in my face. It didn't do any damage at all, but it was unpleasant. And that's how these aristocrats challenged each other to duels. I noticed that these duels were, as a rule, to the death, but there were cases when they might be interrupted. The victor, for example, didn't have to kill the defeated one.

Of course, had the challenge been uttered out loud in words, the duel would not be to the death. But being hit in the face with energy was a means of humiliating someone, as if to say "look at all this energy I have, punk! I can toss it about just like that, so I can crush you!"

It was fun seeing the viscount and his changing moods. He so wanted to humiliate me, make me afraid, but something was wrong. I'd simply agreed, my face impassive. I didn't think it would be so simple. I'd come here to get Victoria, but now, I could accomplish two tasks at once. I love it when things work out so easily. Well, maybe not two things. From what I could tell, the way our Family had been treated lately left something to be desired, but this duel was my opportunity to change everything. Of course, I realized they'd never love us. But I hoped they'd think twice before they crossed our paths. Really, this was perfect.

All the local aristocrats gathered around, talking about what was happening, and anticipating a show.

"Is that the new head of the Bulatov Family?" a pretty girl with a glass of wine in her hands asked, clearly surprised.

"Yes," said her friend, adding, "He's cute! Where did he come from? I didn't think they had an heir."

"I heard that the former count, being in desperate straits, gave his ring to a commoner," another voice was heard, and the crowd quickly picked up this rumor.

"Exactly. It's clear that he's a commoner. And now he thinks he's a count..." a boy of about eighteen pointed at me right before his father whopped him on the head.

"Didn't they teach you anything?" said an older man dressed in military uniform. "If you give the ring to a commoner, he will immediately die from the release of energy," he shook his head.

I paid no attention to all this gossip. Many were indignant that the viscount had challenged a defenseless healer to a duel. Others speculated that I wouldn't even last ten seconds. Let them have fun. What did I care?

"Time and place?" asked Snegirev, smiling maliciously, "It is my understanding that you don't want it here and now?" -- he hinted that I would postpone the duel until the last minute. Ha!

"But why not? Let's do it right here and now," I shrugged, and the smirk disappeared from his face. "You have to take out the trash right away, otherwise it starts to stink. Yes, I think it is best to get it done with. You must understand that your insults are cause for war, but as we're already in one, let's get down to it."

"How dare you..." he sputtered, and then said with a scowl, "You don't even have a weapon."

That was true. The mercenaries had stolen most of the things of value, and anyway, I didn't feel like, as a count, I needed to walk around with a sword. Anyway, I was better off without one than with one. I wasn't going to disgrace myself with a cheap blade.

"I see that you have one, though," I said, pointing at his evidently costly sword. "I'll make it mine once we start the duel."

I found that there was no end to how much I could anger him. After every word I uttered, the veins on his forehead swelled more and more. Maybe I didn't even need the duel to take him out? I might be able to give him a stroke just by talking, and then I'd simply withhold treatment. That would be a fitting end to the war between the

Families.

But no — he had a pretty strong Gift, and so he wouldn't die quite so easily. And I'd have a hard time altering his body on the sly, so I had to fight him fair and square.

"Is it customary in Arkhangelsk to challenge those who are weaker to duels?" I heard a commanding voice behind me, and I turned to see who it was. The crowd parted a little, and I saw a young woman in obviously expensive clothes. Hmmm...That face was familiar. Right...it was Princess Ryazantseva. I wonder how she'd ended up here? Meanwhile, she cast a contemptuous glance at the viscount and continued. "Is this how you're asserting yourself? In Moscow, they'd despise you for this."

Good for me yet again. I wasn't wasting my time back at the tavern when I studied all of the princes and their families. You always need to know by sight the powers that be wherever you make your home, and, indeed, you need to know them well.

"Dear princess, whatever are you saying?" Snegirev's face immediately changed. "How could you think so poorly of me? I seek to exercise the right of substitution."

He bowed almost to the floor, while I silently stood there. He was fawning so much that it was sickening to behold.

"I shall nominate Pavel Petrunin, my servant, in my place! He's just the eighth rank, so the forces will be equal," Snegirev continued to fawn. But the princess just shook her head and sighed.

Whispers were immediately heard from the crowd, saying it was a servant against a count. To die at the hands of a commoner, especially in a duel, was almost the highest degree of shame for any Family.

Meanwhile the viscount was beaming. He was glad that he could try to get at me like that. Too bad he was so sure his servant could defeat me. I'd already conducted a full diagnosis of the guy, and he didn't have a chance. I'd have to hold back if I didn't want to finish him off in seconds. Probably I needed to make a show of prolonging the encounter a little. Otherwise they'd suspect something was off.

What was really unpleasant is how weak his servant was. And yet everyone around us thought that he had a chance! The viscount was actually confident he'd win.

"Here!" Snegirev took the sheath from his belt and handed it to Pavel, the servant. Pavel bowed deeply, and gingerly accepted the weapon. It was quite valuable, in fact, custom made, no doubt. What was nice is that after the duel, the victor got to keep his opponent's weapon. "Finish him off fast, Pavel, and I'll give you a bonus."

Pavel beamed with happiness then, and bowed yet again, and entered the dueling circle. I was already there. They fenced off the dueling circle with ribbon, keeping the spectators outside so that there'd be no danger to them and no interference in the fight. That being said, the spectators were all pretty strong, as this was what mattered most in high society.

"I have a spare sword in the car," smiled the viscount. "I want a fair duel," he said a little louder so that everyone could hear.

"Keep it for yourself, you will need it later," I smiled in response. "Why do I even need a weapon if I am against a coward who chooses to sacrifice his servant?" Everyone heard this, but the viscount managed to keep a grip on himself, and maintain his smile.

Still, it was evident how furious he was. He was doing his best to intimidate me, but I kept my cool. Really, what did I have to be nervous about? The viscount, though, didn't understand how it was I could be so confident.

"Mikhail..." a quiet voice said, and, turning around, I saw Victoria. "I understand that my blade is a woman's, but it's still better than fighting with your bare hands," she took the sheath from her belt and handed me her sword.

I appreciated her gesture and noted it. She didn't yet know me, and what to expect, even. But she saw how seemingly unjust this fight was, and wanted to clearly show whose side she was on. That being said, it would be reasonable to want me to die, since for all she knew, I wasn't out to help her.

Indeed, it was a woman's sword. It was made for her smaller hand, the guard narrow and the blade thin and elegant. It was a good blade, strong, and it could conduct energy well, but...

"No, no! Wait!" a young man burst out of the crowd, clearly tipsy. He had an unfinished glass of wine in his hands, but that was quickly corrected. He gulped down the rest, and called for the waiter again. "Heavens, though! What the hell is going on here?"

The guy looked around the crowd, then looked at the dueling circle, and walked towards us with an unsteady gait.

"Here!" He tore his sword from his belt. I could tell right away it was costly. "Take!" he thrust it in my hands. "Sorry, but I can't bear to st-st-stand by and just watch! No c-c-count should have to fight with a lady's blade!"

"No worries, count..." I looked at him carefully, but his face was unfamiliar. Still, along the way I'd only managed to study those who lived in Arkhangelsk or nearby, along with the princes. Thanks to the Internet, this was easily done. Clearly this guy wasn't a local count.

"Count Cherepanov!" he introduced himself. "Nikolai Leonidovich Cherepanov! And yes, I'm passing through here, I just stopped by the ball..." with these words he handed me his sword and immediately stepped back. "Don't disgrace us counts! I don't want to hear about it!"

"But your sword is worth more than the life of the viscount and all his servants combined! Why spoil this sword using it against them?" I called after him, but he just waved his hand.

"I don't care, at least I'll see how you wield my weapon," he took another sip of his glass, and realizing that he was too drunk, activated his Gift. I watched him, and I have to say that this guy was very cunning. He could control water, and quite skillfully. In a matter of seconds, his blood was clear of alcohol. He was now merely lightly intoxicated.

The young count stood with the others to observe the fight as he enjoyed his wine.

"Count, don't worry," Snegirev turned to Cherepanov, and even bowed his head as a sign of respect. "After the duel, we will agree on a price, and I will not charge a high ransom for the blade!"

The count merely waved at the annoying viscount and continued sipping his beverage. He cared about wine much more than he did about Snegirev. And he wanted to watch the fight.

He didn't have to wait long. All of the preparations were completed, and so now I stood facing Pavel in the middle of the circle. We then shook hands.

And as soon as we did this, a roar of indignation swept through the crowd. Really, how could a count shake hands with some commoner? I didn't care, though. Pavel deserved respect for even daring to stand against me. And what did it matter if he was a commoner rather than a king?

"I've killed many, but this is the first time I'll be taking out a count," my opponent said quietly, producing a nasty grin. I could see that he enjoyed killing. "I thank you for this opportunity to add your scalp to my belt."

"Have you killed a lot, then? Did you

slaughter some pigs for your master's barbecues? Well, that doesn't count," I grinned, and took a few steps back.

I marveled at how pathetic this man was. He wanted to impress his master, and since he took pleasure in killing, this, what, gave his life some kind of meaning? Okay, I am often cynical, because I've seen a lot in my life, but this was, well, how very sad.

Just then, someone announced the start of the duel. Show time! Later, I didn't even want to recall how it went down. Pavel was confident he could kill me, and rushed into the attack. One swing, and then another. I simply dodged these two blows, letting the sword swish over my head and past me. The servant then tried to throw a sweeping roundhouse kick, but... who does that anyway? And why? Okay, time to finish with him. The tip of my blade pierced his ribs and entered straight into his heart. I didn't even have to use my strength; it was really quite easy.

"Next!" I said to the viscount, wiping the blade off on the now-dead Pavel's clothes. My voice echoed throughout the spacious hall, and everyone heard it. After my swift victory, a ringing silence reigned. "You have another sword, it seems. And after my victory, I will ask you to make a public apology for your bad behavior."

"A-ha!" Count Cherepanov was the first to break the silence. "I knew it! He's a count! Haha! Good man, this count! He didn't disgrace us, no! He's one of us!"

Behind him sounded a roar of voices then. It not like everyone thought I didn't stand a chance, but no one could imagine that it would end so quickly.

I issued the next challenge for a reason. It was my right according to the rules. The viscount could challenge me again, but after winning this round, I had the right to refuse. But why should I? I hoped this time he'd fight me himself instead of sacrificing another of his servants. As bodyguards weren't allowed inside the event, he'd have to make it another servant.

"I accept the challenge!" shouted Andrei Snegirev. "Pavel was unprepared, and it was my fault, too, for telling him not to fight with all his might, so as not to disgrace Count Bulatov," he began to tell everyone why his servant had been so easily defeated. "I put forth another servant. He won't hold back!"

And then a man of about thirty-fiver entered the dueling circle. I could tell right away that he was far stronger than Pavel. What did I say about bodyguards? This was one, I'm sure. He was just pretending to be a servant. I placed him at the sixth rank, at least.

"It seems to me that this servant of yours is much stronger than the previous one..." the princess said with suspicion — she was still watching us. "You think this is a fair fight?"

"He's eighth rank!" said the viscount. "There are documents that will confirm this! But they're back at my mansion..."

"You can refuse," the princess turned to me. "Your honor will not in any way suffer."

"Thank you," I smiled politely. "But I expect to finish him off, too."

The hall was again filled with a hubbub of voices. And if last time they immediately "buried" me, now they even started rooting for me. And Cherepanov was completely jubilant, every now and then shouting not the most flattering phrases at Snegirev's bodyguard. But it was, of course, all within the bounds of decency.

"You can take a rest for half an hour," the second, an elderly man who served as a butler, came up to me. It was he who announced the beginning of the fight last time.

I knew the rules, though. It's true that I was entitled to rest, but I wasn't going to take advantage of it.

"Thank you, but I'd rather wrap this up rather quickly," I shook my head. "I came here to spend the evening with Victoria and enjoy the delightful hospitality of our hosts, but I have to deal with this nonsense first. So I'd appreciate it if you'd announce the start of the duel."

The butler bowed and approached the other participant. And I just stood and watched what was happening around me. The servants quickly ran to the viscount's car and brought the spare sword. It was far less costly, I had to say. And this is what he had earlier proposed I fight with? Clearly this was another attempt at humiliating me. Oh, well.

Once his servant had the sword, Snegirev gave him some instructions, and then stepped out of the dueling circle.

“Don’t make Petrunin’s mistake!” shouted the viscount. “Give it your all!”

Um, so had Petrunin, but what good did that do him? But all this was for show, I could tell. The viscount didn't want the spectators to know how much stronger this guy was.

Just like before, we stood in the center of the circle and shook hands. And whilst there, the servant decided to talk some trash.

“I’ll tell you a secret,” he said quietly with a nasty smile. “When you die, and your Family is transferred to the viscount, he promised us the countess. For three days, to teach her a few things...” Oh, how much confidence there was in his words. But what was the point of telling me this? Did he want to shake me up so that I'd rush him in a frenzy?

“I’ll share a secret, too,” I said, pouring a lot of energy through his hand. “You don’t need women anymore. Even if you somehow survive, you’ll never get it up again. I know. I’m a healer,” I said, smiling ominously. And he...believed me. Right away. Although not every healer could do this, I launched several harmless processes in his, um, nether regions, and he felt it.

“You..you...!” his eyes widened in horror.

“I...I...! ” I smiled.

This time the duel turned out to be a little more interesting. But although my opponent was stronger, he clearly lacked skill. His only ploy was to attack head on using his Gift.

Sadly, it would take him at least thirty or forty years to have a chance at hurting me. Meanwhile, I'd been honing my sword skills for over a century. I'd studied with the best masters, and spared no time and effort to become the most advanced healer to wield a blade. In my world, every healer must be excellent with weapons. After all, what other Gift could alter the capabilities of the body so much?

Whatever, I had to really hold back during this fight. I didn't want to reveal how strong I was, especially given how skewed the local thinking about healers was. Did they, for example, expect healers to know how to use cloaking? Or imbue the weapon with your power so that it penetrates the enemy's defenses without encountering any resistance? As it was, I stuck to fighting the old-fashioned way, without even cloaking myself for protection. My opponent took full advantage of this. Each of my blows bounced off the impenetrable film around his body, but gradually his reserves of strength were depleted, although he could still dance around. At first, the viscount's bodyguard rained blows on me, but I simply dodged or deflected them to the side. I didn't have the strength to simply block everything, and anyway didn't see the point in doing so.

I'd scanned him when we shook hands. He had old injuries that were plaguing him, and in addition to impotence, he would automatically fall on his right leg. I could take advantage of this, not to mention the recently injured tendons in his left hand. Perhaps he'd slipped, or he simply fell while drunk. I'd noticed a lot of little things, and now, thanks to this, I could easily defeat him. Knowing one's opponent's weaknesses was the key to success.

Meanwhile, I noticed how the spectators were looking at us. Obviously with interest, because no one expected me to hold out for even ten seconds. But the battle dragged on, minute after minute, causing the crowd to make more and more noise. The aristocrats clearly liked it. The drunken count shouted especially loudly. True, before the fight he removed a lot of alcohol from his body so as not to miss a single detail due to being dead drunk.

"I declare, this is no commoner!! What kind of moves is he making?" said a man in a strict black suit.

"Those moves strike me as cat and mouse," his comrade in an officer's dress uniform grinned. "Look..." he pointed at me. "Did you see? He could have dealt a fatal blow, but for some reason he didn't."

Looks like they had me dead to rights. Time to end this farce.

Swish! The bodyguard's blade swept right past my face. But I'd drawn near on purpose, because then I inflicted a hail of strikes on him. He couldn't parry any of them, and gradually I depleted his cloak, and then, with a sweeping blow I pierced his throat. As he'd been leaning on his injured leg, he couldn't even retreat. And he'd slowed down, as well. He was a strong one, no doubt about it. But that alone wasn't enough.

Silence reigned again, but this time it was interrupted by applause. It is not often in this hinterland that people got to see such spectacles, and therefore the aristocrats were very happy. I looked at Victoria, who was still standing in one place batting her beautiful eyes, not understanding what had just happened.

Yes, she'd experienced a lot in just fifteen minutes. Just recently, the viscount forcibly tried to marry her, then a new head of the Family appeared, and this new head had already won two duels. But the first thing I did was approach Cherepanov, who was again getting drunk. Now he didn't need to focus on anything, and so the glasses flew into his mouth, one after another. Should I improve his liver? Ah, but he is strong and Gifted; simple diseases didn't harm him.

"Oh, surprised, amazed!" he shook his head, taking the sword from me and clipping it back onto his belt "You and I simply must drink to the victory!" he raised his glass and snatched another from a passing waiter. "Yes, we simply must drink!"

The waiter had been heading for someone else, and sighing, he turned and headed back to the bar.

"Are you really a healer?" the count narrowed his eyes, but it was all in jest. Just in case, I showed him a clot of green energy. "Yes, yes, it just can't be! Your brethren never take up arms, everyone knows this."

Ah, yes, I myself read that somewhere. It's something of a given that healers never fight. In fact, it's that kind of tripe that compelled me to throw that book on the art of healing into the fire. Allegedly, the healer's Gift is weakened during fights. I needed to find out where that notion came from. Seriously. It was strange, indeed, and could be attributable to the local healers being unaware of how to purify the energy from heavy combat. When that happens, the excess energy settles in the channels, your membranes become clogged, and yes, you can eventually lose your Gift. But processing alien energy is child's play. In any case, for whatever reason in this world, it was something of a given that healers never fight.

After chatting a bit more with Cherepanov, I again thanked him for the sword. It truly was a fine weapon. Perfectly balanced, but most importantly, made of high-quality offworld steel. If I had used my Gift, which the sword would have held without resistance, the fight would have taken a split second.

As other aristocrats passed on their congratulation to me, I headed toward the butler serving as the second. All this time, the old man had been waiting for me, clutching my two captured swords. One was cheap, but the other, which had belonged to the viscount himself, looked valuable. Speaking of, he was nowhere to be seen. I wasn't surprised, though. The humiliation I'd heaped on him had to be dispiriting. What a shame, though, that I wasn't able to fight him. But perhaps it was just as well. I'd have had to reveal many of my secrets to defeat him, as he was far more powerful an adversary than were his servants.

"Where shall I deliver your captured swords?" asked the butler.

"Give them to my driver. He should be outside with the others," I said, nodding at him. I felt certain that the swords would make it to my car. Under the rules, ensuring the transfer of the captured weaponry was an obligation of the organizer of the duel. So it was time for the owner of this mansion to do his part.

He, however, had yet to appear, which was understandable. In recent times, the Bulatov Family was seen as outcast, something of pariahs. I needed to get to the bottom of this. I was at a loss as to what compelled the viscount to be so viciously bold in attacking my Family. Clearly someone else was behind this. Whoever it was, well, they were above him, and I needed to find out more. And this included uncovering the reasons for it, because the war between the Families didn't start all on its own.

The dead body was swiftly carried out and the blood wiped off the floor. Now, nothing remained to remind anyone of the duel. The crowd dispersed as well, but everybody was talking about, well, me. In particular, how could I, a healer, the new head of the Bulatov Family, defeat someone with a Gift in a fair fight? To them, this was strange. What can I say?

Meanwhile, I was finally able to turn my attention to the main thing. I headed toward Victoria, who was heatedly discussing something with her servant.

* * *

Countess Bulatov was still reeling from recent events. She felt like she'd left her body, and was watching events from above. In the span of minutes her world had been turned upside down. Although she'd long suspected that her father was most likely dead, now she knew for this sure. And yet, even so, he'd done what he could to save the Family — he'd somehow found a worthy successor. At least, he seemed worthy. She'd stop questioning his strength after his first duel. But he was a healer, just a healer, and this didn't bode well for a Family in the midst of a war. But her father...he was intelligent, insightful, and wouldn't have made a mistake.

When she heard that Mikhail was a healer, she'd wanted to fight the duel in his stead. But the rules forbade this. And then, after the first fight, she realized why he was so confident, so calm. And the second fight, well, after that, she was full of questions. She had honed her skills from a young age. And thus, she easily discerned the oddities in Mikhail's behavior. It was as if he was deliberately dragging out the second duel. From time to time he could have struck and killed, but he didn't. He even created difficulties for himself. He made crazy thrusts with the sword, and then suddenly, a flawless move. To fight like that, well, he'd have to perfect his technique over years, if not decades. And she wasn't the only one who'd noticed. And then, the healer seemed to realize the game was up, and so he wrapped up the kill in a few swift strokes.

Now that the fight was over, as the winner discussed matters with the second, she thought about how this evening had gone from a major mistake to a pleasant surprise just like that. Indeed, for the first time in ages, the countess even smiled, which was amazing given how difficult the past six months had been. She'd especially enjoyed observing the fury of the viscount, who had to somehow control himself before he exploded. He needed to do what he could to save face in front of the other aristocrats.

"Do you know what's going on?" she asked her servant, who'd been standing slightly behind her all this time.

"Nothing more than what you know, madam," he said with a smile. He'd been smiling for awhile now. "But your late father knows how to surprise you. I couldn't be more astonished."

"But now what? What should I do now?" Victoria was almost pleading with him. On the one hand, she was very happy about this new turn of events, but on the other... The girl had no idea what awaited her next. What was this guy about?

"How should I talk to him? Maybe I should leave the ball? But I can't wander about forever..."

"I don't think you should worry," her servant smiled. "Snegirev has slithered out the door already, so you have no reason to leave."

"What if it's a trap..." the girl said quietly, "Well? What's up with you?" The old man was still smiling, but now he was looking over her shoulder. "Is he...standing behind me?" he nodded, and she turned pale. She realized right away that she needed to talk, yet again, about her future. And she had no idea what to expect from this guy.

* * *

Meanwhile, on a road in the country
Viscount Andrei Snegirev's car

Andrei left the ball as soon as he realized that his bodyguard was doomed. He saw how skilled the little punk turned out to be, but there was nothing he could do about it. And no way did he want to remain at the ball, so he leaped into his car and sped out of there.

Thoughts crowded in his head, and he was at a loss as to how this could even happen to him. Just a few minutes ago, the title of count, the remains of the Bulatov estate, and the countess herself were within his grasp. His plan was impeccable, and that was because he'd thought it all out to the smallest detail. Only he hadn't expected someone new to enter the game. The stranger looked like a loser, but then, against all odds, he'd emerged victorious. The viscount couldn't wrap his mind around it.

"A healer...healer!" he moaned, and yelled, "It can't be!"

It was especially discouraging to lose to a pathetic healer. Healers weren't fighters! No! Even those who were truly Gifted, they couldn't hurt a fly. None of them knew how to use weapons, and their Gift, well, they could only heal, right? In aristocratic circles, such a Gift was regarded as more of a curse, because healers would never be strong enough to lead a Family. But that little punk had tried to force him to apologize. That wasn't all, though. Here he, Viscount Snegirev, was driving himself home, and all because of the new head of the Bulatov Family. That was his driver who'd perished in the second duel.

"To think, I could've fought him, killed him..." Andrei Snegirev shook his head. But then again, that healer was a strong fighter! Who knew? As it was, had he fought the stranger, it would have damaged his own reputation, which had anyway taken quite a hit. Anyway, he'd thought that his servant could finish the kid off. In that case, the Bulatov Family would've been humiliated.

"Look where you're going, bitch!" he snarled at a woman pushing a baby stroller, who jumped out of his way just in time. She stared aghast at him as he sped away -- he'd barreled right through a red light.

"Hello! Makar! You bastard, why aren't you

picking up?" he muttered into the phone. "Why didn't I find out about the attack from you? Huh? Rot in hell, creature! Got it?"

A continuous stream of abuse and threats poured from his mouth, but the man on the other end of the line simply remained silent as he listened to his master.

"Sir, the attack happened only three hours ago," the servant answered after waiting for the viscount to finish yelling. "But we have already sent a team of fighters out, and they'll deal with the situation."

"What kind of f*cking team are you talking about? Do you know the forces he used to friggin' capture the castle to start with?" the viscount roared, and again a stream of abuse rained down on the servant.

"Um...Hmmmm..." the servant sounded cowed, and hemmed and hawed some more. "The castle?" he eked out in a falsetto. "I was talking about the village of Zaitsevka..." he faltered, and commenced to clearing his throat.

"Aaaarrgh!!!" Andrei could no longer contain himself, and he started smashing whatever was at hand in an impotent rage. He then grabbed the phone again, and wanted to break it too, but he changed his mind. "Call the mercenaries! I want them ready in half an hour! UNDERSTOOD?!" he yelled into the phone, and the stuttering servant responded, "A-a-as you wish, mast-t-ter!"

CHAPTER 3

I WALKED UP BEHIND VICTORIA, who was in a heated discussion with her servant. She didn't notice me, even, and I could have listened in, but I didn't. I instead was focused on catching what others were saying. I wanted to hear the chatter about me, and also the gossip about the Bulatov Family, in general. How astonished everyone was that a new figure had entered the scene — a successor to old Count Bulatov. I'd certainly surprised them. But of course. How could it be otherwise? It's not like this kind of thing was a common occurrence. Rather, with lesser aristocrats, it was more likely to happen, but not when it came to a count's Family! As I stood there, the countess's servant alerted her to my presence, and alarmed, she looked around.

“Good evening,” I smiled. She said nothing,

and simply stared at me in disbelief and alarm. I, too, was at a loss for words.

"Good evening..." Victoria said hesitantly then. "I take it we're going to have a conversation?"

"Yes, a conversation is certainly in order," I nodded. "But why does it have to happen now? Would you like to dance? I've been too busy to relax in recent days. I assume that you've been occupied, as well?"

Victoria smiled rather sadly at that, and then, after a pause, she extended her hand to me.

I immediately took it, and felt... Ohhh... necrotics. And not weak. All this time the lady looked at me intently, trying to discern my expression. Was she now testing my feelings about her being a necromancer? Ha, no worries. For me, those with such a Gift were almost relatives.

However, I was surprised. Where did Gregory Bulatov get a daughter whose Gift was necromancy? Had his wife been a necromancer, and such a strong one as to pass the Gift on to her daughter? I note here that necromancers had a hard time finding mates. Both in my world, and here, it was the same when it came to necrotics. Many were repelled by this Gift, especially those who have not encountered death. For hundreds of years, though, I'd lived side by side with the Grim Reaper. He was more my friend than he was an enemy.

Victoria was clearly surprised when, instead of disgust or fear, a smile appeared on my face. After that, we commenced to enjoying the evening.

Some were surprised to see us, while others took it all in stride. Whatever the case, the local aristocrats were, generally, a little wary of our Family. They kept away, while those who weren't local came up to us to congratulate us on our performance in the duels, and compliment me on my skill with the blade though I be a "mere" healer.

Again, the low expectations of healers here. Why? It's like even a crippled commoner was expected to best a strong healer in combat. That's what I gleaned from what I heard that evening.

The countess was rather thoughtful all evening, but a couple of times, whatever she was thinking caused her to smile. I could tell she was eager to talk, but something was holding her back. She was excited about something, but nervous, as well. Meanwhile, her servant stood aside and beamed with happiness as he looked at us.

"Oh! Bulatov!" Having finished dancing, we had gravitated to a table with hors d'oeuvres. There we encountered Count Cherepanov. By then he'd probably downed his umpteenth glass of wine, and had been chatting with a couple of pretty young ladies. When he saw us, though, he came right over. "Let's have a drink then!" he said, producing another glass of wine from nowhere. Then he noticed Victoria, and fished out another one for her.

"I have to refuse," the girl smiled, but I accepted a glass. Oh! Finally, decent wine. Since arriving in this world, I'd come across nothing but a pale imitation of it. Fortunately, this wasn't universal. You just had to know where to go.

Of course, this wine was a far cry from the fruit of the vine in the distant Balian Kingdom, but it was like nectar compared to what I'd sampled in the port district. Looks like I had some spending to do. I needed not only books, but supplies for the castle's wine cellar, as well. Actually, I could consume a lot of wine, since, as a healer, one of the most basic of skills was that of cleansing alcohol from the blood stream.

Cherepanov and I chatted for quite awhile. He was clueless about the status of the Bulatovs here. He'd traveled to Archangelsk to oversee his father's production and transport company, provide security, supervise the process, and so on. Judging by how much he was imbibing at the local balls, he didn't need to spend too much time at his duties. Or maybe nobody wanted to tangle with a strong Family from the capital.

The ball eventually started winding down, and the guests began heading towards the exit. In fact, we were among to first to leave. Our car was already waiting for us near the exit, which surprised Victoria. She'd been one of the few to arrive by taxi, so she was pleasantly surprised to see the posh SUV. I smiled and shrugged, and opened the back door for her, and then slid in beside her.

"Hmmm...Makar Petrovich," the countess's servant extended his hand to Timothy as he slid into the "shotgun" seat.

"Timothy Valentinovich," he responded as

they briefly shook hands. And off we went, heading for the castle.

Victoria kept sneaking glances at me, but was in no hurry to talk. I, too, wasn't in a hurry. I wanted to get back to the castle first, and then have a real conversation in peace and quiet. I'm sure the countess was full of questions. As for myself, I felt like I had a good handle on things.

"The springs are creaking..." Makar noted, if only to break the silence. "Front right."

"Those are the torsion bars," growled Timothy

"Ah, yes, torsion bars..." repeated Victoria's servant, realizing his conversation starter was a non-starter.

Meanwhile, I admired the views outside the window, even as I cast occasional glances at Victoria. I guess I could've tried to make small talk with her, but besides asking her how she was, I couldn't think of much to say. And so silence reigned in the car as we anticipated arriving at the castle. In fact, I pulled out my phone to pass the time. I checked out the latest news, read up on the Cherepanovs, and was surprised that such a powerhouse of a Family was even out here in the hinterlands.

We finally arrived at the castle. Once we pulled up, almost all of our guys ran out and lined up. As we exited the car, they stared first at me, and then at the countess. They didn't know who to greet first. I was the head of the Family, and they owed me a lot, but then, Victoria was the one they knew the best. The countess, meanwhile, froze in surprise. I'd forgotten to mention that I'd brought some of her guards back. And I'd cured them, as well.

The countess well remembered the shape these guys had been in, as she'd been paying for their treatment. Each of these men was very dear to her, and right then she looked like she was ready to cry. She'd known some of them since she was a child. For almost a minute, we all stood there, silently looking at each other. Valery, the commander, looked at me questioningly, and as soon as I nodded at the girl, he immediately broke into a smile.

"Attention!" barked the commander, and the entire formation fell in. Everybody struggled to hide their smiles as Valery launched into a report. "Countess Bulatov, we have demolished the enemy occupiers. The castle is clear, and we are at your service!"

I still wasn't up on the protocol amongst the aristocracy. No time to read up on it yet. But the resounding cry of "Hurrah!" uttered three times by the recovering castle guards sounded like it could finally bring down the shaky walls of this castle. And curiously, for whatever reason the commander neglected to mention that I'd been the one who'd done the heavy lifting in recapturing the castle. No big deal, though. Nope. These were great men, and deserved the admiration of the countess, who still looked like she was about to burst into tears. She had great composure, though. Even after finding out her father was dead, she'd kept it together.

"Let's go inside, Victoria," I said, indicating the door, and inside we went, where, miraculously, a fire still burned in the hearth. I guess someone had kept it going. Fire was always calming, making even the darkest room cozier.

I recalled a dark magician I knew in my old world who'd gone totally bonkers. He built a black castle, corralled some slaves to serve there, and ruled over his little fiefdom like a dictator. At that time my brother, the king, was not yet married, and was still a decent ruler. He came to me and asked me to help deal with the problem. I never refused my brother, plus I was intrigued by the crazy dark magician. He thought he was the almighty, and that he could build his own Evil Empire. He'd been doing whatever he wanted, forcing his henchmen to plunder the surrounding villages, and in this way gradually expanding his influence. In the end, we brightened up his castle once we set it on fire. Ah, yes, fire. It brought peace, really, to even the darkest, most depressing spaces.

"Well, what comes next?" Victoria's voice pulled me out of my reveries. I wondered what it looked like from the outside when I sat like this smiling as I gazed at the fire.

"Basically, it's business as usual," I shrugged, spread out in an armchair with an imperturbable look.

"No," the girl shook her head, "By the will of my father, you are now the head of the Bulatov

Family! But this is also *my* Family, I am a Bulatov by birth...”

“Are you afraid that I will take your Family for myself and drive you away?” I laughed. Now I got what was troubling her.

“I don’t know your motives,” she looked serious. “Maybe your plan is to sell the Family, or you could even be colluding with Snegirev. Healers aren't like you. Healers don’t fight, giving it their all, and yet I saw it with my own eyes.”

“In cahoots with that piece of shit?” I was taken aback. “And why would I want to sell the Family? Do you think I need money?”

I actually had to regulate my breathing a bit, calm down. Victoria looked at me rather angrily then. Hmm...Maybe I ought to tell her about myself.

“You’ve seen what I can do...And I don't have difficulty procuring funds. Tell me, can your healers bring a person out of a coma and put him back on his feet in the span of a day?”

“What do you mean, “our healers?” she said as the truth dawned on her. “You’re...”

“Yes, I’m from another world!” I nodded, “Are you surprised?”

“It can’t be,” she shook her head in disbelief. “We understand each other. If you were an offworlder, we’d be speaking in an alien tongue. Come up with a plausible story, please.”

She actually thought that I must be joking.

“No, I’m not from an Interface!” I exclaimed, realizing what she was thinking. Again, I had to breathe in and out and start all over again. “I am Archmagister Mikhail of Vernicia, son of Emperor Rekar of Vernicia, conqueror of three worlds, destroyer of Interfaces. It is worth noting that I am the first to reach the level of Archmagister before attaining the age of two hundred. And I arrived here of my own free will, having completed the ancient soul transfer ritual. And no, I didn’t choose this world!,” I exclaimed, realizing what she was thinking.

And then I explained to her why I’d come here, to her world. About how my brother went to war against me, wanting to eliminate one he saw as a contender to his throne.

This, despite the fact I wasn't even vying for it! The last thing I wanted was the crown, as it was truly such a pain in the butt to rule over people. There were far more interesting ways to occupy time in my world. Such as meditating, for example, or drinking expensive alcohol. And then there were women. Really, I lacked the lust for power, and everyone around me understood this — everyone but my brother’s new wife.

Before he got married, my brother was fully engaged in the affairs of the kingdom, and everybody was happy. But as soon as he fell in love...He was a fairly strong mage and she was his equal in this, but still, they understood that I was far stronger than them. I don't even want to recall what happened next, because I’d once vowed to my father that I would help my brother to the best of my ability, and thus, I didn’t wield my powers against him. I simply initiated the soul transfer ritual and found myself in this world. Initially, all I'd wanted was to avoid raising a hand against my brother, but now I was rather pleased with my lot.

"I have to say that this world is quite interesting. And to make settling in here more convenient, I agreed to your father's offer to take over the Family," I said, shrugging as I wound up my tale. "Actually, that's all there is to it. I have no reason to take your Family away from you. And what would I gain, anyway? Your servant?" I chuckled as I looked at old man Makar. He'd quietly tapped at the door, bringing us two cups of tea and some cookies. "Or this rundown castle?" I nodded at the shabby walls of the main hall. "Or maybe a status in society lower than the floorboards?"

I didn't refuse the refreshments. Finally, some tea worth savoring! I had to ask Makar if he knew how to make delicious coffee. I munched on the cookies, and looked at the countess, who was still digesting everything I'd told her. She seemed to believe me, because I was quite convincing and had explained everything in detail. It's not like I could fabricate it all. Moreover, I had a lot of evidence to support what I'd said. There was a reason I'd worked at acquiring strength before showing up on her doorstep.

"Okay. I see...But what should I do?" she said uncertainly. "I can't leave, because this is my castle, and..."

Strange... Why would I want her to leave?

"I don't see why you think you have to leave." I raised one eyebrow questioningly. "I agreed with your father that I would look after you."

"I don't need to be looked after. I myself am..." Victoria sounded heated, but just then I burst out laughing.

"Yes, I see how it's going for you!" I shook my head. "Okay, here's the thing. I promise you that I will not force you to marry anyone. You don't even have to worry about this." In response, Victoria sighed imperceptibly. "As soon as the war is over and the Family is secure, you can do what you want. I'm ready to leave if this is what you want. It doesn't matter to me. By then, I'll have a better understanding of this world, and I'll know how to help you, and also myself. Maybe I'll even gain some status through marriage if there's a worthy girl able to melt my heart." I was joking when I said that, but she didn't pick up on that.

"Aha, right!" she grinned. "The Bulatovs have been at war for twelve years. We can't seem to end it."

"Well, how to tell you...It seemed almost over before I showed up." I said and shrugged. What more was there to say, really? I'd spilled my guts, so to speak, and she just needed to process it all. I'd even shared my plans with her. I had no reason whatsoever to force her to do anything. If she didn't like me much, then I'll keep my word, and leave. I'd study other countries and technologies.

True, I didn't clue her in on the fact that the local Interfaces were harbingers. The real battle would be in a few years or so. But yes, it was inevitable, and times would be tough for everyone. We'd gone through this more than once in my old world, so I knew full well what I was talking about. There will be bloody battles, there will be armies of thousands, all this will happen—these Interfaces are harbingers.

And with that, our conversation ended. The countess was equipped with all she needed to know, including that nobody was going to kick her out. She also knew I wasn't going to take advantage of her Family, or in any way damage it.

As it was late by now, I suggested that she go to her chambers, which was the only suite of rooms in normal condition in this castle. The rest had been ransacked by the mercenaries. She nodded in agreement and, taking her servant, headed off into the recesses of the castle, and I remained in the big drawing room by the fireplace. I decided to just sleep on the sofa there.

That was the plan, anyway. But as luck would have it, as soon as I dozed off, the heartbeat runes were activated, making me jerk awake. It was as if someone was appearing right above me, and this someone was quite small. But as soon as I woke up, the heartbeat immediately disappeared.

"Co-o-ooo!"

"What the hell is that?" I jumped, startled. Really, over the last half hour, I'd even made adjustments to the runes so that every little thing no longer triggered them. But even that didn't help. The strange guest would wake me up and disappear again.

Was it a ghost, or what? No, ghosts didn't have heartbeats, and I clearly sensed one right under the ceiling. Actually, the ceilings here were high, but you could reach them via the stairs. The drawing room was designed for entertaining guests and there were two levels to it.

As soon as the sound disappeared, and I no longer felt life under the ceiling, I was finally able to plunge into the long-awaited slumber.

Co-o-ooo!

I leaped out of bed and rushed up the creaky steps, tracking the source of the heartbeat. But as soon as I got closer, it simply disappeared... Well, that's okay, I can wait right here! I sat down right where the sound had come from before. Once the creature appeared again, I planned on grabbing it.

"Co-o-ooo!"

I just sighed. I didn't know what this thing was, but it was clearly making fun of me. This time the sounds were coming from somewhere down below.

I failed to catch the creature, so I plunged into meditation and again set about configuring my runes. So... Now small animals like birds or mice would no longer wake me up. Also, when Victoria's guards approached, that wouldn't awaken me, either. Easy-peasy. That was done.

Now all I had to do was turn off my hearing, leaving only my sense of touch. If anyone or anything touched me, I'd immediately feel it. But if someone were to come into the room and wander around, that wouldn't awaken me. And if anyone not from the list of trusted persons approached the castle, I would immediately awaken and then I'd explain to them why they were not welcome here without an invitation. With these thoughts I fell into a long-awaited slumber. And after turning around a little, I dimmed my perception of light, because dawn was already breaking outside the window.

* * *

The chambers of Countess Bulatov

As soon as she retired to her room, Victoria could not hold back her tears. She cried until the morning, unable to stop, but as soon as the sun appeared over the horizon, she pulled herself together. This was no time to feel sorry for herself. It was right to mourn the death of her father, but the tears were just a tribute to memory, and Victoria knew that she needed to be strong. She also realized that she was no longer alone. Her father had found a worthy successor, and she no longer doubted this.

Victoria believed Mikhail's words, and was even surprised at how many secrets he immediately revealed to her. The girl highly appreciated his trust. And she had no doubt that he wasn't making anything up. After all, none of the healers in her world had such powers. He'd healed the near-dead, restoring their health in a matter of days. Victoria had seen the shape Valery, the commander of her guard, had been in, and now he was bursting with health, with no trace of the old scars left on his face.

Right, and her father wouldn't give the Family to just anybody, and that meant all was as it should be. Even if she still for whatever reason doubted what the new head of the Family had told her, it was impossible for her to doubt the will of her father. After all, she so respected his memory. Even if there were still some questions deep down inside her, she wanted to believe all this was real. That fact is, if she wanted to be honest with herself, she'd been losing this war.

And something else. Mikhail hadn't cast her out of this, the only decent suite in the entire castle. Instead, he'd gone off to sleep in the rather dreary drawing room by the fireplace. He was trained in manners, courteous, and immediately told that he would not force her to do anything, although he had the right to do whatever he wanted.

Victoria cleaned herself up, left the room and headed downstairs to the drawing room. Mikhail was still sleeping, and did not even wake up when she deliberately closed the door loudly. So the girl approached the sleeping man and studied him carefully for some time. Then, sighing, she adjusted his blankets.

"I will trust your choice, Papa," she said to herself, and righted a blanket that had slipped off the new count.

His "choice," that's right. Victoria knew that

this agreement on the transfer of the Family meant that they were actually engaged, although she realized that Mikhail was unaware of this. So she decided not to mention it to him quite yet. She stood over him for awhile, and then she left, and Mikhail's eyes snapped open.

* * *

Okay, at least I slept for three hours, and that was good. I woke up from someone touching me, but I didn't show it. It was Victoria, fussing around with my blankets. I immediately turned on all my senses, but she just stood there, silent, lost in thought. Then she quietly left. Well, in any case, she certainly had a lot to think about. And I had things to do. So I immediately got up, dressed and went to explore the castle in the light of day.

Yes, there was a lot of junk in this place. Busted up furniture, glass from broken windows, and other debris. But before telling the guards to take it all outside and burn it, I decided to test their combat effectiveness. Yes, they'd gone through combat already back in the village, but I needed to ascertain their strengths and weaknesses. By now, almost all of the wounded were already on their feet -- at least, the ones who had legs were on their feet. There were men still in the ward we'd set up for the sick, and were now eating the food supplies we'd found in the trucks we'd retaken. They needed to eat to regrow new limbs. The process is slow and impossible for the inhabitants of this world. And so for now I didn't reveal it — they needed to get back to good health first.

"Valery, call everyone to formation," I ordered the commander, and I headed for the castle courtyard.

"Everyone? The sentries, too?" he asked.

"Everyone who is free now, and then switch them out."

He roused everybody, and in about five minutes most of the men were standing before me. Some were still on duty, because, after all, we could fall under attack at any moment, although I'd sense it if anyone was to approach, but the sentries would spot them first.

Even Victoria showed up. She looked with curiosity at what we were doing and was very surprised at how quickly the wounded had recovered. Well, there were greater surprises in store for her.

First, I had them run as I monitored their performance. I noticed there'd been some backsliding during their lag time, but nothing that couldn't be dealt with. Outside of the treatment sessions, the guys themselves needed to put in a lot of effort, and do some physical therapy on their own, but no one minded this. Then I checked their combat training, and... How to say? They all knew how to shoot, much better than I did, but otherwise, there was room for improvement. They were strong in close combat, but their technique was wanting, and so it made sense to find a specialist to provide training. Ideally, a wounded or crippled specialist, which shouldn't be too hard. What with how weak the local healers were, there must be plenty of cripples to choose from.

For two hours I ran the guards ragged, and then I told them to clear the garbage out of the castle. And burn it all. Yes, it's true that their only responsibilities were to provide security, but we didn't have any servants to carry out such work. For now, they'd have to do it.

Speaking of servants...

"Victoria," I approached the countess. She didn't mind my putting the guards through drills and such, but she also didn't know what it was all about. "We need to find servants..."

"Servants..." the countess smiled wryly. "That won't be easy. Given our reputation no one wants to work here."

I just laughed.

"Believe me, they'll want to! They'll be lining up outside even."

"Do we have the money to hire them?" she asked, though it was an awkward question.

"Money?" I thought, and made some calculations. "I'll find the money...I'll take care of it."

* * *

Arkhangelsk estate of the Cherepanovs
Early morning

“Oh-h...” Nikolai Cherepanov opened his eyes with difficulty and rolled out of bed, trying not to wake up the two beauties slumbering beside him.

He went to the toilet, washed his face, and immediately headed to the bar full of the finest alcohol. Before his eyes were fully open, he’d grabbed a bottle with one hand, and a corkscrew with the other. All that was left to do was uncork it and kiss the neck, but for some reason, he froze.

“What the hell...” he said. Then he put the bottle down. He bent over and even jumped up and down a little. And he was even more astonished. “Yes, I feel good...how is that?”

What surprised him was that he did, in fact, feel just fine. As long as he could remember, he'd been constantly plagued by pain. In his early childhood, he’d had the misfortune to be near a strong Interface right in the middle of the city. Some powerful mages and steel-clad fighters poured out of the portals and a real massacre ensued. He finished off one strong enemy, but many wounds were inflicted on him in the process. His father threw money at the problem, bought a slew of restorative artifacts, and hired the best healers. They saved his life, but due to the old injuries, he was always in pain. It wasn't sharp pain, but a constant ache that over the course of the day would wear him out. Booze, it turned out, was the best way to dull the pain. And so that is why Nikolai was always reaching for the bottle, and was sober only when necessary. Now, however, this constant pain that was so much a part of him was gone. He was sober, yet felt great. But how? All of the doctors and healers had agreed that his condition was incurable, and he'd have to live with it for the rest of his days.

"What the...? Does this mean...? Should I stop drinking now?" Cherepanov muttered in surprise. He momentarily froze, and then, waving his hand he said, "No, what nonsense!" And he popped the cork.

CHAPTER 4

I CAN SAY THAT VICTORIA got the hang of things pretty quickly. I hadn't expected her to jump into whipping the guards into shape, but she did. I even think she enjoyed it. I learned more about the Family from her demeanor and enthusiasm, and, yes, we made great strides with the men. And once I really got down to it, well, the poor guys, they had no idea what they were in store for. I planned on making real warriors out of them.

We gave them a break for lunch, and I even treated them to a little energy. But once lunch was over, we went at it again. Actually, that's when the countess joined us. She'd changed into a sportier outfit, and even warmed up a little with everyone else.

After the warm-up, I planned on checking out their hand-to-hand combat skills. Yes, there was a time when I, too, engaged in that kind of thing. But even my trainer back in the day said that hand-to-hand combat was invented exclusively for the stupid. What he meant was that for you to end up in hand-to-hand combat you must lose all your weapons, be caught still fighting after expending all of your energy, and then find that you can't, say, even pick up a rock from the ground with which to whack your adversary over the head. To some extent he was right, but the fact is, you should always expect the unexpected, and so yes, you should know how to fight with no weapons on hand.

"Oh no!" I heard a muffled cry and stopped fighting. I turned and saw Victoria looking chagrinned at her sparring partner, who was curled in a fetal position on the ground. I had to help him, as she'd really dealt him a serious blow. She knew it too, by how scared she looked, with her hands over her mouth.

"Mistress..." the guard croaked as soon as I gave him the opportunity to breathe again. "You're much stronger now."

"Forgive me, Vlad!" she exclaimed. "We last fought, what, some six months ago?"

"Yes, m'lady!"

Miscalculating her strength, Victoria had walloped him in the ribs. Fortunately, she hadn't employed her Gift. Had we been using magic in this training session, well, I'd have to constantly dole out treatments. After that, Victoria decided not to participate in sparring anymore. She just stood and watched. I warmed up a little more, and as soon as the last guardsman was gasping on the ground, I announced the end of the day's session. Really, it had gone pretty well, all in all.

"The training is over..." I said, and heard many relieved sighs. "Now let's all get down to cleaning! I promise you that tomorrow you won't be feeling any aches and pains!" I added a spoonful of honey to the ointment. For me it's a piece of cake removing acid from muscles and restoring micro-damage. Anyway it was necessary, or else tomorrow the guardsmen would be about as useful as limp rags.

As for myself, well, I decided to help out with the chores. On the one hand, cleaning is clearly not an activity for an Archmagister, but I didn't see it like that. My new home should be clean and tidy. I could at least burn the busted-up furniture.

But I underestimated how neglected this castle was. We were busy almost until the evening, and Victoria, along with the guards, carried out the trash, heaping it in piles. But our efforts were not enough. Yes, the inside of the castle was now a lot tidier and cleaner, but it was still far from ideal. The mercenaries broke everything they could, as if they'd been on a mission. And there were many other rooms that looked like they'd been the sites of old fights.

But yeah...I'd already tasked Victoria with finding some servants, so it was only a matter of time and money. Once I had the funds lined up, Victoria could hire an army of cleaners for this place.

By the way, about finances. I sat down by the fireplace and took out my phone, and immediately began reading the Family mail. There were a lot of messages, and many of them were not very pleasant. Either the bank confiscated some of our lands for debts, or some Family declared the right to our property by forceful seizure.

I knew things were bad for the Bulatov Family, but I didn't know they were this bad. But all of these dealings were from the last month. The more deeply I dug into things, the more unpleasant the news.

As I delved into the Family business, I asked Victoria if there were any other documents I should see. She sighed heavily and went to her room, and soon returned with a whole stack of papers. This whole pile crashed onto the coffee table, causing it to creak pitifully, as if it wanted to join those heaps of broken furniture in the yard. The table hung in there, though! Alright! Apparently, the tree from which this table was made was worthy, indeed. A druin tree. A hearty tree like that could not be destroyed. But the druin trees were also very touchy — especially if you were to bust a branch off in the forest.

About a century ago, I had the misfortune to meet some of them. I then spent around two years uprooting them from my landscaped grounds. They'd taken over and had no intention of leaving. They crowded out my apple trees and peach grove, not to mention the vineyards. That is when I called the most powerful death mage. There was a time we didn't get along very well, and this is why he charged me a fabulous sum to rid me of my tree problem. I had no choice but to pay it, and then he destroyed all the druin trees. But that was only how it seemed. The druins shifted their malice onto the mage, and so after they were gone from my garden, they took up residence at his house. To the best of my knowledge, the poor guy was still struggling with these immortal trees. How ironic for a mage who specializes in death. He'd by now changed where he lived several times, and yet, each time, as if overnight, the trees moved with him.

Back to the documents that Victoria kindly handed over to me, why was she standing there smiling? Reading the first piece of paper I came across, I realized that the countess was simply gloating. In that look on her face you could read only one thing: "Well, now do you understand what you got yourself into?"

Yes, in fact I did understand it! No need to openly smirk. But in reality, I wasn't at all upset. Yes, we had a lot of debts, and most of our property was lost during the last war. And currently they were trying to completely and irrevocably destroy the Bulatovs. So what? That made it even more interesting! And I smiled, while Victoria now frowned. She probably thought that I was crazy.

After about two hours I put aside a hefty stack of papers and said "Okay, as I understand it, this is a list of what was taken from us. Well, in any case, we'll get it all back," I said with confidence as I met the girl's incredulous eyes. Really, how much more proof did she need? I'd told her my life story already, but she still didn't understand who I was. "And this...it's what we still have?" even I felt a little sad at this point. Because what "this" was comprised a single sheet of paper on the table.

I mean, I was a count! That's the good news. And I had territory. That's a nice thing, too. True, it was completely empty. Which wasn't so very nice. A smattering of villages, uncultivated lands and, you could say, that's it! But the dying count said that his Family had at its disposal several factories, a quarry, production facilities, and even real estate for rent. Perhaps that was all in his head, though. And over those six months in which he lay in prison, well, all of the vermin-like aristocrats got their greedy little hands on everything. The Family holdings had literally been parceled out.

"Vika, can I ask you something?" I'd been poring over the accounts covering the most recent months, and I couldn't understand where the additional expenses came from. It seemed like I had taken everything into account, but a large hole in the budget literally screamed that this was not the case. "Look, this figure here. Where are these funds?" I pointed at the spreadsheet, and she began to carefully run her eyes over the figures.

"Ah, that's a loan payment," she said. "Five months ago I took it out to sow the fields," she said.

“In the autumn?” I raised an eyebrow questioningly. I'm no farming expert, but nothing seems to grow under the snow. Maybe they have snow potatoes? Mmmm... I definitely wouldn’t refuse some right now.

“As soon as the snow melts, the winter crop will begin to grow,” the countess patiently explained to me. “True, it no longer matters.”

“Ummm, say what?” I didn’t understand. How was it that it didn't matter? The money has been spent, which means the crops will need to be harvested.

“As soon as I planted the crops, Baron Yarovitsyn took these lands from me. And there was nothing I could do,” she shrugged. “You see, that was the day Viscount Snegirev attacked the castle again, and I had to urgently withdraw the guard from those lands.”

“So then, this Yarovitsyn will line his pockets at our expense in the spring?” Victoria just nodded in response.

Ya-ro-vi-tsyn. Yes, I memorized his name! That meant that he was second in line, after Snegirev. I decided I should buy a notebook and write down names, or else I wouldn't remember them all. Actually, better still, I should kill my enemies so that I could then just forget about them. Yes, that made the most sense.

Recently, this particular baron had stopped his attacks, as had many others. According to Victoria, this was all one big conspiracy. It was on

Snegirev the other day to deal the final blow to the Family. And so none of the others interfered, because they knew what was going on and that he was playing the main role.

Someone was behind all this, and I definitely needed to find out who it was. And then I smiled.

"Why do you smile like that all the time?" Victoria seemed indignant. "Don't you see how dire our straits are now? We need 30,000 rubles to pay back that loan! I don't have that kind of money, and we have to pay up in three days! I have no idea how we're going to find that kind of money in time."

I just laughed and laughed. Then, calming down, I told her why I was so chill about all this.

"I've only been here one day, and already I owe a debt to someone. And I am sure it's not the only one," I said. To this, Victoria smiled quizzically, as if to ask, "please explain."

"Okay," I said, "Don't worry. I'll take care of this. You can go now. I'll call you if I need you," I said, and again dove into the paperwork. Victoria nodded and headed towards the door.

"C-o-o-ooo!" From somewhere above me I heard that same vile creature that had interrupted my sleep last night. I then heard some wings flapping, but still couldn't see it.

"What the hell is that?" I got up and began examining the ceiling. But to no avail. The insidious creature was excellent at hiding. For whatever reason I couldn't even feel its heartbeat.

"Um, that is..." Victoria froze in the doorway

and looked at me in bewilderment. "That's a pigeon."

"Is it edible?" I asked, which took her aback. "Not that it matters. Can you help me?"

"With what? Getting rid of the pigeon? You need a sixth-rank necromancer to deal with a harmless bird?" she laughed. What's wrong with that? In real life I would not call this creature harmless. We still had to find the vile beastie. It would fly at me when I least expected it, and interrupt when I was in the midst of replenishing my strength. And that sound it made, I could hear it in my dreams."

"Sixth rank..." I said thoughtfully. "So you can't conjure up a necrotic thunderstorm? For this, I think, you need to have attained the first rank, or more..."

"We have nothing above the first rank. The first is the highest, and few around here have attained it," Victoria shook her head.

"Aha, right! Nothing higher, of course not" I chortled. "Okay, thank you, Victoria. I'll get back to working out what to do to restore our fortunes," I said, plopping back into the chair and again diving into the pile of papers on the table.

Indeed, there was a lot to deal with...First, though, I had to come up with the 30K payment for the Morzhov Family. Everybody knew that it was folly to trifle with moneylenders, especially the Morzhovs, who were notorious. I read the fine print listing all of the penalties that we'd face were we not to render payment in timely fashion. They'd take away our castle and all our property, and we needed to stay here. Of course, we could simply stand our ground and not let anyone into the castle. But there were laws about this kind of thing, and we'd be in the wrong. What we needed was to pay this debt off right away and be done with it.

But first, there was a hostile force I had to contend with. To this end, I got my phone out and typed "pigeon" into the browser, realizing I needed some help here. How could a simple bird cause me so much grief?

"Ah, I see..." I shook my head, realizing that I was right. This pigeon was indeed a stupid bird, and a common pest. "So then, is there no way for me to catch you?" I said, looking up at the ceiling. "Just keep on 'talking' to me..."

But the bird said nothing, and I sat there in the silence.

* * *

As Victoria left the room, she couldn't help but smile. It wasn't just because the pigeon issue was funny. Mikhail's words inspired hope and confidence in the future. Even though he was fully aware of the massive challenges facing the Bulatovs, not a shadow of doubt crossed his face. He was totally certain he could handle it all, but...

"Eh..." the girl sighed and headed to her room.

Maybe Mikhail did look like someone who knew how to get it all done. But even if every word he'd told her was the truth, just the same he couldn't come up with that kind of money in just three days. If only he was a gold mage rather than a healer, maybe. But gold mages were the stuff of legends, they were so rare. They could allegedly spin gold out of thin air using only their energy. But they'd all been executed a thousand years ago, as had anyone else who inherited that Gift.

Victoria froze for a couple of seconds, as if not daring to do something. But then, with a bitter smile, she pressed an inconspicuous ledge in one of the walls of her room. She had to exert some force, as the stone was reluctant to budge. But then the mechanism clicked, and with a rumble, the wall first moved back a little and then slid to the side, revealing a small inner chamber. Inside were many dusty paintings, and on the wall hung a sword that once belonged to the head of the Bulatov Family.

It was here that the countess had hidden all of the treasures that she could save. These were items of value to her personally, as well as to the Family as a whole. In addition to paintings depicting former heads and members of the Family, there were also objects that were reminiscent of the past. Mercenaries would see these items as trash, but to Victoria, they held great value. Her mother's favorite dress, that plush cat that was her favorite toy as a child. Really, over time she'd come to realize that to throw these special toys and personal articles out meant discarding memories.

Again she sighed, and then walked over to the far corner of the chamber where a massive safe was hidden behind a mountain of things. To open it, she needed her Family ring. Any other way of opening it was incredibly difficult, and would require bringing in specialists.

Victoria stood there pondering, and then, finally, she pressed her ring into the slot. In a couple of seconds, a small but heavy door clicked open. It didn't hold much, this safe, and inside was jewelry, mostly. Ancient, antique, historical pieces. One of them was a necklace made of black stones that seemed to absorb color. The necklace was her mother's, and seeing it, Victoria couldn't hold back her tears. As she pressed the necklace to her breast, they silently rolled down her cheeks.

"Forgive me, mama..." she whispered quietly, turning aside. "But I have no choice..."

This necklace was worth 100,000 rubles, but she'd get 70,000 at best were she to sell it. Victoria was mortified at the thought, but she'd already been shopping around the Internet to see what she could get for it. Still, she couldn't bear the thought of putting it up for sale. But now that there was a ray of hope for improving the Bulatov Family's situation, she realized that the time had come.

Mikhail impressed her, but she knew he wasn't able to get the funds together to pay off their debt so quickly. Anyway, that was her opinion. She felt like she had to do her part to help. So, wiping away her tears, she exited the chamber, and then, with a quiet hum, the massive wall slid back into place.

* * *

I sat at the table until nightfall, thinking. Sometimes the flapping of wings knocked me out of my thoughts, but I tried not to pay the slightest attention to the vile creature. Unlike the nasty seagulls, it didn't seem to have to shit, and for that I was grateful. But that constant "cooing," and the subterfuge, well, to hell with it. Once I got around to scattering some poisoned grains about, no more bird problem.

I had a lot of work to do. We needed money right away to resolve pressing issues. Okay. That much was clear, and the big picture of what we were facing had formed in my head. What this was a picture of was "shit creek," and we were in the proverbial canoe, without the proverbial paddle.

Well, as they say, solve each problem as it arose. But what happens when you're facing a lot of them all at once? Enough, though. I was simply venting. The situation wasn't actually all that bad. I was telling Victoria the truth when I said that making money was easy for me. I could tell that she didn't believe me, but I had no doubt she would before too long. After all, I'd been totally candid with her.

I'd been around in existence for a long, long time, and so I knew all about making money. In short, to make money in the shortest possible time, there were three options. These included prostitution, robbery, or acquiring trophies. I wasn't into either of the first two, but I could set about picking up some trophies, and that's what I'd probably do.

But actually, I'd left something out. There was one more option for making fast money. But it applied only to this world, and also wasn't something I engaged in.

What this was, if I am to believe what I read on the Internet, was organ transplants. As the healers here didn't know how to restore organs, the aristocrats in need would buy them from commoners. Of course, this was rife with issues that must be dealt with. The donor had to be selected with great care, as both their physical characteristics and energies had to be compatible.

Theoretically, I could grow an extra kidney a day. The heart, well, not worth the trouble since it didn't seem these were subject to transplant here. I could see why, as they contained too many magical channels. No way could the locals deal with the complexity.

So, yes, let's focus on trophies instead. Yes, although kidneys were selling for 10K rubles, I'd essentially be serving as an incubator. Also, even more important, I might easily slip up and reveal my impressive healing abilities. For the time being I didn't want this. My plan was to let them know about my full abilities later, when I was secure enough in this world.

Picking up trophies was, in fact, an honest way to make some money. When you robbed people, you inflicted harm on innocents who generally didn't deserve it. Trophies were a different matter. Anything goes as far as the Interfaces went. They were out to kill you, and you were out to kill them. It was all done by mutual agreement, essentially, where the winner takes all. And these offworlders, well, who asked them to show up? They'd come here of their own free will, after all. They deserved what they got.

I'd been able to find out some fun facts about Arkhangelsk. Generally speaking, portals opened up randomly, but there were three locales where they occurred far more regularly.

In the industrial district, for example, there were portals opening up almost every day. Really, if the offworlders were doing this on purpose, then I didn't understand their motivation at all. Every industrial complex had its own security, as was the case wherever big money was involved. Thus, the offworlders would often emerge only to be gunned down in seconds. Sometimes, security personnel would even go through the portals to explain to the offworlders why they were better off not attacking the factories. And yet the offworlders continued their attacks.

Another area less rich in portals was located outside the city. The offworlders who landed here tended to be small groups of catchers that would find themselves right in the middle of endless forests. They didn't end up catching much of anything out there besides bullets.

But the hottest area for portal action was, in fact, the port district. It was a regular portal party there. They might not be major Interfaces, but you could count on two or three every night. They might also occur during daylight hours, although far less often. I myself can testify to this.

Having made up my mind what I would do that night, I summoned Georgy. It made more sense for me to go there by taxi, as my posh SUV would attract unwanted attention. After all, I'd stolen it from the big boss out there. No doubt he was looking for it, in fact. I didn't want to tangle with his gang of mafiosi tonight, as I was focused on picking up artifacts. Another good reason to have Georgy drive me was that it made sense to give Timothy some rest and relaxation time. He and Marina, his granddaughter, still needed to settle in at the castle.

As I waited for Georgy, I conducted a little research on what it was that the offworlders were after, generally speaking. Maybe if I figured this out, I could use the information to my advantage. Most of all, they were into kidnapping children, and the younger the better. They snatched babies right from the hands of their mothers, and then they'd whoop out loud in delight as they dashed through the portals with them. But that wasn't the only thing. They would take essentially whatever wasn't nailed to the floor. Household items, weapons, equipment — whatever. All they sought was to get the stuff through the portal. That was the gist of it. Besides this, there was nothing else out there about the offworlders.

By now, Georgy had arrived, so I got ready

and headed out.

"Count Bulatov, Sir!" The guard at the door stood at attention.

"I'm off on business if anything comes up. I'll be gone all night," I said, nodding at him. Good to keep them up on my whereabouts.

He nodded in response, and opened the door for me. Then, I plopped down in the back seat of the car, and off we flew to the port district.

I didn't waste any time along the way. Instead of counting crows outside the window, I plunged into deep meditation and began improving my spatial anomaly locator. I wanted to make it more efficient, as right now it took too much energy to maintain it. So I added two new runes, and that did the trick. Now, it would work automatically without my having to focus on it. The Vegula rune would accumulate communication energy.

Really, I'm surprised they knew nothing about runes on this world. These are the basic building blocks of the magical language of inscription, and no, they're not very difficult to learn. Once learned, through trial and error, you could create new symbols and new combinations. Why not? You could then apply runes not only to your bones, but also to your soul and your flesh. And hey, you could put them on castle walls and so on. Like, weapons. Even tattoos, if executed correctly and injected with the right amount of energy, can be quite powerful, and at the same time provide a person with new opportunities.

But then, what was I talking about when their

maximum level topped out at first rank. In my old world, first rank meant the average level for a magister. Strong, solid, but still just a magister. Clearly the ranking system here applied to how developed the source was, rather than the ability to employ their Gift.

Anyway, I was just finishing inscribing a rune, and even managed to test it in action, when the car stopped.

“We’ve arrived!” Georgy turned around. “So when should I pick you up? I want to make sure I’m here on time.”

“Wait...” I closed my eyes and poured a little more mana into the chain of runes. And it worked! “Let us head a quarter mile to the north, and then we’ll be there.”

“A quarter mile,” he repeated. “That’s where the pedestrian path is...Okay, never mind!” He waved dismissively at his thought, and then there we were, near an Interface portal.

“Be in close touch, I don’t know how long I’ll be busy,” I told him and hurried out of the car.

The first Interface was right on time for me! I might be lucky, but then, as I drew nearer, I heard fighting going on.

What a shame! I wasn't the first to show up. Local official anti-portal fighters beat me to it. What are they called? ‘Troops for Managing Offworld Penetration’, that's what they were called. For whatever reason, some people made fun of that name. In any event, they were simply referred to as ‘The Penetrators.’

They were a branch of the anti-portal police, and indeed, their fighters were impressively strong. The portal opened, and, as usual, around twenty offworlder fighters poured out. Right behind them were twenty or so catchers who fanned out in different directions to gather as much as they could from this world. Even junk was valuable to them. But instead of successful looting and kidnapping, they were greeted with a long burst from a heavy-caliber reinforced machine gun. Protective artifacts burst like soap bubbles, and all this carnage took only a few minutes. I took part in it only as a spectator. It was a real pity that so many artifacts were being destroyed in vain.

And I could see why simple protective artifacts were hard to find. These were acquired only if the offworlder was killed by magic. And they only offered protection from physical attacks.

Anyway, then a small assault force entered the portal, while I wandered off. There was nothing to see here and, anyway, the rune script announced the opening of another portal less than a mile away.

Meanwhile, the streets filled up with people again. It was night, and buzzing with activity. But nobody bothered me. Perhaps my cloak played a role. I didn't wear the mask so as to avoid attracting unnecessary attention, but the soft aura of necrotics from my cloak no doubt surrounded me. And people subconsciously probably felt this, especially the weaker people.

As I walked along, I wondered how it came to be that the so-called Penetrators were able to show up at that last portal before I got there. It was as if they, too, could sense its presence. I had to find out how. Also, they usually didn't take notice of weak, small portals. Perhaps they were aided by some kind of artifact that senses only large spatial anomalies. My detector would pick up any signal within a radius of almost two kilometers.

Now, one such signal led me to the slums. I don't know what the offworlders wanted to find here. But there weren't very many of them. Just one warrior in cheap-looking armor, and two catchers. They were armed with blades, and also the standard hooks on ropes.

The portal had very recently opened, and the offworlders hadn't gotten very far. By the time I arrived, one of the catchers had just finished tying up a woman of about thirty years of age, maybe older, and the second was scouring the area. He broke into empty houses and piled all kinds of rubbish near the portal. Meanwhile, the warrior stood there, warily looking around. He spotted me first.

"Get him!" he barked, motioning toward me.

Really, how offensive. I was cut to the core, even. This warrior was, allegedly there to protect the catchers. Meanwhile, the catchers were supposed to kidnap defenseless citizens and drag them into the portal. That was how it was supposed to go down. So how did I qualify as a defenseless citizen? The reason I'd worn this cloak was so that the sword on my belt wouldn't be visible. Did this offworlder really think I was just a passerby?

Although they looked like homeless people, the catchers turned out to be professionals. I'm guessing that yes, in their world they have schools that taught how to properly capture prisoners. The hook whistled towards my leg, but I jumped a little to the side and grabbed the rope, immediately sending a good dose of energy along it.

"A-ah-ah!" screamed the catcher as the skin started peeling off of his palms. "Necromancer! Necromancer!"

Right, I get it. Necromancers can do this too, plus my costume smells like necrotics. Nobody was afraid of healers, so I might as well mess with them by passing myself off as a necromancer.

The other catcher was the smarter of the two, because he took to his heels and ran. Good try, anyway. I ripped the rope out of the hands of the first catcher, and sent the hook into the back of the second one. With one touch, he collapsed onto the ground writhing in convulsions. Weaklings. It was ridiculously easy for me to hit vulnerabilities in the body. I knew about these due to my diagnostic skills.

If someone, say, suffered from epilepsy, for example, I could provoke an attack just like that, virtually free of charge. It took very little energy, even if my victim possessed a strong Gift. As the second catcher was himself an epileptic, I'd taken advantage of it. The single warrior, though, was quite healthy. Bad teeth don't count, but too bad for him, it's quite difficult to win the battle when you have a vicious toothache. And if you had a sword charged with vital energy, it was quite easy to win one. In fact, the warrior didn't even bother to block my blow. He rushed to attack me, and completely relying on his protective artifact, tried to cut me down with his sword, without being distracted by my blows.

"Well, your bad," I said, shaking my head. "Did you not see what I did to your comrades?"

I was sitting on his dead body speaking to him. I didn't need to drain him, as my source now generated energy on its own. I merely took a little, but not enough to harm myself. Too much of other people's energy wasn't good for me. Fortunately, offworlder energy was more concentrated, and this was good as I didn't need as much. I channeled all of it toward developing my source.

As I sat there, I surveyed my surroundings. This was, indeed, a poor part of town. One dilapidated house after another, and the street itself was more like a narrow lane. Though the windows were dark, I could clearly feel the beating of several hearts. Might they have helped the woman? No, I don't think so. There they were, cowering in their huts, and I could see why. With no weapons or Gift, they wouldn't have stood a chance against the offworlders.

Now it was quiet, and a few people were peering at me through the cracks in their boarded-up windows. I assumed that as soon as I was gone, they'd come out to rummage through the junk here. Too bad for them I'd leave with all the trophies.

"Tfft?" a huge rat emerged from behind the trash heap. It stared at me and squeaked questioningly.

"Hmm...okay, you can have a bit of that ear. But no more," I said, pointing at a catcher, and the rat ran over to feast on the magic-infused meat. "Actually, that's cartilage," I observed.

I didn't let the critter eat too much, even though it tried. I had to give the rat a little kick to let it know the meal was over. I didn't want to see it get over-saturated with energy. The rat might morph into a toothy monster.

Next, I searched all the pockets of the three offworlders, and without even looking at what I'd scored, I threw everything into a bag. I'll see what my take was later. I did see that the warrior had two artifacts, one of which was protective, while the other allowed him to release a wave of power. I guess technically that would be protective, as well. It looked like a lighter and needed to be broken in half to activate it. It was disposable, but you could use it to keep back a throng of pursuers just long enough to make it back through the portal. But the warrior hadn't even activated it, as here it was in his pocket. That meant that he never saw me as a real threat. He paid for this.

"Can you manage?" I threw a knife toward the tied-up woman, and set about tossing the bodies through the portal. I didn't bother taking the warrior's armor, although it was worth some money. Time was of the essence now, because I sensed another portal opening. It wasn't far away, just a few hundred meters, but I had no time to lose.

"Why did you kill them?" the woman stunned me by asking. "I... maybe I wouldn't have minded. He had such strong, warm hands! And the way he touched me..."

Damn! That's it. Time for me to leave. Really, unreal! Anyway, I was in a hurry. She continued to complain about the lack of real men in her life right now. Me, I tried to put her out of my mind. Just let go of it, and don't let it trouble you anymore. Don't think about a woman so pathetic that being kidnapped and forced into sexual slavery seemed like a good alternative to what she had going on in her life. I didn't want to clue her in on the truth, which is that the way she looked, she'd probably end up in the mines. A deep, dark mine without a single ray of light. But that would be rude. In fact, it turned out the she herself had approached the offworlders. But whatever. We all had our problems, some worse than others.

I sprinted to the next portal, but was still a little late. There were many more offworlders exiting this one -- five warriors, one of whom was armed with a good crossbow, and the same number of catchers. They'd already captured a girl who looked to be about twenty years old, and were about to drag her into the portal. Maybe she wasn't the first, and I also saw a corpse. He'd been hacked to death by the warriors; he probably put up a fight. Judging by the clothes, he was just a simple passerby, one of the locals.

I had to jump into action. I did my diagnostics of the offworlders on the fly. And then...

Click!

Yes, I used up my new artifact. I was up against strong adversaries, and so I had to give it my best. I'd fished out the disposable artifact, broke it, and also reinforced it with a lot of my energy.

The shock wave caused the five warriors to fly back several meters, and then collapse on the ground. But that wasn't all, because I'd channeled energy into the blast on purpose, and the effect of doing so made itself felt.

"What, are you drunk?" said the one who was apparently the commander. This was all because a fighter had stood up and was shaky on his feet. But as soon as he, too, stood, he realized I'd done something. Yes, I'd cast a dizzy spell! It was all I could do on the fly, but it could be a big help.

As a catcher rushed at me, I attacked the warriors. Yes, they were dizzy, but they repelled my blows, and even tried to launch counterattacks. One warrior with a spear and shield was especially infuriating. I couldn't draw close to him because his comrades were covering him, and he could do me a lot of damage from afar.

Again, what a waste...I grabbed the shaft of his spear and jerked it towards me so that the warrior had to really grip it hard not to lose it. So then...My diagnosis of this guy was that he suffered from a complex lung disease in childhood. It's called pulmonary disease here, and they knew a lot about it in this world. Myself, I hadn't yet studied it much.

Theoretically, though, I could tweak the walls of the bronchi themselves and force them to produce more fluid. Then, he'd start choking and coughing. However, this would take time. I could instead provoke a bronchospasm, or play with the alveoli, that being the cells of the lungs that saturate the blood. Really, the options were plenty.

However, of more interest was that recently, this guy ate a lot of spicy food. So the sudden attack of diarrhea I settled on made him grab his stomach, which is when I pulled him close to me and plunged the sword into his eye. The results were perfect. Why reinvent the wheel when you have such a powerful spell in your arsenal? His ignoble death had a demoralizing effect on the other warriors, and I took advantage of this. Thus, by the time the catchers reached me...

"You're gonna die, offworld scum!" I heard a furious scream and heavy footsteps.

I took a swift look over my shoulder, and saw three big guys in striped sailor's shirts turning down our dark alley. Two held clubs in their hands, while the third was armed with a sword. They all looked at the offworlders with hatred.

The catcher closest to me lost focus for a second, for which he received a sword in the neck. Blood gushed out like a fountain, and the look of surprise on his face spoke volumes.

"Yes, my friend, artifacts don't always work," I answered his silent question as his eyes rolled back in his head.

Just then the portal flashed and two more catchers ran out. One was well-armed with a harpoon, while the second had the standard rope and hook. Right away they noticed the hefty sailors running up to us, and the one with the harpoon fired at them. But one of the big brutes intercepted it with his club. Then, although he'd lost his weapon, the catcher rushed at the hefty sailor, furiously screaming obscenities as he ran.

Meanwhile, I suddenly thought about that crossbow. Where was it?

Ah, there it was, awaiting me. The warrior with the crossbow was protected by melee fighters, but he wasn't able to target me. He simply couldn't aim right, no doubt because of my dizzy spell. And when you're dizzy, it's hard to hit a target with a crossbow. I leaped forward, and plunged my sword into his chest and drained some of his life energy.

Meanwhile, a battle ensued between the sailors and the two catchers. Essentially, they kept each other occupied, while I finished off the last of the offworlders. It was all a pretty simple affair. They would throw their hooks, which enabled me to channel magic through the ropes, which were an excellent conductor. Thus, all I had to do was catch the hook and do whatever manipulations to the catchers' bodies. The trick was in getting each catcher to clutch onto the rope even tighter rather than releasing it before I was done.

I didn't bother helping out the sailors. First, they didn't need it, and also, the battle was in full force over there, and were I to fly into the middle of it, I could get hit by so-called friendly fire. Actually, hard to say how "friendly" such fire would be. We were on the same side against the offworlders, but... Anyway, they were holding their own in a fierce fight. Clearly these were experienced fighters. In no time they dispatched the offworlders. One of sailors, after losing his weapon, swiftly picked up my spear and tossed it at one of the catchers. Then, he finished him off with his fists, pummeling him like a jackhammer so that the catcher was pulp. And so on. One sailor with a sword laughed at a catcher who was clutching a knife. He struck the catcher several times with the side of his blade, breaking his protective amulet, and then he plunged the tip of the sword into him.

And the last catcher, well, he didn't last long. The catcher flailed around with a knife and then his hook on a rope, but to no avail. A sailor clubbed him to death. His club was big and long and heavy. Forget about surviving for long when it came down on you.

Well done, guys! Kudos for not looking the other way when trouble struck. They heard the cries for help from the captive girl and heeded the call, fearless in the face of offworld danger. Even when two new offworlders emerged from the portal, they stood their ground. Now was the time to find out their standing with me — were these guys friend or foe?

"Offworld carrion!" spat a sailor at the defeated enemy, and he even kicked a corpse. "When will you all die..."

"No kidding. They keep on coming," nodded his comrade, tossing his club aside. "Look at that spear! Can I have it?" he asked.

"What do you mean? Why are you asking me?" he asked, surprised. "Look, it's his spear," he pointed at me.

That was good. They didn't seem inclined to take someone else's property. That was unusual in this part of town. Usually, "might makes right" around here.

I'd been standing to the side, but now I approached them whilst still keeping an eye on the still-open portal. You never know. Someone else might emerge with even more artifacts for me. Of course, that would be too much joy. Portals were short-lived, and usually after they deliver a group of offworlders, they begin self-destructing. I expected it to be gone within ten minutes. Meanwhile, I didn't know what to expect from my "helpers." Right now, they think they saved me. Maybe they expected payment for this?

"How do you want to divvy up the trophies?" I decided to just ask them, not putting my weapon away just yet.

"What do you mean?" asked one of them. "It's all about honor; however many of them you kill, that would be your take," he shrugged. "These three are ours..."

Good answer. These sailors were both brave and honest. So, after exchanging a few words with them, I decided to give them the spear. Yes, and the swords too, I simply couldn't carry that many away.

I carried out a full diagnosis, but didn't bother treating them for anything. They were honest and deserved it, but they were also exceptionally healthy. They hadn't even been wounded during the battle.

In the meantime, I was sorting out the trophies, putting the most valuable items in a special pocket of the backpack, and while choosing from what else was there, I chatted with them, and found out why the sailors had come to the rescue.

"Weren't you leery about joining in? After all, you saw that I was holding my own," I asked.

"Yeah, it takes balls, hell yes! But someone needs to teach these alien bastards a lesson. A lethal lesson, ha! Ha-ha-ha!" He laughed.

"They're real f*ckers!" said another one who looked to be around forty years old, and he spat on one of the corpses again. "'Nuff said!"

"Yeah, these bastards stole the son of our friend, and the kid was only eight years old, with his whole life ahead of him! Monsters!" the third one kicked the long-suffering corpse, "What kind of evil are you to steal little boys and girls? They all deserve to die, and until they do, I will not rest!"

They're not going to all die, believe me. Not for

a long, long time, and not until more and more of them show up here. Of course, to be sure of this, I should visit them. See what the world is like on the other side of the portal. I needed to learn a lot more about them, and in the meanwhile, I could pick up quite a few artifacts.

I picked up only the most valuable trophies. Artifacts, gold, coins. A few weapons that seemed particularly valuable. I even bargained with the sailors for coins that they got from the catchers. They were happy to hand them over in exchange for the offworld armor, even though I got the better deal. The armor wasn't, in fact, anything I could use, as it was too bulky and heavy. Of course, I took the crossbow. And also a jam-packed quiver of bolts, and the shooter's shoulder bag, which contained more supplies.

I didn't bother going through the loot here, and simply parted with the sailors and headed for the tavern where I had lived for several days. It wasn't far away. As I recalled, the kebabs there were worth the trouble of dropping by.

En route there, I opened my bag and took a peek at the artifacts.

"I could have retrieved more, of course, but..." I shook my head. "No, why complain?" I'd scored well this night, and could wind things up now.

I paid no attention to other portals. Anyway, the locater was silent, and why look for more? I'd acquired energy, as well, and the money I'd get from these artifacts was enough for now. I'd get plenty for just the protective artifacts, like these animal fangs. They were small, yes, but worth 20K each. I had at least three of them.

I was feeling good from the offworlder energy, as well. My source was working at full capacity. Now that it was fully activated, I didn't have to act like an energy vampire anymore.

I wasn't at the tavern for long. Right away, I ordered some food for myself, and took a few bites, and then ordered a lot, lot more for the road. We didn't have a functioning kitchen at the castle yet, not to mention we had no servants, either. And although we had provisions, they were simple products, though good enough for the guards. I, though, wanted more than oatmeal and potatoes.

I continued my repast as I waited for Georgy, and looked around at the others in the tavern. It was rather quiet in here right now, but this was only natural as it was almost dawn, so the drunks had all passed out by now, some in the street, and others in their rooms.

I also noticed the waitress I'd treated while staying here. There was no longer any trace of the necrotic disease, and she looked like she was on the mend. She needed no more help from me. True, she looked at me askance, no doubt recalling how rude I'd been, clutching her hand and scolding her for a minor chip on the plate.

Right now, I was even missing the tavern. It wasn't like a posh place, but I liked it here. That being said, the castle was far more interesting. So much fun in store in terms of the Bulatov affairs -- attacks to repel, income to find to keep the castle afloat, war to wage with other Families.

"Hello, count!" said an obviously sleepy Georgy as he sat down at my table.

"Would you like to order something? Are you hungry?" I asked.

"I want to sleep," he smiled. I got the hint, so soon there was no trace of his drowsiness left. Just a tiny shot of energy, and he was as fresh as if he'd been sleeping for a week. Of course, in ten or so hours, he'd be exhausted, as his body would demand payback.

Until then, I had plans for him. As soon as he completed my tasks, he could sleep as much as he wanted.

In the meantime, I finished eating and off we went to the castle. Along the way, again I saw little out the window. True, it was still dark out, with only streetlights to be seen, but even that was interesting. A wealth of questions came to mind, such as how they managed the infrastructure around here. I'd already learned all about how electricity was generated, but just the same, it seemed like magic to me. The magic of those who were ungifted...

Then I took a closer look at what I'd scored on my hunt for trophies. An artifact for healing cuts. Disposable, but still worth something. Three small protective artifacts, one of which I kept for myself, and another which I planned to give Victoria as needed. Money was one thing, but more valuable than *moolah* was protection from stray bullets. Later, I'd find something even more powerful.

Yes, should a bullet penetrate the reinforced bones of my skull, in all likelihood, it wouldn't kill me. I'd invested a lot of energy into ensuring my longevity, and so in the event of a critical injury, all of the reserves I'd dedicated to this would immediately activate with the aim of urgently bringing me back online. This, in fact, is the main focus of the Diamond Armor spell. It wouldn't protect me as much as everything else altogether, but should something happen and I needed it, the effect of the spell was unparalleled.

Looking at my loot, I decided the rest wasn't worth keeping. I'd just give it all to Georgy and see what he could get for it. There was also that handful of coins, as well. Coppers, kopecks, change. All good.

"Georgy!" I said to him as we drew near the castle. "Take this stuff, and after you sell it, subtract your usual cut from the total."

And I handed him the rather crumpled bag. I'd used one in which food had been packed. That was the only one I could find.

"Ohhh..." Georgy immediately became serious when he saw what exactly was in the bag. "You do know that stuff like this is usually transported in reinforced armored cars with multiple locks?"

"Really? Who knew?" I said, scratching the back of my head thoughtfully. "Anyway, that bag will suffice. Sell what you can and take your cut. And don't worry so much, there's nothing much there," I laughed, and grabbed boxes of food as I got out of the car.

I had so many boxes of to-go food that I had to use my chin so that they didn't all fall out of my arms. Fortunately, the guards met me at the gate and helped me with my precarious load.

"Thank you!" I nodded at them "All good here?"

"Yes..." one of them said, and his stomach rumbled loudly.

I had everybody covered, though. Half of the trunk of the car had boxes of to-go delights in it. So I let them have most of it, but asked them to leave me and Victoria enough for breakfast, which wasn't far off.

At night, the castle looked rather sinister. Inside, you could walk along the endless corridors and feel like you were all alone there. The plus side of necrotics were that they kept the mice away. But that pigeon, well, what was that about? For a stupid bird it sure was adept at hiding. I got the feeling that what that thing was under the ceiling in the main hall was something creepy.

But casting such musings aside, I lay down on my ad hoc bed and fell asleep right away. A full stomach and an eventful night did their job.

And I dreamed... Scraps from my past life, luminous, full of color. There I was in my tower drinking one of the most expensive wines. Around me were lovely damsels, the best in the kingdom. They were practically fighting for the opportunity to dance in front of me. But one of them, the most beautiful, with one slight movement of her hand unfastens a clasp, and her airy gown starts sliding off her onto the floor...

"C-o-o-ooo!"

"Scum!" I jumped out of bed, and without even seeing the creature, I fired a shot from the pre-loaded crossbow. The bolt whistled upward, and...

It lodged into the ceiling.

No way had I missed. I felt exactly where the heartbeat was a moment ago, and now, there was no one there anymore. I definitely didn't miss... And I couldn't have imagined it either.

And yes, that creepy cooing from somewhere to my side confirmed that the creature was real. Again, I heard the flapping of wings, and then silence.

"It's okay, I'll get you..." I said quietly, reloading the crossbow. Next time I wouldn't even have to sit up, since now I clasped the crossbow to my chest. I'd fire straight off, and the creature would be toast.

"C-o-o-ooo!"

Now the sound was closer and louder, but my second bolt again went nowhere.

I stood up to reload the crossbow. And then, as soon as I again closed my eyes, I heard the self-satisfied cooing.

This scenario played out again and again, until dawn. That's when the creature itself fell silent, probably tired of our game. I managed to get a couple of hours of sleep in before the aroma of coffee wafted into the room.

Time to get up. I had a lot to do, and my stomach was empty. Hunger gnawed at me, so how to sleep? I'd collected a lot of energy the previous night, and used it right away to further develop my body. I reinforced my bones, and improved the blood supply to my muscles. I even developed my heart such that I'd best not let local doctors examine me. They'd see right away that my heart was not quite the same as anyone else's. Generally I was just like the locals when it came to all my other bodily attributes, except that my blood supply is far denser. I wanted it to be like this so that I could accelerate its operations without having to worry about ischemia. When blood-borne substances are in short supply, that's what happens — tissue starvation.

Then I headed into the dining room. Yes, we actually had a dining room, and entering it, I was impressed. Yesterday it was filled with rubble, but now, the guardsmen had whipped it into shape. True, all we had in the way of furniture was a table. And it was barely big enough to hold the food I'd brought from the tavern.

"So then, what smells so good?" I heard as I was digging into a hearty breakfast. Victoria then entered the room. Imagine her surprise when she saw trays with "food for commoners." At least that was she'd called the shish kabobs.

"You should try it before turning your nose up at it," I grumbled as I devoured my portion and moved onto another meat dish and something that looked like baked pigeon. I enjoyed the latter the most, imagining that it was that bastard that had kept me up again last night.

For some time the countess hesitated at the door, and then she asked her servant to make her coffee. I asked him to make me some, too. I was intrigued at the range of this old man's skills.

"Sit down, I brought it yesterday," I pointed to the dishes placed on the table. True, I left everything in the to-go packages — why not? Anyway we don't have a lot of dishes.

"You brought home the bacon, though," Victoria smiled. I just shrugged. No big deal, right? Yes, though, I'd scored us some bounty. "So you went out for food last night?"

"That was part of it," I smiled, recalling my adventures. They included clearing offworlders out of the port district.

Meanwhile, Victoria's aristocratic soul couldn't stand it any longer. So no more turning her nose up at it, she sat down at the table. I could hear her stomach rumbling.

"Mmmm..." she murmured as she tried a dish. "Pretty tasty," she agreed. "But where's this food from? The packaging looks cheap."

Ach! There's no pleasing the girl!

Once, I was at an expensive restaurant that served seafood. And guess what? I ordered some exquisite dish for that cost fifteen rubles, a real delicacy. And they brought me raw oysters. Thank you, at least I didn't have to crack open the shells -- I might have broken my teeth trying. I didn't even know if I wanted to eat the raw oysters.

First I made sure they didn't have helminths in them. Only when I knew it was safe did I try them, and they were strange, but delicious.

That being said, this kebab tasted a hundred times better. Not to mention how much better cake was.

We ate in silence, then Makar brought coffee, and also in silence we began sipping it. Everything was too tasty for conversation. For future reference, I should keep in mind that I'd better not order anything tasty for serious meetings. Not if I wanted to discuss business.

"Okay then. That was great, but...Let's get down to business!" I put my cup down and looked at Victoria. "I need a list."

"What?"

"A list of the property recently stolen from us. I know it's somewhere in the documents, but the information is hard to unbury, and I need to compile it all together," I nodded. "Don't forget about the servants. We also need a list of everything we need for the castle. Not everything, really, just the necessities. We'll get more later."

"Shouldn't we have a list of the lists that we need?" she smiled, but seeing how puzzled I was, she looked serious then. "Okay, I'll make you your lists," she said.

"And also the guards. We have too few of them now, we need to make a list..." I watched as she began to giggle again. "Well, have them put the call out. Have those who left come back."

"Sure, they'll all come running back!" she

grimaced a little then. “No doubt.”

“Tell them it's an order. Come to the castle, and as soon as possible. I understand that hardly anyone will come, but still.”

“Actually, there are some who would return to duty, but they’re still in the hospitals. I’m guessing that there are around twenty of them. Quite a lot, “she said thoughtfully. “I placed them in different hospitals to make them harder to find.”

“That’s smart!” I nodded. “If all the guards were in one hospital, the viscount would quickly eliminate them. But does this mean that I have to run around all of the hospitals in the city?” I said, thinking about how long that would take.

“Not only in the city...Also in the countryside,” she said sadly.

“Is there any way to somehow gather them together? Here, for example,” I suggested, and in response Victoria shook her head.

“That would cost a lot. And we don’t even have anything to pay off our debt yet. Although, I have a plan. You don’t have to worry,” she smiled. “You’ll see, all I have to do is...”

“Don’t bother,” I interrupted her. “I’ve already done something that I think will cover the debt. There will be money in the evening, and it should be enough to bring the wounded here, too,” I waved my hand. “So you can start tracking them down.”

“Are you sure you can cure them all?” she again looked at me dubiously. Really. I’m glad I was done masticating food. I’d definitely have choked on it, hearing her doubt. That would be the funniest death of the Archmagister of the Healing Arts since the beginning of the Universe.

I didn't even respond, at least not right away. I simply picked up a knife and ran it across my arm, producing a deep cut. Ah, yes, my bones were definitely stronger. I didn't even have a scratch on them.

"What are you...Why!?" Victoria said, alarmed at the sight of the blood gushing from the wound. I was actually pumping it out to make it all the more shocking. "But...but.." she then said as the wound began to heal right before her eyes. In another ten seconds, there wasn't even a scar left.

"So there you have it," I shrugged. "Have you forgotten that I'm a healer? Would you like me to run diagnostics on you? I'm thinking you may have issues with your memory."

"I have issues with trust," Victoria shook her head. "And forgive me! After all, lately I've been completely alone, completely unaccustomed to trusting people..." she lowered her eyes and plunged into her thoughts. "I'll do it all. I'll get the guards to the castle, although not all of them at once."

"Wonderful," I said, clapping my hands and smiling. "You'll see. I'll make them good as new. Even if they're missing limbs. Bring them here. I can grow them new ones, better than before!"

Hearing this, the countess didn't know if I was joking or not. You see, in this world, limbs didn't regenerate. And yes, what a pity! I myself have lost both arms and legs more than once. Really, how could anybody live without them? It'd be a chore. Of course, on this world they used prosthetics. That would be well and good, but how to put runes on them?

"However, the money issue remains open," Victoria reminded me, but when she saw the look in my eyes, she immediately raised her hands in a conciliatory gesture. "Yes, okay. I got it! Loud and clear! In the evening we'll have money. I remember. No need for diagnostics or whatever you're thinking."

And on this, we finished breakfast. I returned to the drawing room, meditated a bit, and pored over some paperwork. I even searched the Internet for information on why the local so-called pigeons were dangerous. From what I read, they really weren't. In fact, they were completely harmless and do not pose any threat. So what, was I being gaslighted? I'd spent too many hours when I should be sleeping trying to finish that bird off. I'd even caught a glimpse of it, but only briefly. So here I was in a castle inhabited by a pigeon. It was fat and mean. But it was also so elusive and arrogant that it seemed immortal. I didn't see how it could be so impudent if it was a mortal pigeon.

I sat at the table until the evening. Then I retired to the library and read a couple of books. I enjoyed the smell of ancient books and leafed through them. Yes, for the sake of such a library, I was ready to sacrifice the entire guard of that viscount, and it would clearly be worth it. I found books on magic, technology, the history of different states. And fiction, well there was an entire shelf devoted to it in the library. I had a lot of reading to do, and for me, it was always worthwhile to pick up new information through books. My pleasure was interrupted by a phone call. Apparently Georgy had sold the artifacts and coins and was on his way to the castle.

"Ehh..." I sighed heavily, putting the book back in its place. Why, though, was everything so dusty here? But no, better not let anyone clean up the library in case they damaged something. I'll clean in here, at some time. While I'm at it, I'll put some protective runes on the door, walls and ceiling.

Maybe I should just move into this room? Okay, I'll decide all that later, but now I had to meet Georgy.

* * *

The castle courtyard

"... yes, I understand that it's unlikely... But you still call them," Victoria put her hand on Valery's shoulder, and he sighed sadly.

"As you wish, madam. But they left when you were having a hard time. I won't forgive them for this," he said firmly. "But, of course, I'll issue the call and order everyone to show up. As soon as possible, just like you said."

"Thank you, Valery," Victoria said with a

smile. "I don't know what I would do without you. Thank the Almighty that you're back on your feet."

"The Almighty would be Mikhail, then," he grinned. "I don't know who he is, or how your father was able to convince him to accept the Family, but..."

At that moment, the sound of an engine was heard in the distance, and the fighters immediately took their places.

"Report!" the commander barked into the radio, and he was immediately told that everything was fine. The taxi, already familiar to them all, was approaching. So the fighters relaxed a little, but kept their weapons ready.

"Calm down, he's here for me," I said, walking up to them at the castle gates. "What are you doing out here, by the way?"

"We were talking about summoning the guards," Victoria waved her hand. "Are you going somewhere?" she indicated the taxi.

"No," he shook his head and walked up to the yellow car that had stopped nearby, from which a young man of about twenty had just emerged

"Hiya!" he waved at the countess and the guards. "I've done as you asked, sir," he said, and handed me a shopping bag.

"The countess is standing right here, and you're chewing gum, you idiot," I reprimanded him. The boy immediately swallowed his gum and looked serious.

"Please forgive me, Madam Bulatov!" he said, "I didn't recognize you right away!"

"Won't that hurt him? Swallowing gum like that..." asked Victoria.

"We'd have to be lucky. But I won't treat his intestines, so that he learns how to look after his health..." I muttered, accepting the package from the boy.

The package turned out to be simple only in appearance. In reality, it was much more complicated. First, I unwrapped one package and found another one inside. And then yet another. And so on until I unfurled all seven layers.

"So it's just to be on the safe side," the taxi driver shrugged. "And here it is, safe and sound!"

Victoria tried with all her might to see what the guy had brought. And she soon saw, and her eyes widened.

"Ten... thirty... Sixty? That's it?" I asked Georgy, and he nodded affirmatively. "Have you taken your cut already?"

"Yes, exactly what you said, two hundred rubles," the taxi driver said contentedly. "Well? Is there anything else I can do for you?"

"Well..." I handed the money to Victoria and reached into my pocket as my phone rang. As did Valery as his phone rang. "Uh-huh... I'll be right there" I nodded to the voice on the phone. "Actually, Georgy, you'd better leave. Right away."

"I don't quite understand..." Georgy said with a broad smile. But just then an explosion thundered in the distance, and he grew serious in a flash. "Okay, I hear you!" He wasn't a fool...A fool would not have understood, but a second later,

Georgy was peeling out after executing a U-turn, and soon he sped out of sight.

"Well, gentlemen and lady! It seems that another profitable night awaits our Family!" I said, smiling grimly.

CHAPTER 5

"COUNT BULATOV, ENEMY FORCES have entered the village of Sinyutino. They seem to be mercenaries," said one of our guards over the phone. I hung up and stared at Valery.

"Well?" I asked. "Where is this village of Sinyutino? And what would it be that they blew up there?"

"It's not far," he said, calling up a map on his phone and showing me. "It's abandoned. It's been a long time since anybody's lived there. But I don't know what they blew up there."

"Maybe they just wanted to draw our attention?" suggested the countess.

Actually, that made sense. An act to intimidate us, as if to say "We're in power here. You just hunker down in your castle and keep your head down." As if I'd do that!

I listened to a couple more reports from our sentries, but they lacked details. They just reported that equipment and a fairly large detachment of mercenaries had entered the village. But no one knew how many mercenaries were in the detachment.

Victoria was for not confronting them, as they were a strong force and why should we risk losing any of our people? Anyway the village was empty, with nothing of value. The mercenaries were many in number, plus they were well-armed, while we had forty guys at most, and they weren't even all in full health. As for weapons, we were woefully lacking in arms.

"So what you're saying is abandon the village? Okay, but you said that we don't have weapons," I was indignant. "What better way to get them if not from these mercenaries?" I produced my devilishly handsome smile, and only then did Victoria get what I was driving at. "According to the reports from our intelligence, the mercenaries are bringing in reinforcements, even."

"Do you think they're planning on staying awhile?"

"If they're setting up a base there, then we'll always have to be on the alert for attacks on our castle. We can't run away from confrontations forever, so it's best that we strike first," I summed up. That made sense -- I didn't think our enemy was stupid.

It was, in general, not wise to underestimate these guys. Even if they did something profoundly stupid, it was always worth considering the reasons why. We all wanted to live, and none of us wanted to lose. Thus, they must have set up in this abandoned village with one goal in mind, and that was to await reinforcements, and to then strike. Or else maybe they wanted to take one village after another until we were surrounded. In that case, we'd best make it clear right away that such an undertaking was doomed to failure.

"Okay then. We're attacking first — the decision is made," I said. "How about you, will you be joining us?"

"What a question! Of course!" exclaimed the countess. "Only I need corpses, but if they're old ones, completely damaged, I'll have to expend a lot of effort."

"Don't worry about the corpses," I smiled. "There will soon be as many as your heart desires."

I decided to take a dozen of our troops with us. I didn't see the point in taking any more, as we needed forces to guard the castle, and a larger group would be harder to manage. Were I to take too many of my men, some would likely die, and I didn't want to lose any of these guys. These ones were our most loyal, after all.

As soon as the sun dipped low and darkness was descending we set out. It's such a pleasure traversing through a snow-covered forest under the cover of darkness, and we succeeded in approaching the village unnoticed.

"Wait for me here," I ordered my people to stop a couple of kilometers from the village. "I'll do the reconnaissance, while you keep a lookout. If anything happens, you can reach me..."

I gave my final instructions to the guards, told them to protect the countess, and if needed, head back to the castle. It was always good to have a backup plan. Off I went to the village. Already I could hear them yelling, lining up for roll call, and then some cussing and the usual for these kinds of lowlife mercenaries. I saw their insignia on their cars, and, indeed, these were the same mercenaries who'd taken the castle before my arrival. I knew for sure who'd hired them. But just the same, I felt I should interrogate a couple of them. They might even know who was behind Snegirev.

That would help me form a complete picture of what was going on. Otherwise, it was as if the entire world suddenly declared war against our Family. And not just our world was out to get us, we had the offworlders to contend with, too.

"Right-o," I said to myself as I wound up my reconnaissance. I'd looped the entire village by then and procured a head count of the enemy forces.

Sixty-two people, nine of whom had average Gifts. Considerable reserves of ammunition and weapons, and quite a lot of equipment. There were six Svyatogorsk vehicles, altogether.

An interesting means of transport. Had I my way, I'd always ride in one. They weren't at all comfortable, but the technology was fascinating. Hefty wheels, that powerful armored angular body, and the design was nothing short of aggressive. Not to mention the heavy machine gun on the roof that was controlled from inside.

I'd recently read an article on this car, and now knew all about it. It was popular in this country, for good reason. But there was only one thing I didn't understand. I'd heard a lot of disparaging remarks about domestic technology. Everybody griped about how wretched and backward it was, but right now in front of me I saw these vehicles, all of which were manufactured in the capital. I saw nothing wrong with them.

The enemy forces were well equipped, apparently. In fact, they had enough weapons here for a hundred people. So I showed up just in time, right when I should have. Perfect, really, because where else could I acquire so many arms, so much gear and equipment absolutely free of charge? I didn't neglect amplifying my hearing on this reconnaissance trip. Taking a peek isn't always enough. Eavesdropping is usually worth the effort.

This time, though, I didn't find out much. These men mostly chatted about the women they'd hooked up with in their free time, and boasted about their "feats," which had nothing to do with the capture of the village, or anything like that. But not all of the talk was a waste of my time. After about an hour of listening to various conversations, I heard two sentries complaining.

They were unhappy that they were stuck rotting in this lousy village when the main attack would take place only in three or four days. Like, what was the point of establishing a foothold here, digging trenches and installing weapons, when you could immediately invade the castle? Then, it would all be over.

Worry not, fellas. It will all be over before you know it.

I returned to the forest by retracing my route to the village. There was one big disadvantage to the winter. Unless it was snowing outside it has hard to cover your tracks. All they had to do was spot footprints in the snow to find out there were people in the forest.

I briefly met up with my crew. I didn't explain everything in detail, and told them only how many mercenaries there were, and about how much weaponry they had. Yes, while I could count the living and be spot on, this wasn't the case with any weapons they might have hidden. I also told the others about the enemy's plans -- at least, what I'd managed to overhear. Victoria realized right away that I'd been right about their motives. It was irritating to her, wasn't it, that I was right virtually all of the time? The secret to my success in this is to always expect the worst.

I ordered my men to wait, grabbed my crossbow and bolts, and went hunting. The night was long, and we still had time, so I might as well reduce their numbers. And as I walked, a good plan was developing in my head. If all went as I expected, the mercenaries were in for a big surprise. Of course, they wouldn't be able to appreciate it for long.

* * *

Five minutes later
The clearing in the forest

"Is he for real?" asked a guardsman who had recently been captured by Snegirev. "He's taking a crossbow against an entire army??"

"Forget about it already!" Valery frowned. "He got you out of captivity, and there were guards there too."

"No, commander, I don't mean it like that!" the guardsman immediately raised his hands in a conciliatory gesture. "It's just strange, they can cut him down with one machine gun burst. Even if he has artifacts, it's still too dangerous. If only he had some backup, or a sniper, just in case of a firefight."

"Backup? What good would that do against six Svyatogor tanks and some sixty fighters?" laughed the commander.

"That's my point! He went alone against all that... With a crossbow!" the guard didn't let up, but Valery shut him down with one look.

"He ordered us to wait, so we'll wait," he shook his head. "Yes, he's unconventional, but I'm sure he has a plan. And it won't be something our enemies expect," he added with a wicked smile. Indeed, Mikhail loved to surprise the enemy. Valery was very interested in what the surprise would be this time.

* * *

There was a reason I wanted the crossbow, especially one that was from an offworlder. The bolts absorbed my energy like a sponge, so I was able to put a new spell into each shot.

In my world this spell I was going to use was called "Last Breath." In fact, it is extremely complex, and few people employ it. The energy consumption is colossal, and the discharge is sometimes questionable. But I needed information, and I need it now.

I also put another spell in each of the bolts that I fired at the unwary. Strangely, this was a healing spell. So these were healing pellets aimed at the skulls, necks and hearts of enemy combatants. Totally complete compulsory treatment devoid of red tape, waiting your turn, and delivered right to you. This treatment plan was only part of my scheme.

I fired off the first bolt almost as soon as I got to the village. I followed one of the mercenaries for a couple of minutes, and when he ducked behind a hut I fired off a shot. As soon as his body fell onto the trampled snow, I dragged it off and covered it with snow.

I don't understand at all why the mercenaries wore black uniforms that were easy to spot against the snowy landscape. It's not like they couldn't wear white in the winter, right? But perhaps they had some kind of rules about their wardrobe.

Anyway, I didn't even need to see them. I could sense their heartbeats, and with a little extra mana channeled into the chain of runes, I could tell exactly where they were.

Actually, the village was quite nice. I checked it out as I hunted. Although, yes, one village looked pretty much like another. Take the one where Snegirev had kept the prisoners I'd sprung. It looked identical to this one. The same log cabins, roofs made of metal sheeting, small windows and doors. Not that there was anything wrong with it. It's just that they were all the same. The village comprised a single street lined with about fifteen houses, no more.

My second victim wasn't hard to find. The sentry decided to leave his post to relieve himself, and that's when my treatment overtook him. The bolt entered his heart, and immediately healed the wounds, though he died anyway. Yes, I healed him so swiftly that the poor guy didn't even have time to scream. Thus, I wandered around the village, melding into the darkness. Yes, they had their spotlights set up, and headlights switched on in their vehicles, but this didn't help them, not at all. Of course, I didn't march down the single street of the village.

In an hour and a half I'd shot six people. I did it so quietly that no one noticed anything. I didn't bother the ones standing at their post talking on their radios. If they were to raise the alarm, my plans would go down the drain. But if it worked out, and if I was careful enough, I'd end up with six perfectly preserved bodies at my disposal. Thanks to the healing spell, everyone's faces were intact, and there wasn't a drop of blood on their clothes. A couple of them did end up with marks on their necks, but I easily removed all this with a blood splitting spell. Next, I tied all these bodies together, and dragged them into the forest as if I was hauling a barge.

"Is that what I'm thinking it is?" Victoria said as soon as I approached. Of course, she could see for herself. Or were the necromancers here as weak as the healers? "How did you manage to keep them in this condition? They're not even frozen!"

She was impressed, I could tell. They were quite intact. It was as if they were alive. But was I or wasn't I a healer? Yes, I'd ensured that no corpse spots marred their skin. After all, it was important to my plan that they look alive.

"Can you raise them?" I brought six of them for a reason, and didn't look for more. I figured she'd be able to handle that many.

"Hmmm...I think so, yes. But there may be a problem with managing them," the countess said thoughtfully.

"Leave that to me," I smiled at the way Victoria looked at me.

What of it? Is it that I'm a healer, was that it? I wasn't supposed to delve into any other kind of magic?

She was always forgetting that I am an Archmagister. At this level of energy mastery, whether you want it or not, you can control other elements. Sure, not as good as she could when it came to the dead, but still, in my world, it was a normal practice for two or even three mages to join forces.

I remember one day our kingdom was attacked by an army of the dead. Powerful necromancers from a connected world raised a huge army of zombie puppets and sent them to the largest cities to create even more dead people. And Kisarin, an Archmagister from the Order of the Flame, happened to be visiting my tower. And so the two of us set out to take care of this problem. I don't even remember how many dead people we encountered. Twenty thousand, I think. And all of them were strong, complex, charged with necrotic energy to the max. But if you combine the magic of fire and life, you get an explosive cocktail that can destroy hordes of the dead raised by necromancers, and in a matter of moments. "Cleansing Flame," that's what we called this spell. And then, as if nothing had happened, we went back to tasting a couple of barrels of wine that Kisarin had brought me as a gift.

Generally speaking, the combination of two elements sometimes produces fascinating results. What a pity not many know how to combine them. How nicc that it is to be one of the chosen few.

Thus far, all was going according to plan. I was sure of this, because the spell embedded in each bolt I'd fired allowed me to expand the picture a little.

The" Last Breath" was more like mental

magic. At least that's what ignoramuses from this world would think. In fact, healers work not only with the body, but also successfully influence the mind. This spell allowed me to see the memories of a dying person. However, it consumed an incredible amount of energy, and so I could only discern a couple of seconds of the memory of each of my victims.

"Well, six is good," Victoria concluded. "I don't understand how you finished them off totally unnoticed, but I don't expect you to tell us."

"Why not? I can give you all the details. For example, this one," I pointed to one of the dead. "I shot him with a crossbow. But his comrade, well," I pointed to another. "That was more complicated. However, I also shot him with a crossbow. Would you like me to tell you how I killed the third one?"

"Let me guess...you used the crossbow, right?" smiled the countess.

"Your insight has no limits," I spread my hands. "So you see, there's nothing to tell. I finished them all off in exactly the same way, I just walked up, fired a shot and then dragged the corpse off."

Why did this seem so hard to comprehend?

It took nothing to revive the corpses, and within a minute we all set off like a rather motley crowd towards the village to begin the operation I had planned. As Victoria correctly noted, I only killed six, and there were many other mercenaries in the village. And this majority would soon notice the disappearance of their comrades and raise the alarm. The search would begin, but instead of their friends they'd be finding us.

I was still lacking forces and gear. I can't right now go up against an entire army, and so I had to use stealth and wits. I didn't feel badly about that, though, in light of who our enemies were.

We approached the outskirts of the village. I and Victoria left our twelve fighters there, ordering them to not attack under any circumstances until I gave the signal.

"How will you signal us?" asked Valery as we were leaving. I and Victoria both looked back at him.

"What do you mean?" I was surprised. "When we took the castle, don't you remember the signal?"

"Yes, half the city noticed it..." he remembered the cannonade of shots that broke out when I was discovered in the castle.

"Well, this time my signal will be visible from space," I grinned, and the commander sputtered in surprise.

Victoria and I and the six zombies went to the far side of the village. There, I had to expend a little effort.

The countess cast her magic on the corpses, taking control of them. All I had to do was clear their minds so that they would acquire at least some intelligence and recall some of their memories. Victoria could not yet create intelligent zombies, so I had to help.

"Can you give me control?" I asked, after

finishing with the last one.

"What? You'd have to ingest some necrotics," she said in surprise. "Only necromancers can control the dead without harming themselves."

"Only necromancers... and one healer," I smiled, "Don't worry about me, everything will be fine."

Victoria stood there for a couple of seconds, but then shrugged and put her hand on my chest. I immediately felt the threads of necrotics stretching from the six dead men straight to my source. But I quickly blocked it, isolating it from the rest of the energy in my body.

The manipulation is not the easiest; it can only be learned at the magister stage. Unless this was done, the energy would mix with mine and harm my source. It would be a deadly sort of problem, so to speak.

Anyway, as I'd kept these corpses in excellent condition, it wasn't hard for me to cleanse their brains of death and enable them to function at a tolerable level. In the end, their memories were sufficient to allow me to issue simple commands to them.

They all immediately headed towards the targets I indicated, and then another, rather simple, but very important task on my behalf awaited them.

"All done! Now we just wait," I said, sitting down in the snow and closing my eyes.

"Wait for what?" the countess asked, sitting down next to me. "That signal you mentioned? Will we see it from here?"

I didn't respond. I just looked at her reproachfully, and she fell silent. Meanwhile, I concentrated on the dead under my control. I could no longer influence them in any way; only necromancers could do that. But I could observe their actions. They were following the orders I'd given them.

Ah, yes, they were doing my bidding. That's it, let the fun begin!

* * *

Meanwhile, inside a house in the village

"Report!" an officer sitting at the table barked as he looked at the soldier who entered the room. "Well?"

"The equipment has been tested and is ready for battle. We do have some problems with fueling and lubing, but they can wait until the morning." reported the private.

"What about the fortifications? Is the perimeter ready?" asked the officer. He was a young, clean-shaven man in a pitch-black uniform. However, everyone here had a black uniform, and there was almost nothing to distinguish between officers and privates.

"Yes sir! The fortifications have been erected, the barracks are occupied; guards are stationed at the ammunition depot!"

"You're free to go!" the officer waved his hand,

and the soldier stepped back out into the cold.

"Listen, Lipov, what is it that we're missing here?" As soon as the private left, the other officer picked up their conversation. "The boss called me, offered me double the price, and told me to show up, but didn't really explain anything."

"We're going to finish with this countess. They say that some new bloke showed up there with a surprise," the bald man waved his hand. "And they also dug up some guards from somewhere, so tomorrow or the day after tomorrow we'll go to the castle."

"That's what I thought. Back to the castle. But why so many guns?" asked the third guy. "There's enough for two hundred fighters, and which is more than we need."

"Tomorrow another group will be brought in, and we'll equip them..." Lipov wanted to say something else, but the front door swung open sharply, and a fighter entered the hut.

"Makarov, damn you!" growled one of the officers. "Close the door, you idiot! It's cold! And why aren't you on duty?"

The fighter just stood there, looking straight ahead with empty eyes. They kept on cussing him out, but then there was silence. This is because the fighter suddenly tossed a bundle of dynamite on the floor. And then he fired at it with his pistol. Before anyone could come to their senses, the house was blasted apart. Along with everyone in there, as nobody had time to activate their shields. Just then, five other powerful explosions occurred outside, and all hell broke out.

* * *

"Ooof!" I had to cover my ears.

Victoria also covered her ears and hunkered down on the ground. Otherwise, she'd have been blown away by the sound.

My plan, though simple, was a good one. The "Last Breath" spell gave me access to fragments of the memory of the mercenaries I'd killed. A couple of seconds is all, but that provided a wealth of information.

For example, I knew where these guys were stationed. Thus, I was able to "behead" the enemy first, leaving the scattered groups aimless, without leadership. Now all that remained was to finish off the strays fleeing in horror, and then our work here would be done.

What I'd done was access the zombies' memories about how many of their guys were on duty, and how many weren't. Out of sixty men, only twenty were still on active duty. I sent three zombies with explosives to the off-duty men. The other three zombies made their way to where the sentries were stationed, simultaneously blowing them up. The only place I left alone was the shed with all the gear and supplies. Although it was rather heavily guarded, I didn't want to blow up my property.

I'd manipulated the memories of the mercenaries' brains for a reason. I needed them to remember what explosives were and also how to activate them. Actually, I'd assumed they'd employ grenades, which I'd recently become familiar with myself. But by the sound of the explosions, the dead men had come up with something even better. Judging by the power of the blasts, these guys had been preparing to turn our castle into rubble.

Actually, this wasn't exactly an original plan, employing zombies this way. In fact, in my world, necromancers were essentially all alike in their tactics. They'd all raise bands of zombies, give them explosive artifacts and send them forth to greet the enemy. Effective, right? It made sense to do likewise here.

"What was that?" Victoria asked as the blasts died down.

"That would be the signal," I shrugged. "Now we fight!"

And I flew around the corner and started firing at a man fleeing in panic. He didn't know what hit him, and collapsed on the melted snow. I didn't bother draining any energy from him. No time for that now. Not what with two other mercenaries rushing at me. I tossed my crossbow aside, and drew my offworld sword, imbuing it with energy.

But just then Victoria flew past me and launched into an attack. The thin blade of her sword had a barely discernible haze, and with a swing, she sliced open the stomachs of each of the astonished would-be attackers. She moved swiftly, with grace and skill. Clearly she'd trained under a real master. And she'd trained hard.

The mercenaries were in real trouble, alright. To die at the hands of a necromancer is not the most enviable fate. Most likely, that meant more than the death of the body. If one's soul was weak, then the mage of death could destroy it, too. In any event, both of the mercenaries died in terrible agony. But before they could even fall to the ground, Victoria took control of them and sent the now zombified mercenaries into attack against three of their former comrades.

This trio had just emerged from the ad hoc barracks looking bewildered at the chaos around them. Too bad for them. I plunged my blade deep into the chest of one of them, piercing his heart and other vital organs. My sword, imbued with power, cut through his bones like a hot knife through butter. With two quick swipes, the other mercenaries also fell lifeless onto the snow.

“Aaaurgh! You sons of bitches!” I heard the scream of fury as a tall, hefty bald man busted out from under some rubble. His clothes were burnt shreds, and some rebar was sticking out of his stomach, but this didn't stop him from tearing to pieces the two zombies Victoria sent his way as she dealt with a third mercenary.

“That one is mine!” I warned her and rushed to attack. She was, of course, strong, but just in case I wanted to handle this guy.

Not to mention, but going up against a strong opponent was also a bonus for me because it was a great way to develop my source — the best, even. Indeed, this guy was powerful. He'd survived one hell of an explosion.

Although he didn't possess any magic, clearly he was endowed with an above average Gift. A powerful physique, for sure -- his Gift enhanced his physical assets, allowing him to strike more powerfully, move more swiftly, and withstand far more damage than what was normal.

He'd noticed me, as well, and we both rushed toward each other. He'd even pulled his sword out from under the rubble, although it was somewhat mangled by the explosion.

"Grrrr!" he growled as he made a sweeping blow. I jumped back, but managed to nick him with my sword. All I could do was scratch him, but that was all it took to carry out a full diagnosis.

He'd be dead in two hours. His intestines were a such a mess that the contents were seeping into his abdominal cavity. Any normal man in this condition would be lying on the ground groaning in agony until they died, but this guy was strong enough to carry on fighting. He was also sporting numerous other injuries and fractures, but none of them were yet a problem.

During our brief moment of contact, I released a little energy into him to increase his sensitivity to pain. This caused him to momentarily freeze, and that's when I struck him again. But he managed to block my blow, and kicked me in the chest, and I found myself tumbling head over heels in the dirty snow. I felt like I'd been hit by a train. Powerful... My ribs immediately crackled as they fused back together and I rose to my feet. I'd also torn several ligaments in my shoulder, but that was no big deal. Really, all in all I was fine, with no other damage.

By then, my opponent was ready to swing at me again. I dodged his blow, and was about to attack him again when...

**Thwack!*

The crossbow bolt dug into the warrior's chest, and the black haze that enveloped the projectile was instantly absorbed into the resulting wound. With a look of horror, the big brute collapsed onto the ground. I ran up to him and activated "Last Breath," but his soul was too strong. I tried to find out who hired them, but he was able to ignore the question and instead revealed completely different memories. They were not at all of interest to me.

What a shame! Oh, well. By now, our forces had finished off the rest of the mercenaries. It wasn't too difficult, since the explosions had taken out most of them. Valery showed up and reported that they'd taken two prisoners.

"Sir!" my commander seemed concerned about something, and after reporting he made a request. "We have four wounded, one of whom is about to die!"

"Why wait to tell me?" I hated losing people who were loyal to me. So right away I went to tend to the wounded.

Indeed, one of ours was in a precarious situation. He'd been hit in the back by a short burst of gunfire. A quick diagnosis showed that his lungs were punctured in several places and his heart sac was in bad shape, but the heart itself was completely intact, at least for now. But he had bullet fragments in the heart sac, and that was the problem.

I had to stop and think about how to deal with them. Meanwhile, Valery told me how this had happened. It seemed that this guy had shielded his comrades from the machine-gun fire. He'd thrown himself into covering them, which was, of course, commendable. But the consequences were troublesome. I pondered how to extract the bullet fragments, and also how to retrieve him from the other world.

"You start collecting the equipment and anything else of value. I'll be here awhile," I told Valery. "If you need help, summon it from the castle. I don't want anything of value to remain here."

The commander immediately ran off to carry out the order, and I began treatment. First, I slowed down my patient's heartbeat, and next I started blocking the damaged vessels. Only then did I start removing the bullet fragments. I recalled as I worked all of the various instruments and gear that were used in the local hospitals. I could've used some of them, actually. It would've made all this much easier.

The healers here were a different breed, but

they did have at their disposal countless auxiliary methods for conserving energy. However, they would throw all they had into their treatments, wasting resources. What for? If, for example, the goal was to heal a damaged artery, what point was there in dispersing your power throughout the body? If the energy wasn't applied carefully and with precision, you could run out, even.

Thus, I concentrated specifically on spot treatment. No, I couldn't put this guy on his feet right away, but at least I'd have almost no deficit in my energy expenditure. Still, if I had some instruments, I'd spend even less energy and could benefit greater numbers of the wounded.

All in all, it took me about an hour to do what was needed. Meanwhile, reinforcements arrived, and they loaded all of the ammo and weaponry into the armored vehicles as Valery prepared a detailed report on the loot. I was pleased, indeed I was! Not all of it fit into the trucks, so I don't know how the mercenaries got it to the village to start with. We had to use the vehicles we already had at the castle to transport it all.

"Valery..." I said thoughtfully, approaching the guard commander. "I was thinking, wouldn't it make sense to build on our success?" And my smile as I spoke caused Valery to grow pale. "Aren't those great assets to our fleet?" I indicated the Svyatogor armored cars.

What a name. I already liked them, and as I stood next to the armored Svyatogors, I felt like trying them out.

Valery had nothing to say in response. I sensed his lack of enthusiasm, but he didn't want to openly object. And so I soon had nine fresh fighters with me in three captured vehicles. One drove, the other manned the machine guns, and the third was the backup.

"Victoria," I called out to the girl who was helping the soldiers load heavy boxes of ammunition. Her help, of course, consisted of advising them on how to pack them. "Can you wrap all this up by yourself?" she nodded. "Then we'll meet later back at the castle. In the meantime, I'll be paying Snegirev a visit."

Victoria was busy, and didn't register what I'd said right away. Before it sunk in, I jumped into the car, shut the door, and ordered the driver to get moving.

"Mikhail! What did you just say?!" she shouted after us. "You're not really going to..." we were too far off for me to hear the rest.

Er, no. I wasn't going to his estate, as that would be suicide. Instead, I found a checkpoint on the map where the viscount's guards ought to be stationed. Actually, Valery confirmed this, saying it was an outpost Snegirev had taken from us some six months ago. I assumed there would items of value there, too. But if not, in any case we could send a message to Snegirev.

The operation didn't take long. We were there in just half an hour, stopped nearby, and simply fired on the sentry booth, and then on the rest of the buildings, with our machine guns. I myself directed the shooters in this, as I could sense exactly where the enemy was hiding.

Of course, before this we'd scouted and made sure that there were no civilians around. Not that there could by any. This checkpoint was a small fortification, right on the side of the road, with a couple of houses in which the guards lived. There were only six people stationed here, who were manning the fortified sentry booth in shifts. Theoretically, such checkpoints were there to prevent the enemy from drawing near undetected. The guards were supposed to repel any attack until reinforcements arrived. That was the idea, anyway. But we clearly surprised them, as nobody even fired a shot at us. Two were left alive because they raised their hands and surrendered. Good decision. Really, the others should have done likewise. But for some reason they didn't, and they had to be killed.

And then, in the span of ten minutes, we went through the buildings, collecting all the weapons and equipment, and headed back. According to the prisoners, reinforcements would be there within an hour, as they'd sent out an alert. Why wait for them, as we'd done what we set out to do? I felt that I'd sent a strong message to the viscount.

It took about an hour to get back to the castle, and all this time I looked out of the small window in the armored vehicle. I had no reason to strain my source. I'd fought a good fight this night, fed it energy and now I simply needed to assimilate it. Actually, a good sleep would be nice. And this was my aim upon returning to the castle. It was bustling there, of course, with all of the equipment, the newly acquired vehicles, ammo and so on. We even had some of the mercenaries' uniforms, which, who knows, might come in handy. You never know. Maybe when we faced off against more of them, we could sell them their clothes.

Finally, all was done, and I lay down to sleep. I was drifting off into dreamland when...

"C-o-o-ooo!"

The feathered bastard was cooing right into my ear. I drew out the crossbow hidden under my blanket, and fired at the gray blur as it rose into the air. I know I shot it!

"Well?!" I was perplexed and angry as I jumped out of bed and reloaded my weapon. "I hit you, didn't I?!"

I did see some fluff in the air, and yet the crossbow bolt simply struck the wall. Meanwhile, the pigeon was gone. I even rubbed my eyes and looked for its carcass on the ground, but no, the creature again, somehow, evaded my shot, though I know my aim was true.

I felt incredibly sleepy, but I decided not to go to bed. I felt like that would be futile as the bastard bird wouldn't allow me to sleep. I could turn off my hearing and turn down sensitivity and the chain of runes, but maybe that was what this creature wanted. Then, once I was defenseless, it would peck at me. No, this was untenable.

"What do you say to this?" I said through

clenched teeth as I finished drawing lines of runes right where the ceiling met the wall.

This had taken me hours, and the sun was almost up before I was done.

I'd created magic nets right up to the ceiling, and also where I'd seen the bird before. It wasn't possible to avoid them. As soon as the bird showed up again in this space, it would immediately fall into one of the traps. No, it wouldn't kill the bird, but it would paralyze it, and it might even fall to the floor. Then it would get what it deserved!

But it was too soon to celebrate. I returned to my bed and climbed under the covers as if nothing had happened. I didn't even bring my crossbow with me.

Now, smiling, I closed my eyes, ready to hear the bird thrashing around in fear and consternation. I'd poured enough energy into the runes to shock a large boar. Or even a bull.

But as soon as I was snug in bed, I heard the flapping of wings. I clearly felt the familiar heartbeat, but the bird continued flying. Even where I'd placed my nets. It flew near them, but didn't fall into them.

"C-o-o-ooo!"*

"Scum!" I screamed as the bird again screamed into my ear. But then, as soon as I opened my eyes, it was gone. Even the heartbeat disappeared. "Uh-h..." I sat on the bed and began to think. Really, maybe I should move? The goons from the local gangs would visit me in the tavern, but I could handle them. But this, well...

Maybe I should activate my" Universal Diarrhea" spell? That should do the trick, but I'd spend all my energy on it. And yes, everyone in the castle would suffer. But that pigeon was such a cunning creature, it could possibly use the ailment against me somehow.

So that left me waiting with my crossbow in my arms. But there was a plus in this. I recalled all of the simple attack spells for healers that I hadn't used for a couple of hundred years.

For example, there was the "Calm" spell. The target would calm down, their heartbeat and breathing would slow. Simply put, it would remove adrenaline from the blood and prevent more from developing. Even if the target tried to run off, he wouldn't be fast enough to get away.

The problem was making the spell work over the entire area. This reduced the effectiveness of the spell, but it wasn't like I was inflicting "Calm" on a giant monster. It's a pigeon! That's it! Although I'd love to sic this pigeon on the viscount. That would be like killing two birds with one stone, pun intended.

At some point in my vigil I managed to get the crossbow bolt to release energy upon impact whilst covering an area with a radius of a meter with my "Calm" spell. But the cursed creature simply disappeared then, only to reappear in another space.

I'd been tormented by the bird for hours on end. My nets didn't work, nor did all the bolts I'd fired at it. I'd wasted something like twenty bolts on trying, using up almost all of my supply.

"This is war! Yes, war!" I said quietly, and then, finally, I fell asleep.

* * *

Two hours later
Same place

I woke up because someone had been standing outside the door for about forty minutes, fidgeting. He did not dare knock, but he was in no hurry to enter. It was Valery. I recognized him right away.

At least I'd caught some sleep.

"Ohhh..." I peeled one eye open, only with the help of magic. "Two hours..." I leaned back on the pillow. The creature had tortured me until morning, and now it was already noon. "Come in, Valery," I croaked, and the door quietly opened.

"Good afternoon, Sir!" he said briskly, but seeing the expression on my face, he reworded his greeting. "Good morning, right?"

"Nothing good about it...Hello alone will suffice!" I rasped, as I got up. "Why have you been hovering outside my door for almost an hour?"

"I didn't want to wake you up..." he said, scratching the back of his head. "I've got a serious matter to discuss."

How I love serious matters, especially right when I get up. Maybe he's clever enough to resolve them while I'm still too sleepy to realize it? Okay, let's listen first, and see what's up. So I waved my hand, inviting him to speak up.

"I want to step down as commander of the guard," he blurted out in one breath. I wasn't even surprised. He clearly realized what I'd come to understand.

I'd noticed that he wasn't yet ready for the responsibility. He was taking losses far too much to heart, and was reluctant to send men out to certain death. He'd rather die himself than order others to perish. For a commander, though, this was unacceptable. And there had been a lot of such moments. No, this was a good man, and an excellent fighter, but not a commander, unfortunately. He was still too young. Give him another decade to mature. Yes, he was clearly trying his best, but he was suffering in the role, and forcing himself to do what was needed.

"Hmm..." I thought. "Right now our Family is at war," I said, grabbing a bottle of water and drinking some down. "So here's the thing. How am I to understand what you're saying? There isn't anyone to take your place, so you want to abandon the guard, leaving it without a commander? Is this cowardice or betrayal?"

"No, how can you say that?" he exclaimed. "Sir, I would never betray the Family."

I knew that, but I wanted to see his reaction.

"But I'm not a real commander. There was someone else... far better. A world-class man, a strong warrior and an excellent leader. But, officially, he died four years ago during the storming of the castle of the Belozerov Family," he said.

"I've heard about him. But would you mention him if he had really died?" I understood what he was getting at.

"Yes. I've seen what you're capable of. And he didn't actually die -- the old count registered him as dead to protect him. And I don't believe what the healers back then said..."

Actually, all of this was really interesting. I even spent some energy to fully wake up so that I could properly take it all in.

Previously, the Bulatov family had a different commander, everyone called him Chernomor. He was the same age as the old count, and his best friend, although he was a mere commoner. He was a fourth rank warrior, a physical god, essentially. Very strong, fearless, and most importantly, fiercely loyal to the Family.

He suffered significant brain damage during a battle with the head of the Belozerov Family. The count spent a lot of money trying to restore Chernomor's health, but in vain. He was now what they call a vegetable, unable to react to anything. All he could do was lay there like a log, and the only thing keeping him alive was medical technology. Fascinating. I'd have to see what was wrong with him.

According to Valery, Chernomor was now in a special institution, where he is monitored day and night by the best specialists in the place. No, none of this was cheap, but the Bulatovs have been paying for it for eight years now. Count Bulatov just couldn't allow his friend to go to the next world, and until the end he hoped for a miracle. And so, a miracle in the form of the Archmagister was now going to visit Chernomor and bring him back to life.

And the Belozerovs were added to my list of targets. True, in the four years since they'd taken out Chernomor, they'd never fully recovered. It's a pity that back then, Chernomor failed to put the Belozerovs to rest for good. That would mean less for me to do.

"Okay, I'm interested. I'm free right now," I nodded towards the exit. "I can't relieve you of command yet, but as soon as I find a worthy successor, I'll immediately demote you to the rank and file. Agreed?"

"Thank you, Sir!" Valery bowed and left the room.

I sat for a while thinking, and at some point I smelled the aroma of coffee coming from the corridor. Ah, that would be just fine right now. After a couple of mugs, I wouldn't have to expend energy just to stay alert.

I followed the smell into the dining room, where I ran into Victoria. She was sitting there, drinking coffee, and, to my surprise, there was another cup on the table. Was this for me? Was I that predictable?

I sat down and picked it up, and immediately took a sip. Ugh...So strong!

"Oh! Sir, Madam, sorry for disturbing you!" her servant, Makar, appeared at the door, shot me a mean look, and immediately disappeared.

"Was this coffee not for me?" I guessed.

In response, the girl just smiled. Yep, I guess I stole his coffee. Oh, well, he can make more for himself. He was good at it.

"Why didn't you tell me about Chernomor?" I asked Victoria after I was done with my coffee. Hearing my question, her expressed turned stony.

"He's dead!" she shook her head. "And nothing can be done about it. Not even you are capable of bringing him back."

"What makes you so sure of this? And why don't you want me to even try?" I didn't let up. She should know by now that there was no healer stronger than me to be found in this world.

"Mikhail, do you think that I don't want him back?" she said with sudden tears in her eyes. "He was examined by the best doctors, the best mentalists. And they all agreed he was brain dead. There is no soul in his body, only a shell remains in which a semblance of life is artificially maintained. And you think I wouldn't want to cure him? He was like a second father to me!"

"The best healers," I grimaced. It revolted me to think about it -- I fully understood the kind of mediocrity she was talking about. "What do mentalists have to do with his case? If the soul, for example, is concentrated in the area of the source, how can they impact it?" I looked at her, but saw that she'd understood nothing of what I just said. Okay, time to get down to basics. There are many places where the soul could hide such that no one would find it -- no one but me, that is.

“It’s hopeless,” she shook her head. “There's no point in even trying.”

Oh, of course not! The most loyal and bravest of them all, but no, let's not even try, right? Okay, Countess, I give up on you.

I nodded goodbye, and left and immediately summoned Timothy. He came right away, and I told him to get the car. Soon I heard the engine roaring outside.

As I made my way outside, I got the address and room number from Valery, and then, two hours later, Timothy delivered me to the entrance of this institution. Even from the outside, you could tell it was a heavily fortified, solid kind of place.

The grounds were encircled by a massive fence, and armed guards were stationed at the entrance. Above the gates hung an ornate sign announcing the name. I thought it was a hospital at first, but it wasn’t like a regular medical establishment. The name spelled it out.

“Anatoly Fukoff Institute for Managing Muscular Atrophy.” Yes indeed, a suitably technical sounding name. No doubt everyone referred to it simply as the “Fukoff Institute.”

It was located far outside the city, in a lovely, park-like setting. And yet, the nearest village was at least thirty kilometers from here. The guards were wary, but they let me in without any questions as soon as I showed them the Family ring. Apparently only members of the Families on the list they had were allowed inside. I didn't need his room number at all. The guard escorted me right to him. Really judging by how expensive this place must be, I had to say that the Bulatov family must have had a whole lot of money. There were medical personnel and healers, along with all of manner of medical equipment inside.

The guard stood outside the door and I entered the room. Indeed, Chernomor was completely safe. No one could get into his room unless they were thoroughly vetted. Not unless they blasted their way in or something.

Once inside, I looked around. It was quite spacious, with a hospital bed in the middle of it. I heard some hissing sounds, and clearly the mattress under the old man was somehow moving. Interesting... My guess was that this was so the patient's muscles wouldn't atrophy, or his tissues collapse over time. The mattress forced his body to move.

Yes, so interesting! Along with so many other things in this world. I never imagined how their inability to develop the Gift of Healing would inspire so much inventiveness.

I carefully examined the equipment, and then turned to studying the patient. He looked like an old man, but in fact he was only forty-five or fifty years old. What was remarkable was that, although he'd lost some mass, he still didn't look like a shriveled mummy, as I would've expected. I could tell that he'd been a strong man, and still was, in a way. I was impressed at how he'd weathered the years he'd spent here. But yes, it was his mind that was the issue...

Ah, just what I expected -- his soul was still in his body, but locked deep inside. It would be a little more difficult than I thought, and I'd have to make a couple of more trips here. I couldn't do it all at once.

“But you can hear me...” I smiled, and his soul responded with a slight burst of energy. “Well, Chernomor! Are you ready to return to duty and again serve the Bulatov Family? Do you want to destroy the enemy?”

The response was a new burst of energy. But the torn face of Chernomor didn't move a muscle.

“Well, stop lying there, Chernomor,” I smiled, and my eyes filled with green light. And in my hands a ball of concentrated vital energy began to grow. “The Family is in danger, and you're just lying here!” At this, the ball of energy flashed green, and I drove it into Chernomor's chest.

Phew! I hope I didn't overdo it...

CHAPTER 6

THE BALL OF VITAL ENERGY flashed a bright green as it entered Chernomor's chest, and right away his eyes snapped open.

"Well, about time!" he boomed so loudly that he made the walls vibrate. "Glad someone could do something!" Clearly he was disgruntled.

I was surprised that he could do that much after lying here for so long. I also didn't expect his awakening to happen like this. I thought it would take him a few minutes at least to come to the realization that he was no longer imprisoned in his own body, and that he would then rejoice, maybe shed a few tears of happiness. But no, the first thing Chernomor did was voice his unhappiness over the local healers. To him, they were all idiots and dumbasses, and hearing this, I felt like we were going to get along. We clearly agreed on at least a few things.

"Ugh..." he groaned as he struggled to sit up. His ossified joints naturally creaked, and his stiff muscles didn't want to obey him and produced acute pain, but it was as if he didn't care.

"You should still lie down," I advised him, but he just shook his head.

"No more lying down! I have something to say!" Chernomor gritted his teeth, and then sat up. Of course, he couldn't stand up, but at least he was sitting. "So then!" He said, glancing at me. "Tell me, who are you? Get to the point; spare the details."

"The new head of the Bulatov Family," I shrugged. Chernomor immediately looked at the ring, and convinced of the veracity of my words, he sighed heavily.

"Understood!" And his thick eyebrows drew together, shielding his eyes. "So... Gregory and his daughter are dead," he lost himself in his thoughts for a couple of seconds, and only his heavy breathing could be heard in the room. "So..." he said loudly again. "How did you acquire the Family?"

This was no fool, and he knew full well that I could not have taken the ring by deception or through any other nefarious means. He wanted to know how it had happened, though.

"Gregory gave it to me," I said. How else could it have happened, really? "In fact, he offered it to me."

I told him briefly about how I became the

head of the Family. Without leaving anything out, I told him about my agreement with Gregory. Chernomor listened intently, sometimes stopping me to ask questions. He also wanted to know what had become of some of his comrades from past battles, but I couldn't always tell him much. I wasn't here back then, after all. The old man had been out of action in the Fukoff Institute for some time now. Although, how old was he, really? At the age of fifty, life was just beginning, and the fact that he now had a thick gray beard reaching to his chest didn't make him an old man.

"Oh, and Victoria is not dead. She's alive and well in her castle," I said, winding up the recap.

"Great. That means the war isn't over yet," nodded Chernomor, his face grim. Although, what was I talking about? That stern look was his default, I expect. Still, what he said sounded harsh.

"Actually, I'm here, too," I reminded him. "In addition to Victoria there is at least one more Bulatov, I hasten to remind you."

He heard me but said nothing, and again plunged into his thoughts. And after a couple of minutes of reflecting on things he seemed to reach some conclusions and, slapping his hands on his bed he spoke, his deep base tones again causing the walls the vibrate.

"Right! It's time for me to get up," he said and began struggling to rise.

"Where are you going, Chernomor?" I almost laughed. Here he'd just opened his eyes for the first time in years and yet he wanted to get up and go, maybe even off to battle, judging by his demeanor.

"I don't care!" He said stubbornly, straining to get out of bed. "I want to leave. Now."

"Sleep, come on..." I put my hand on his forehead and activated the "Pacification" spell, plunging him into a deep magical sleep.

His massive frame immediately slumped back onto the bed, which creaked in protest — it was a miracle he didn't break it. I looked at him and shook my head. Stubborn as a herd of sheep, but I liked him. Clearly this was a leader, and just who we needed to serve as the commander of the guard. Later, I'd straighten him out about who was boss.

That would take a little more time. I summoned Timothy and told him to go back to the castle and bring a couple of our men back, and in the meanwhile I went to see the head of the Fukoff Institute.

He was a man of about forty years of age dressed in a formal suit, over which he wore a white doctor's coat. I found him in his richly furnished office. All of the medical doctors and such here wore those white coats. I had to find out why. Really, how to get blood out of them? They just weren't practical. Our healers wore red, or, in extreme cases, blue coats. These were bright, easy to spot, and our enemies knew they'd best turn tail and run when they saw them.

"Unfortunately, we won't be able to return

your money," he said with mock regret, as soon as he heard what I wanted. I'd told him I'd be taking Chernomor with me, and he didn't even object. "We drew up a contract for eight years. It's all there in print."

I had the time, so I picked up the contract, and carefully studied it. This, although I never expected that we'd get any money back. I'd come here with a specific goal in mind, and I'd achieved it.

And so, after signing various documents absolving the Fukoff Institute of all responsibility, I went outside. I didn't have long to wait by then, and in some twenty minutes I heard the roar of the engine and saw the black SUV heading toward me. The guards opened the gates right away, and the staff rolled Chernomor out on a gurney, and loaded him into the car's back seat.

I was glad I'd put him to sleep. No fuss this way. Indeed, he looked as if he'd never been awake at all. Lethargic, diminished and helpless. But this was only how he looked. In a few hours, after the treatment finished healing him, I'd bring him out of the magic coma. I wanted his body to be ready first.

Timothy drove as fast as usual, so we were back at the castle in no time. He flew down the road, which was fine with me. In fact, I told him he could go faster next time. Yes, it might be dangerous, but after all, I'm a healer, so no worries.

Victoria was awaiting us at the entrance. She

looked aghast as she saw them unloading the seemingly lifeless body of one so dear to her from the SUV. She went with us to the hall I'd set aside to serve as a ward for our wounded. It was quite a spacious hall. Our guards had hung up a lot of lamps and made it comfortable for their wounded comrades. True, nobody was ever here for longer than half a day.

Then I want straight to the drawing room with the fireplace that served as my study and bed chamber. I still had a lot of other affairs to tend to. For example, I needed to peruse the lists compiled by Victoria of lands and possessions that had been taken from us. Even more important to me were the lists of what we'd procured from the mercenaries.

Valery told me a couple of hours ago that they'd counted everything and compiled a spreadsheet listing what we'd scored, and I was looking forward to finding out how rich we were now.

"You mean, ammunition from other weapons?" I asked, after Valery told me the figures.

"Well, most of the ammunition doesn't correspond with the weapons that were confiscated from the mercenaries," Valery reported to me.

"Confiscated... that's a good word," I smiled, "We have to do some more confiscating, then."

"Yes we do," he said, also smiling. "It's not like we want to rent this stuff."

That was too bad about the ammo, but it wasn't a big deal. All it meant was that this was just the start. There must be more soldiers with lots of guns and equipment heading our way. This ammunition had been brought in for them, it seems.

What, then, should I do with it? Most of the boxes of ammunition were of no value to us. But we could sell them. Even though trading in weaponry and ammo was strictly regulated here, we could do it on the sly.

Besides the useless ammunition, there was lots of other loot, including six Svyatogor cars. Of course, two of them were damaged by explosions, but Valery said they could be repaired at low cost. The other four were in mint condition, and we had ammo that fit the machine guns, so we could use them against the enemy.

Two good trucks, several dozen small arms, machine guns, rifles, automatics and more. I didn't know much about these firearms, but Valery explained the differences between them to me. I mean, I could certainly tell a pistol from a tank, but yes, I still had a lot to learn.

We'd also collected a lot of bladed weapons. Swords, knives, and stuff like that. Their value was questionable, but in any event, they could always be sold. Now, our guard was armed to the teeth, and we were no longer facing a shortage of weaponry.

Better still, we now had a lot of explosives. It would be sinful to sell such a lovely find. Clearly the mercenaries had been planning to level the castle to the ground, they'd brought so much dynamite with them. We'd be using all of this loot in the near future, only against them. Yes, we'd done well with this haul. The outing had been profitable, and on top of that, we'd left a couple of surprises in case the mercenaries decided to go back to the village.

Once Valery left, I again plunged into my research on the Internet, along with my perusal of documents. It didn't take me long to ascertain that there really was no way to sell ammo and weaponry on the black market. It just wasn't possible. Period. The only way to offload this stuff was through official channels run by the Empire, or else I could give it all away, which would be the same thing, were I to try to sell the ammo officially. The Empire paid peanuts, because they could get away with doing so. Ah, well.

"Georgy?" I called up my taxi driver. "I have a question."

"At your service!" he sounded cheerful and alert. "If you need me, I'm nearby and can be there in five minutes."

"Can you sell ammunition for heavy weapons?"

I heard him suddenly start coughing. Time for him to quit eating or drinking whilst on the phone. He could choke to death.

"Um, please excuse me, but I want to remind you..." he said after a long pause. "I'm a taxi driver! Just a taxi driver, I get people from point A to point

B, and all that. I'm not the head of an underground cartel; I'm just a taxi driver."

"So can you sell the ammo or not?" I interrupted him.

There was silence on the phone again, but this time not for long.

"I can..." the guy sighed resignedly.

"Send me your email then, and I'll send you the list," I said with a smile. Really, and he'd been saying he was just a taxi driver. As if.

He then muttered that he didn't have an email address yet, but that he would in another five minutes. He had to figure out first how to create one. I said nothing to that, and hung up to await his message.

Yes, I definitely appreciated this techno world. Once, my old world experienced an Interface with one such world, but it was nothing like this one. That one also had mechanical transportation, but it was steam powered. Everything there was powered by steam, and where they got that much firewood remained a mystery to me to this day. Small surprise that they stole firewood from us. If a portal opened in a forest, they would celebrate. And then, they'd clear the forest in two or so hours, and be on their way.

As I reminisced, Georgy managed to figure out how to set up email, and then he sent me a message via my phone. I then sent a hefty list with the types of ammo, the quantities, and everything else.

Now that these must-do items were off my

agenda for the day, I decided to take a walk around the castle. Time to check out how things were going. Yes, it was still practically a ruin in places, and we needed to hire some servants ASAP. We had the money, and we'd soon have more, so I saw no point in delaying. Vika should have already dealt with this matter and yet I found her sitting by Chernomor's bedside. She was stroking his gray hair and quietly talking to him. No, it didn't look good. She still didn't believe in me, that's what. She didn't believe that I'd cured him, and so she thought I'd brought him here hoping for a miracle of some sort. But, oh, well. He'd be awake again before too long. The restoration process was almost complete, and all that remained was to apply some finishing touches and then wake him up.

Next, I walked around outside and checked the sentries at their posts. The guardsmen were at their stations in the castle towers, and had set up some nice firing positions for themselves. Since we'd procured some two-way radios from the mercenaries, Valery had also sent men out to patrol the forest.

"Don't forget to check on the village, as well," I reminded him. "The mercenaries could well go back there, and then we'd have to pay them another visit."

"Of course, sir," he nodded. "All of the surrounding villages are under constant surveillance. Patrols check them every hour, although they don't go too close; otherwise you never know."

I nodded and headed back to Victoria. She had to hire those servants. That was important enough that I had to make sure she was on it.

* * *

An inconspicuous building on the outskirts of Arkhangelsk
The mercenaries' station

The man in a business suit sat in a chair listening attentively to the speaker. He was having a hard time maintaining his composure. In fact, the throbbing veins in his forehead betrayed his thoughts about what he was hearing.

"All?!" he asked the man in the black mercenary uniform reporting to him.

"All of the forces have been defeated. All of them. Several prisoners have been taken," the underling bowed his head. He, too, was at a loss at how the assault detachment could be demolished by such small forces.

"But..." the boss began, rubbing his temples. He had a hard time keeping calm when a host of dire thoughts were overwhelming him. "Could it be that our client wasn't forthright with us? We're talking about something like twenty men, almost totally unarmed. How could that be?"

"No, he told us the truth," responded the mercenary underling. "We double-checked, sent out reconnaissance, and they said the castle didn't have much in the way of forces. And not much in terms of mages, either. The necromancer girl... and this healer," he shrugged, "They must have some powerful artifacts."

"Wait," the boss raised his finger. "You said they took prisoners. How do you know? After all, none of our people escaped from that village, did they?" This immediately seemed suspicious to him, because, traditionally, the Bulatovs did not leave any witnesses.

"Well," the mercenary scratched the back of his head. For a couple of seconds he tried to find words and muster up courage, but then he blurted out. "They've already demanded a ransom. Double the usual. Two thousand per person..."

The boss's face was now impassive, except that his temples were pulsating like crazy, and a capillary in his eye burst, causing it to turn red.

"Leave now..." he hissed to his subordinate. The latter didn't have to be told twice, and he was gone in a flash. It was like he'd morphed into a gaseous state and seeped out under the shut door.

Once he was gone, a furious scream sounded from the office, along with the crashing of furniture being flung around.

"F**king hell! Mother** asswipes!" the boss yelled, while the subordinate and the boss's secretary simply stood outside waiting for the storm to abate. A couple of minutes later the door opened, and the now calm, even gallant man appeared on the threshold. "Merkov, agree to the ransom! Bring those men to me right away! We need to find out how these Bulatovs were able to overpower us."

* * *

Well, what a shame. I'd wanted to interrogate the prisoners, but that was off the table now. Yes, I told Victoria to ransom them, but I didn't think the enemy would buy their guys back so quickly. This was even though the countess had doubled the price, she said, to prevent the mercenaries from rushing into a decision. However, they agreed to our terms in the space of ten minutes.

It would be wrong now to torture them, or to interrogate them. Under the law, they no longer belonged to me, and within twenty-four hours I must deliver them to a special agency that dealt in matters such as ransom. They collected a small percentage, but they would guarantee the fairness of the transaction. I'd get my money, and the other side would get their men.

Well, alright, I was pleased. Money was good, and these funds were as if out of the blue. We'd have to make a point of taking more prisoners. They were worth more than corpses, it seemed.

Why did I entrust this to Victoria? I wanted to test her ability to conduct business and negotiate. In battle, she'd shown herself to be a middling, yet persistent mage. She needed a little practice and study, and only then would she amount to a real force. As for how she'd do when it came to business matters, this had yet to be seen. Well, now I knew, and I was pleased with the result. She'd done what was needed swiftly and transparently and had gotten the most from the enemy. Thus, I could give her more to handle without worrying about it.

There was no point in waiting, so the guards set about preparing to transport the prisoners. Even though the intermediary agency guaranteed the security of the transaction, just the same, anything could happen along the way. Mercenaries, after all, weren't aristocrats, and they didn't have reputations to worry about, thus you could expect them to fight dirty. And so I deployed two Svyatogors on the mission to deliver the prisoners and collect the ransom, along with a dozen heavily armed men from our guard. Should there be trouble along the way my guys would be ready for it. There was just one thing that bothered me as they were about to leave.

"Wait, stop!" I said to one of the men, and he froze in place, and looked alarmed. He was worried at how closely I was looking at him, and also how suspicious I was. "Damn..." I shook my head and put my hand on his chest. "Enough! You're free to go!" I said after a couple of seconds in which I neutralized the necrotic substances that had accumulated in his body.

I had to do that same thing to the other fighters. These were all guys who'd trained with Victoria in hand-to-hand combat.

Truly, the girl still had a lot to learn. Indeed. This, then, was one of the side effects of serving a necromancer. She couldn't yet fully contain her powers, so some of her necrotics infected the bodies of those who served her. It didn't kill them right away, and many wouldn't even notice until the concentration was enough to cause problems. But everyone around her would age a little more quickly, have worse resistance to maladies, and they'd end up growing tired more quickly. These were little things, but still, not pleasant.

On the other hand, maybe that pigeon might die from the necrotics in the castle? Hmm... If so, I might want to leave everything as is.

Before the armored cars had cleared the gates, my phone started beeping. What a handy thing, the alarm clock. In fact, it was time to awaken Chernomor. It wouldn't be good for him to sleep too long. Now he needed to move about, because otherwise the energy from the vital forces distributed over the muscles and joints might simply dissipate.

I went straight to the treatment room, stopping by the countess's servant on the way, and asked him to bring three cups of tea. I knew from him that Victoria was already there. If Chernomor didn't want a cup, I'd drink his and mine. And if Victoria didn't want hers, I'd drink that cup of tea, as well.

"I'm glad you're here already," I smiled at Victoria who sat at Chernomor's head. "Well then, are you ready to talk to him?"

"Mikhail, really, you don't need to give me false hope. I told you how dear he is to me..." the girl began to speak, but I quit listening. I put my palm on Chernomor's mutilated forehead and his eyes snapped open.

He looked furious. It was like he wanted to beat me up. Or at least try.

"You..." he said in a deep voice, but suddenly noticed Victoria's surprised face. And he immediately softened. "Vika," he mumbled into his beard. "Vika, my girl..."

"Uncle Chernomor!" she exclaimed and grabbed him, causing him to groan. Really, it was a tight hug.

She didn't let up for a couple of minutes, but as Chernomor's strength gradually returned to him, finally he was about to tear the girl off of him. He gave her a somber look, and then, without further ado, began interrogating her. Mostly about me.

Victoria was taken aback at first, but began to answer his many questions. She told him all about the many events that occurred over the years he'd been in a coma. About the wars with the different Families, and how the neighbors grew ever bolder and how they then began to divvy up the Bulatov assets and fall en masse upon them. Not much good to report about those years, and Chernomor's eyebrows frowned more and more as he listened.

"And then Mikhail showed up. I can talk about how we met and more until dawn breaks, but ..." She looked at me with gratitude in her eyes. "He recaptured the castle all by himself, got the best of our guard out of the hospitals, and literally saved me at that ball."

"Got it," he raised his hand, saying he'd heard enough. "I understand, and so I trust him," he nodded to himself. "But if he offends you..." Chernomor looked at me meaningfully and showed me his huge fist.

"Oh, well, may you need another nap," I said, shaking my head and sending him back to the kingdom of dreams. He plopped back onto the bed and passed out just like that. "He's threatening me with his clenched fist..." I muttered. I was none too pleased.

I waited a couple of minutes and then brought him back to his senses. This time he looked even more furious, but at least he was silent.

"Well, have you calmed down?" I smiled. "Right off I'd like to point out that you and I are not equals, and my powers are anything but simple. Henceforth my supremacy must not be challenged in any way. I hope you understand me now? Well?" I might as well show him who was boss while he was weakened by that coma. Who knows? In another two weeks he might be uncontrollable.

He was still glaring at me and sniffing into his beard. For a full minute he said nothing.

"Chernomor, did you enjoy your long sleep?" I took a sip of tea and stepped towards him.

"Yes, I heard you, I heard!" he said, still grumbling, and turned away. "What's there not to understand..."

“That’s good,” I smiled, sitting down in a chair and putting the cup on another chair next to me. “Now you need to start moving, but very carefully. You need to walk around more before you can think about going into battle.” Hearing this, he clenched his teeth, but said nothing.

And then, Victoria and I both brought him up to speed on recent events. We told him in detail about what we were dealing with, and speculated about what would happen next.

Makar kept running in and out of the room bringing us tea and cookies, although I got the impression that he and Chernomor were not on the best of terms. One reason I thought this was because the cookies he gave Chernomor were dry and tasteless — all but inedible.

Our men also started dropping in to visit their newly awakened commander. They were clearly happy to see him. I could tell that he'd earned their respect and unquestioning obedience. I didn’t think we’d have any problems with our guard under Chernomor's leadership.

As evening fell, I returned to my fireplace in the drawing room, while the others remained with the old warrior. They were reminiscing about stories from their past, sometimes laughing, other times they were somber when the conversation touched on losses and fallen comrades. I saw no point in being there. I checked on how his recovery was going, and after ascertaining that all was well, I left to peruse more documents and then get some sleep. At least, that was the plan.

That night, again, the pigeon tried to plague me. But this time I'd loaded new spells into the crossbow bolts. It might have helped, because the vile bird seemed to calm down.

The next day was boring. When I woke up, I was actually surprised at the lack of messages on my phone. Then, once I learned from the guards that nothing had happened over the course of the night, I decided to devote the entire day to meditation. It was, in fact, long overdue.

My source had been developed quite well lately. I felt I had to acknowledge this. But in fact, I was now only at the ninth rank. Let me remind you that the worst is the tenth. But there was no reason to despair, because I'd started the strengthening process, and all that I needed to do now was keep on training, and carrying out treatments, and most of all, I needed to participate in battles. Of course, the ninth rank, this is in reference to my source -- my energy reserves, recovery speed, and so on. That kind of thing. But my primary advantage was my rich store of knowledge collected over several centuries in a far more magically-advanced world.

I returned to the drawing room, made myself comfortable, and plunged into deep meditation. I could be brought out of it either with a touch, or if the chain of runes for detecting heartbeats was activated. Even that would wake me up only were strangers to enter. But nothing happened until the evening, so I was able to devote the day to strengthening my own self. I distributed the accumulated energy throughout my body, and also did some light work on my magical channels. I also improved the speed in which I could pump energy through so-called magical depots. And I didn't neglect my defensive capabilities, either. Neither my Diamond Armor, nor my energy reserves were panaceas -- not at all. I also further strengthened my skull bones, tweaked the structure of the bone fibers, and did some work on the seams between the fixed bones.

Anyone from my past life would not have believed that I'd be engaging in this kind of thing. Just the same, to mock tending to one's body like this, well, that would be stupid, regardless of how many other defensive techniques the healers in my world employed. It was far from superfluous to, say, make your skin so strong that a spear, even one charged with energy, would be unable to pierce it. I also devoted several hours to increasing the elasticity of my heart sac. I couldn't do this to the heart itself, however now the tissues surrounding it were impervious to bullets, even from a rifle. To do this, I had to create a magical combination that was passive in effect. I'd have to spend energy maintaining it, of course, but safety first, as they say.

And just when I was finishing my meditation, and checking on my work and all of my upgrades by sending energy through the channels, my phone rang.

It was my one of my men reporting that the mercenaries were back in our area. This time they'd used two different detachments to capture a couple of villages. The lookout reporting this didn't know how many troops were in each detachment. However, he estimated that there were now one hundred and fifty of them in the village we'd just cleared, but they didn't seem to have a lot of hardware with them, except for two tanks.

Tanks, yes, I'd read about them not long ago, and immediately wanted to ride in such a marvel of machinery, touch it, fire the cannon. Be careful what you wish for, right? I guess that, one way or the other I'd get up close to one tonight! In the other village, it was the opposite scenario, where only fifty men had established themselves. These numbers were only rough estimates, but just the same, unpleasant.

The timing was a problem...I thought we had a couple of days before they'd be back. This could all be because of that prisoner exchange. They could tell that we didn't have a large force at the castle, and this had emboldened them.

And here I was, about to ask Chernomor if he was ready to again lead the guard. Maybe I should wait, though.

"Bang"

The door burst open, and Chernomor strode into the room.

"Where's my sword?!" he roared, causing plaster dust to fall from the ceiling. "Where's my armor?" After him ran Victoria and Valery, and I asked them, "Who told him?" They glanced at each other, each one looking guilty. I sighed. “Grandpa, go lie down! We’ll handle this ourselves...”

“I’m ready! Where are my weapons and artifacts? Where did you hide them?” He couldn't calm down.

“Here's the thing...Chernomor, they’re gone. We had to sell some things, and other items were lost...” clearly Victoria hated telling Chernomor this, but he had to find out sometime.

A wealth of emotions crossed the old warrior's face, but then he nodded, indicating he got it. After all, he’d spent years in a coma, so why hang onto his things?

“Well, give me something to fight with! And I can’t make my way through the forest with a bare ass!” he growled, and I laughed. “Let’s go out there and recapture these villages. We need to teach them not to trespass on our lands! Are you ready, Vika?” He turned to the countess, but she shook her head, saying “Don’t ask me.”

“Why not?!” Chernomor was surprised. “We’ll rough them up and be done with it, short and sweet!”

“The head of the clan is Mikhail,” she pointed at me. “And he will make the decision. Don’t you remember what father said?”

Chernomor was about to protest, but Victoria spoke first. “Only one can be the head of the house. A team can’t have multiple leaders.”

Hmm...Good stuff, that. I thought more and more highly of her every day.

“You’re right, Vika,” Chernomor nodded.

"What are we going to do, Mikhail? Just don't tell me to sit this one out. I've done my shared of that in my time."

I thought about it, and quickly reached a decision.

"Okay then," I smiled wickedly. "Gather the guard! We'll take ten men with us, and have the rest ready as backup."

As Valery set about putting together the strike force and setting up a defense here at the castle, the countess, Chernomor, and myself drew up a plan. We gave Chernomor a large, if not the best quality, sword. It wasn't easy to find something that would fit, but we also managed to come up with a uniform and set of armor from the loot we'd already scored from the mercenaries. And, of course, we decided to bring along one of the machine guns, and not the smallest, either.

This time our plan was simple. Not that our last plan was terribly complex, either. In any event, we didn't waste time on strategizing. We piled into the armored cars and set off, but in half an hour or so we stopped. You see, I sensed people in the forest.

"Ah yes, they've grown some smarts since last time," I said quietly.

"What are you talking about?" Victoria asked.

"This time they have groups of patrols. They're watching the perimeter of the village, and also the surrounding territory."

And indeed, a full kilometer from the enemy base we regularly spotted small teams of two or three enemy patrols set up. Each of them had radios, and I heard them responding to a roll call, and thus, should one of them fall under attack, the base would immediately be alerted. So even if we took out the patrol, their base would know about it within five minutes.

And in the village itself there were, indeed, one hundred and fifty men. Actually, one hundred and fifty-six in total, and among them quite a few with above-average Gifts. No doubt the strongest were earning a handsome salary out there. I was certain that the prisoners had told them all about our capabilities. They were definitely better prepared for us now. But it could be worse. Since I wasn't able to interrogate them, they had no idea what my abilities were. So even if we couldn't dislodge them from the village this time, I could at least inflict damage.

I spent the next two hours scouting. I tracked the enemy's patrol routes, and took a good look at the base. Having done so, I decided we should strike, but first, I had to make some preparations — in particular, I created a pile of corpses for Victoria. You see, that plan was to again have Victoria create zombies for us, and again we'd use them against the mercenaries. How fun!

Actually, that was the gist of our strategy. I returned to the others and told them what the lay of the land was, and they all agreed that the time for action was now. Victoria took half the fighters and disappeared into the forest, Chernomor took the other half, and went to the far side of the village, while I moved further out.

I made a wide circle around the village, shooting down patrols, one after the other. I didn't even try to hide. On the contrary, I made a point of making sure I was seen by at least one of the patrols before killing them. I wanted to make sure they had time to call for reinforcements. I'd killed four patrols before hearing the roar of engines, at which point I hid in the forest. Fortunately, hiding at night was easy for me. I saw well in the dark, whereas regular people didn't. I then radioed Vika and told her to launch her part of the plan.

Meanwhile, a detachment of thirty mercenaries and two armored cars were sent out after me. They didn't know where I was, though, and went to where I'd killed a patrol and started looking around in the woods there for me. I waited until I heard explosions on the far side of the village, and as soon as the detachment was about to head back in response, I fired my crossbow, hitting one mercenary.

The others rushed back to kill me, but I was already gone. All they found was a mess of footprints in the snow. Meanwhile, as they bumbled about looking for me, I headed to the agreed upon rendezvous.

Another half hour passed as the fighting continued, and then first Victoria and her men and then Chernomor and his appeared. No one required treatment, although some had suffered minor injuries, but generally, all was well. We'd all decided to not risk engaging in combat this time.

Instead, we'd retreat once we achieved our objective using the Zombies.

Victoria's men were fine, since essentially all they'd been doing was escorting her to the corpses. She then did her thing with them and sent an army of the undead to attack the mercenary fortifications. Once she sent out the first batch of zombies, she gave another batch to Chernomor, who then created more chaos with the undead troops.

"Well?" I asked him. "Happy now?"

"And how!" he said. "But I'm weak. Very weak. There was a time that I'd have scattered their forces all on my own. Sending that kind of rabble to the Bulatov castle is a slap in the Family's face!"

"Down, boy," I smiled. "Just watch, they'll come after us in hordes now."

And indeed, according to Victoria, he was at least fourth rank. But he'd been weakened by the years in a coma, and right now I'd say he was closer to the sixth or seventh rank. But he'd mastered a lot of skills and experience, and once a pro, always a pro. It wouldn't take him long to get back his former strength. With a little training, and some serious fighting, in no time Chernomor would again be a mighty warrior.

"So what do you think they'll do next?" I asked him, after checking out the aftermath of our efforts. We'd killed quite a few of the enemy — about sixty men. Now there were less than a hundred of them in the village.

"Well, they have three options," he replied.

"Either they'll attack the castle before long, or they'll dig in even deeper in the village and wait for reinforcements. The third option is that they'll get the hell out of here! I think the latter scenario is the likeliest, but the first two cannot be ruled out. It's a pity that we didn't take a single prisoner -- then we could have found out more about the enemy."

"Okay," I nodded. "Now they're ready for us, so we can't repeat our performance, so let's get out of here."

"Well, wait a minute..." Chernomor said thoughtfully. "There's that other village..."

"Didn't I say we were heading back home?" I smiled. And then, for the first time ever, Chernomor the Grim smiled at me.

* * *

The village of Sviridovka

"Commander! The first detachment is under attack!" reported a soldier covered in sweat as he flew into the headquarters. "We've suffered serious losses, but the enemy has retreated!"

"Keep me informed," the officer nodded and motioned to the soldier to carry on. "Ugh..." he rubbed his bald spot, and shook his head. "Well, they won't attack us again today."

"True!" nodded another officer sitting at the table eating his now lukewarm dinner.

As they'd only just settled into this village, he

hadn't had a chance to eat yet. But now that they'd set up the defense, placed men at the posts and stationed others in the barracks, they could finally relax. So the officers were ready to enjoy a quiet dinner, and maybe play some cards. And the news about the attack on another detachment rather pleased them. You see, according to intelligence data, the enemy didn't have a large force, so they wouldn't be dispersing them.

"So yeah, tomorrow we'll drop by the castle, and let the countess entertain us" one of them laughed.

"Ideally, she'll already be naked," snickered another.

"Right, have you actually seen her? If you like the scary type, okay," said the youngest of the officers. "I'll take a close look first. I don't share my talents with just anyone."

"You're crazy, kiddo. When else will you get to do it to a countess? Even if she's a witch with warts, well..." before he could finish the door swung open, letting in a blast of cold.

"Perelepenko, you bastard!" the commander immediately growled and stared at the soldier frozen at the threshold. "Why the hell are you standing here? Get out of here!"

"Brrrr..." the solder just stood in place. "Urrrrgh.."

"Perelepenko?! Drunk again? What the hell?! Have you no idea the kind of trouble you're in?" the commander rose from the table and headed toward Perelepenko, who meanwhile pulled a bundle of dynamite out from under his coat.

Just then, a powerful explosion thundered somewhere in the village, and then a second, and a third.

"Brrrr..." said Perelepenko again, and then he activated the detonator.

CHAPTER 7

I FELT RATHER FATIGUED. It wasn't too bad, but still, I didn't like it.

I'd had to put a lot of my energy into the last sortie, but at least we'd cleared the village with no losses of our own. Yes, some of my men were wounded, but this didn't cost me much. Most of my energy expenditures were on treating myself. After all, when a detachment of mercenaries armed to the teeth is on your tail, you don't count the costs. I spent resources on reinforcing my muscles, and others on further hardening my skin. I would have liked to devote more to these two areas, but I also had to deal with some damage here and there simply from the heavy demands I'd had to make on my body. Unless a body is developed, it simply cannot handle excessive quantities of energy poured into it. Over time, muscles and ligaments begin to tear, joints lose their flexibility, and tendons stretch, and are thinner. Thus, this all requires maintenance. But in this recent foray, I'd only taken a couple of hits, with no damage to critical organs.

As we drove back to the castle, everyone was sunk in their own thoughts. I was, overall, happy about the trophies we'd scored on our outing. The men, meanwhile, were pleased that we'd come across some nice food supplies. They were all happily exclaiming over it as they loaded the huge boxes of provisions into our trucks -- our newly acquired trucks, of course.

Victoria was also smiling. I think what made her heart sing were all the corpses we loaded into one of the trucks. It was full of them, and I gave her carte blanche to do whatever she wanted with the dead mercenaries. I didn't expect that she'd ever have to worry about running out of them. What she needed to train her Gift showed up right at her doorstep with enviable regularity.

In fact, I thought it was odd that the mercenaries hadn't yet blocked the road to the castle. That's what I'd do. I'd simply cut the castle off from the outside world. Then, they'd just wait for our supplies to run out. Of course, now we were unloading two big trucks stuffed with provisions for the castle. And yet another was still heading this way. We could actually hole up for quite awhile.

Although, yes, I do believe I'd read somewhere that the roads all belonged to the Empire, and so the Emperor had forbidden anyone from messing with them. They all had to be kept open. No doubt the mercenaries had no desire to provoke the wrath of the Empire, although this law was, apparently, a rather new one. It was instituted after an incident in which hostilities between two Families resulted in a road blockage that extended over several hours. It so happened that this occurred when a powerful healing artifact was being transported to the heir to the throne, who was in dire need of it. Every since then, anyone who messed with the roads was swiftly and severely punished. That put a stop to further blockages.

I wasn't the only one who was tired now. Victoria had spent a lot of her energy raising and keeping the dead in their "undead" state. And Chernomor had thrown himself into the fighting with such gusto that I was worried he might fall back into a coma. Our fighters, too, had spent the entire night rushing about in the snowy forest. Once we got back to the castle, we all headed right for the dining room. We were all ravenous — I could barely restrain my stomach from trying to consume itself.

"Mikhail! Are you wounded?" asked Victoria in surprise as soon as I took off my jacket. I was wearing a light shirt under it, and now a large blood stain in the shoulder area was visible.

"Nothing to worry about, Victoria," I said, casually pushing aside the edge of the torn fabric. Under the saturated material of the shirt, my skin was absolutely unblemished — no sign of a wound. This, despite the fact a bullet had clearly pierced my shirt there.

"Sorry, I should know better," Victoria said, chastened. "I'm still not used to your, well, powers."

"My tricks?" I laughed, guessing what she wanted to say. Well, yes, it was a sort of sleight of hand.

Meanwhile, Makar flew into the dining room, took one look at our hungry faces, and flew back out.

"All will be ready in a minute!" he shouted as he left. As soon as we all sat down at the table, we heard the rumble of trolley carts being pushed down the hallway. Then Makar entered with one of them laden with dishes with sparkling silver covers. "What you see here is no worse than what you'd find in the best aristocratic houses of the Empire!" said Makar with pride.

Uh-huh. It reminded me of when I sampled an oyster served to me in an expensive restaurant for aristocrats. The waiter first arranged the tableware, setting cutlery next to the dish, and then he proudly removed the silver cover to reveal the dish. It was underwhelming.

"Sorry, Makar, but why such ceremony for serving these rations?" I asked. "And why is it I'm eating worse now that I'm a count than when I was residing at the tavern?"

"Count, you're not being fair," said Chernomor in a deep voice. "These aren't just any dry rations. Do you see the emblem?" He turned over the sealed box and showed me an insignia on it.

I didn't know what it meant. Yes, I saw a coat of arms. Okay, nice.

"So what?"

"Here's what," said Chernomor, "Imperial dry rations are nothing to turn your nose up at!" he said, and then he began unpacking his box.

The others hadn't waited even, and were all digging into the food in their meal boxes. I looked at them and shrugged. In the end, any food was better than nothing at all.

"Hmm..." I threw the first piece of mystery food into my mouth. It was kind of like a cut up candy bar... the piece I just ate was brown.

"Well? Tasty, eh? Now try the porridge!" Chernomor boomed approvingly.

In fact, I couldn't stop eating. No matter that the food really was delicious, despite its nondescript appearance. What mattered was what my scan of this food revealed.

The bar I was eating contained as many nutrients as what a huge meal at the tavern provided. And it wasn't bad tasting for a candy bar. Once I'd consumed it, I turned to the porridge, which was outstanding. I had no idea how they'd manage to cram so many vitamins into it, but by now I was ready to shake hands with the creators of these rations. Clearly, the Imperial Army cared about its soldiers. I didn't want to think about the amount of research that went into putting these meal boxes together. I asked the others what was in these dishes, and Chernomor grinned and again pointed to the back of the box.

"This is Meal No. 305. Do you see? That number indicates how often the composition of the different dishes has changed.

Really. Yes, decades of painstaking work went into these rations. And we now had a truckload of these boxes, which should last us for quite awhile. These meals were designed to be consumed by people who engaged in grueling physical activity. And when the body is provided all of the nutrients and other elements it needs, healing processes go much faster. I knew I'd have to spend less energy on self-healing.

"Okay," I got up from the table. Victoria and Chernomor were again delving into memories and I saw no point in sitting around eavesdropping. "I have digested the information. And now all that's left is to digest this food. If a war breaks out, call me."

I waved farewell then and headed for my drawing room. Right, we still had a lot of work to do in the castle before I had a dedicated space for myself. In the meantime, this drawing room would suffice as both a sleeping space, an office, and whatever else I needed. It was rather a shame, in light of all of the other rooms in this edifice. But we still had to clean them, furnish them, as well, and, where needed, carry out repairs. A person could spend the rest of their life on house maintenance, really. Who had the time for it? Not me. It'd be a waste for me to spend my resources on, say, fixing the staircase, or even plugging the leaks in the roof.

That night, the pigeon let me sleep. Like usual, I was prepared for him, just in case, with my ceiling traps, and my loaded crossbow, but this time there was no need. Had I actually killed it with one of my spells? Hopefully I had. And with these thoughts, I drifted off into a sleep that extended into the morning.

"What kind of demon are you?" The question arose deep inside me. Yes, that night the creature had left me alone. And so for the first time in what seemed like ages, I slept well. I almost felt like thanking the pigeon, except for one thing. When I awoke the crossbow by my bed was covered in bird shit. I felt like tossing it out.

Right, it was high time we acquired more servants. No way to avoid this fact. Time to get the guards into helping out. This, too, was a war of sorts.

I downed a couple of cups of coffee, rubbed the last vestiges of sleep out of my eyes, and got down to business. I reviewed our bank statements and saw that Victoria had paid off the loan, and that the funds had reached the debtor. So that matter had been put to rest. No need to worry about any more payments. Now it was time to formally change the commander of the guard. In fact, this had been on yesterday's agenda.

To this end, I approached Chernomor. I found him in a small room which he'd staked out for himself with a small window. What struck the eye was the heavy machine gun that was pointed out the window. And the room was chock full of all sorts of weaponry, whilst grenades were strewn all over the bed.

"What's all this here for?" I indicated the bed, but Chernomor just waved dismissively. He sat at a desk on which was stationed yet another machine gun. He was either cleaning it or repairing it.

"I was massaging my wooden muscles," he said in a deep voice. "I ended up sleeping on them. I mean the grenades."

Hmmm...I'd clearly neglected to treat any lingering brain damage.

"Okay," I shook my head, resigning myself to the oddities of the future guard commander. "Are you ready?"

"Again you ask me, count!" he exclaimed, and it was only now that I noticed that he was attired in his full dress uniform. It was still a bit too big for him, but he didn't seem to mind. He'd ironed it and it had been cleaned, as well. He had apparently prepared in advance for his appointment as commander of the guard.

I didn't even have to say anything. We both silently walked out into the castle courtyard, where we found the guardsmen, all lined up in a row. Valery was standing before them, with a smile on his face.

"I present your new old guard commander!" I said, indicating Chernomor. "Since you all know him already I don't think I need to introduce him." I could tell by their expressions that they were all pleased by this change in command. They knew Chernomor well, and had already served under him. "By the way, the former commander asked me to make this happen," I nodded at Valery, and he confirmed my words.

I wanted them to know that I hadn't forced Valery's demotion. I didn't want anyone to think less of him for this.

"Ha! Putting the operator of a B-K unit in charge of the guard! Real smart move, that one!" Chernomor said, looking pointedly at me. I just smiled and shook my head. Whatever he meant, he was aiming his barb at the wrong guy.

"Actually, it was father's idea," said Victoria quietly. "He singled out Valery as a man of impeccable integrity and loyalty to the Family."

"Harrumph..." Chernomor cleared his throat, realizing that his nasty barb was a big fail this time. As for me, I had no idea was B-K was.

I found out that it was simple. This was an abbreviation for a mechanized combat suit. In the past, the Bulatovs had a couple of them but they were too costly, even when the Family wasn't facing hard times. One of the suits was lost in battle, and the other broke down and they sold it, as to fix it would have cost them far more than it was worth.

So why did they even mention the suits? The base line price for them started at two hundred thousand, and ended at several million. Not to mention the maintenance costs for batteries, fuel, and more. All this made me want one, just to have it.

Chernomor stood before the men now and began talking to them about something. He'd already been working on a training regiment, and now was "delighting" them with the details of the grueling drilling he had in store for them. All good stuff. They should train. The new commander had my blessings for developing the men's combat skills, even if they incurred serious injuries in the process. Of course, that should only be when I was here at the castle and able to immediately heal them. This kind of hardcore training was the best, though, as it mirrored real-life conditions.

I had Victoria join me in my drawing room. I'd told her to do something, and there'd been no results yet, though days had passed. We needed servants, so where were they? It was wrong to ask the guards to do that kind of work. They needed to train, and also guard the castle rather than waste their time on such menial matters.

"It's a problem," the countess said with a shrug. "I've contacted servants who are seeking work, as well as hiring agencies, and no one wants to work for us. They all say that it's too dangerous."

"What about the ones who used to work here?" I asked.

"I spoke to them too..." the countess said, sounding a little sad. "They're deathly afraid of returning. I even offered them a higher wage, but they still refused."

"I see," I nodded. "Then I'll recruit the servants myself, don't worry about it."

Victoria chuckled then, as if to say "Good luck. A lot of good that'll do you."

"I called everyone," she reminded me. "Don't think I didn't try."

"Aha!" I smiled, "But you don't know how to motivate people. I'm not going to promise you the moon, but by tomorrow we'll definitely have some servants."

Victoria clearly didn't believe me, but I didn't even feel offended. I'll just surprise her, because, yes, I had a foolproof tactic for recruiting personnel. It never failed, and, moreover, it cost nothing at all. No, it wasn't like I was going to make anybody work for food. They'd all be paid a fair wage.

Victoria left to her chambers and I dialed Georgy's number. He picked up right away, as if he was waiting for me to call. The first thing he said was that he hadn't fulfilled my latest task yet.

"Let's not discuss this on the phone. But just so you know, I haven't yet found a buyer for, um, the items. But I'm still looking, and I have a couple of ideas..." What was he talking about? Oh, yes, that ammo! My bad, I'd forgotten all about it. Well, what mattered was that he didn't forget.

"I'm calling you about something else," I said after a pause. "Why don't you drop by and we'll discuss everything then."

How odd, though. As I recall I'd asked him

about the ammo via the phone, and at the time he didn't seem worried about it. Something must've changed, such as some new information, or something. Anyway, I had even more ammo to sell now — Valery already drew up a new list.

When Georgy arrived, he was immediately shown to my drawing room, where I was already sipping a cup of tea over a plate of sweet treats. I had no idea why the mercenaries needed such a big supply of candy and pastries, but I appreciated it. All the more so as they'd delivered them directly to one of my villages.

"Good afternoon, Mr. Bulatov," Georgy nodded to me, and I motioned to him to take the seat opposite me. "All the way here I've been dying to find out what it is you wanted to talk about with me," he said, scratching the back of his head. He seemed rather nervous. "Do you have still more weapons to sell? Or military equipment? The Svyatogors? That would be too complicated for me. I don't even know who to contact. It could get dicey, like I might find myself in cement shoes, or worse..."

"Can you find me a cook and a cleaner?" I cut in, and after he digested my request, he breathed a sigh of relief.

"It'd be better if they were facing difficulties or were disabled. You see, ordinary servants are afraid to come here."

"Hmm..." he thought. "Mind if I make a couple of calls?"

I just waved yes, of course I don't mind, and

took a bite of a chocolate truffle.

Georgy made several calls and then told me that he'd found at least two candidates. I'd have to talk to them and definitely meet them. The main thing was that both of the women had ailing children who were terminally ill, and so if I healed their young ones, these two women would be my most faithful servants. They were both tentatively interested, but didn't believe I could perform such miraculous cures. They lived in the port district, and anyway I wanted to go back there, seek out some Interfaces, and enjoy some delicious food at the tavern. So yes, this dovetailed nicely with my plans.

We also discussed offloading the ammunition. It turned out this was no simple matter, as ordinary gangs didn't use this kind of heavy-duty weaponry. These were Imperial models in terms of the firearms and delivery systems. Indeed, it struck me as strange that ordinary mercenaries were armed with this kind of weaponry. Where did they acquire them? Oh, well. I'd find out sooner or later. I'd simply soften them up first, using physical means, and then they'd give up their superiors, whom I'd handle more harshly.

As we were talking, Victoria entered the room, but seeing that I was talking to Georgy, she turned to leave; I saw her throw me a puzzled look. Yes, I'm sure that it looked strange to anybody else. To her, after all, Georgy was just a regular taxi driver. She had no idea what he was doing at the castle, much less having tea and sweets with me.

However, I saw no need to explain anything to her. Sooner or later she'd see for herself the value of cultivating faithful people. Moreover, Georgy really did have a talent for handling issues that needed attention.

He and I immediately headed to the port district, and along the way Georgy kept calling somebody and would then engage in an animated chat with them. I didn't listen in, and instead meditated, so the time flew by in useful fashion. Before I knew it, we stopped near a nondescript three-story apartment building.

"Sir, if you don't mind, could you wait here for five to ten minutes?" Georgy asked, turning to see me. "She lives in a communal apartment, so there are always a lot of people around."

I nodded that it would be no problem and stepped out of the car. I wanted to breathe a little fresh sea air. Georgy went inside as I looked at where we were.

This was a standard poverty-stricken neighborhood. Narrow streets, apartment houses as if stuck together. The mismatched balconies hung above us looked like they could fall off into the street as they were all fashioned out of cheap materials supported only by the unshakable faith of unknown builders.

"Okay, they're ready to see you!" Georgy's voice pulled me out of my thoughts. "You don't need your mask."

My mask, that's right! I brought it with me,

but forgot all about it. Okay, if Georgy said the coast was clear, then I wasn't going to worry about it.

The first patient was on the third floor, and although it was empty on the streets, inside the building there were people all over the place. What a crowd! Now I knew what he meant by communal apartment. We turned down a long corridor lined with doors into cramped rooms. There was a single shower for everyone, and only one bathroom, as well.

Now there were about twenty people sitting in the corridor, and everyone was blindfolded. They muttered complaints, but as soon as Georgy raised his voice, they all shut up and waited to be allowed to take off their blindfolds.

"Wouldn't it be easier if they were all in their rooms?" I asked Georgy, and he just shrugged.

"One of them might step out just as we were walking by. Or else they could peek out at us."

He was right, actually. It was better that we could see them, but not vice versa.

In the last room a woman sat on the bed, and she, too, was blindfolded. On her lap lay a child who looked to be around seven years old.

The little one was as skinny as a skeleton and totally bald. Yes, her malady was most unpleasant, and could deprive the child of her life within the next six months.

"Is it...you?" said the woman, hearing us walk into the room "Can you save my baby? Please, I beg you! Do everything in your power! If you cure my child, I will serve you for the rest of my life! I... am an excellent cook, I have thirty years of experience! I promise..."

"Let's discuss everything later, okay?" I said, placing my hands on the child's weakened body. The child seemed to be a girl, but it's not like I could tell by just looking.

My diagnosis took less than a minute, and I found out what the poor little girl was suffering from. Yes, it was a tumor, and not just one. The infection gradually spread throughout the weakened body, but the biggest problem was the blood. In short, I'm talking about the blood-forming organs — spleen, liver, lymph nodes, which are primarily found in the bones. But for me, this was a simple matter, and in my world, even weak healers who ranked slightly higher than students could cope with such maladies.

All this required was a background in anatomy, and a comprehension of the processes associated with such infections. As such tumors are usually located near the main magical channels, they weren't difficult to manipulate. But this wasn't fast work, because if one were to kill the infected cells too quickly, the results could actually kill the patient. All in all, the process took me around half an hour. I didn't spend much energy, actually, but in the end, her body really got a jump start.

"Do you have anything to eat around here? Preferably something tasty," I added. "The girl is going to be extremely hungry."

"What? Trina just hasn't had an appetite lately," said the woman.

"Mommy... but I *am* hungry, I want to eat..." the little girl squeaked in a weak voice, causing tears to trickle out from under her mother's blindfold. Of course, by "jump start" I meant a huge charge of vital energy directed right where it was needed.

"Well, then, show us your cooking skills! Otherwise, I'll order delivery from the eatery on that Street of Three Sluts," I decided to scare her.

"No, we don't need that slop! I'll make us something right now!" And with trembling hands, she began untying her blindfold. Georgy moved to stop her, but I shook my head. I knew that she'd be my cook for sure.

"Trina, baby," the woman said tearfully. "What would you like? Porridge? Some pie?"

"Meat! She needs meat!" I said, after conducting a short scan. Any food would do for the time being, but what she needed to rejuvenate was meat. "So then, contact Georgy later and he'll bring you to our castle later, in the evening. Agreed?"

She almost threw herself at my feet, she was so grateful. But I didn't need that kind of thing. I told her that the best way to thank me was to work at the castle. And my work here done, I left. She needed to collect herself, feed the child, and wind things up. As we drove to the next address, Georgy gave me the rundown on the cook's professional skills. Sounded like she was something of a real chef. There were some fine restaurants both in the port district and in the city center, and she wasn't a simple prep cook.

Well, I'd find out for myself once I tasted her cooking. But based on what Georgy was saying, I wasn't going to be disappointed. Now, though, I had to figure out what to do with the little girl. I hadn't planned on building a daycare center in the castle. As it was, I left little Marina, the knitter of hats, to her own devices. Already she'd made hats for every single one of our guards, and exacted payment from them. She was quite the little entrepreneur.

Next, we sought out a cleaning lady. We had a lot for her to do at the castle. She'd need helpers, too, but for now we'd start with her.

The cleaning lady lived in a separate apartment, so this time we didn't have to have everyone wear blindfolds. She met us outside the building and led us inside and then to her son's room. I see... This is the same issue that plagued Timothy, my driver now, before I treated him, except that this patient was much younger, and so it would be much easier to heal him.

The boy was hit by a gangster's car half a year ago. They'd slammed into him and ran right over him as they sped off. As a consequence, he'd suffered even more fractures, and yet, miraculously, he somehow survived. True, he could no longer move or even speak, and his mother was feeding him through a special tube. She worked like a slave to pay for everything —

otherwise, they'd be starving now. The head of the family bailed out, and ran off to work on a merchant ship. He couldn't take it, and so he abandoned his loved ones.

"Georgy didn't really explain anything," she said. "You're not a black healer, are you?"

"Why would you think that? Do I look like one?" I was surprised. Judging by her expression, I guess I did. And yes, my cloak did reek of necrotics, so I guess I could see why she was worried about it. "No, I'm no black healer, don't worry. Did Georgy tell you what my conditions were? Are you willing to work for me at the castle?"

Even if she wasn't ready to agree to this, I felt sorry for the boy. He still had a lot of life before him, and without my help he was doomed to spend the rest of his days in bed looking at the ceiling. But he wasn't brain dead, and so he'd be fully aware of everything. All he could do, though, was move his eyes. Not to mention the constant pain, about which he couldn't even complain.

Well then, this case was more difficult. My diagnostics revealed a lot of hidden damage, all of which needed to be dealt with. I set to work after sending Georgy out to get us something to eat. And I got to know Zina a little, that being the child's mother. As I conducted my treatment, she could see the changes in the boy's condition taking place, and that's all she needed to believe in me and my powers. I worked until late in the evening, and so I arranged for the new servants to start work tomorrow.

As I still had things to do here, I let Georgy go, and, donning my mask, I set out on a stroll. What else could I do since my spatial anomaly locater remained stubbornly silent? But then there was one weak signal. It was about a kilometer away — a portal had opened. By the time I made it there, all the fun was over, and now the official forces were gathering up any artifacts and tossing the corpses into a special vehicle. What a shame, but yes, this was a little bit like fishing. I wanted to make a catch, but instead I ended up eating some shish kabobs. I enjoyed every bite, so, really, it wasn't a total bust.

I decided I didn't feel like hunting for portals until the break of dawn. I had the feeling this would be a waste of time. And so I summoned Georgy again, and had him take me back to the castle. Of note that night was that I'd had an interesting discussion with some sailors. They'd intercepted me on one of the main streets and tried to force me to serve on their ship. Like, "the pay is good, loser, you can earn enough money for your bread." I got the impression I should buy some new clothes.

"So, no new loot today?" smiled Georgy as I got into the car. I'd noticed how tense he was whenever I showed up with new items for sale.

"Not today. I wasn't lucky," I said, and, hearing this, his smile was even brighter.

He had no other questions, as we'd already talked about everything else. In the morning he'd deliver the new servants to the castle -- both of the women were ready to swear fealty to me. They even found somewhere to place the children for a little while until they settled in. I didn't ask where. The main thing was that finally we'd dealt with the matter of the servants.

I got back quite late, but Victoria was still up and in my drawing room. She was seated in my favorite chair, meditating. I was glad, as I wanted to run a theory I had about the pigeon by her.

"Victoria, might I ask you something?" I said, interrupting her meditation. "Since you're here anyway, meditating..."

"Hmmm...?" she opened her eyes.

"I'd like to switch bedrooms, just for tonight, okay?" I knew this wasn't very gentlemanly of me, but I needed a good night of sleep.

The countess was surprised, but then she shrugged and said she'd have Makar make up a bed for me. I thanked her right away and headed for her chambers.

"Ahhhhh..." I moaned in pleasure as I stretched out on the most comfortable sofa. My consciousness immediately began to fall into a sweet slumber, and behold, bright flashes of memories of my former life, my youth appeared before my eyes.

I once again found myself in the Academy of Magic under the auspices of the Imperial Family. Only the very, very best future magicians of the Empire were allowed to study there. An image appeared before me of how I first stepped over the threshold of this academy. How I was introduced to my peers, and then I saw her...She had the Gift of Flame, and had a personality to match. Damn, she was hot! In more ways than one! Everything spun around me with lightning speed, and then, she and I were alone, and she looked at me, and licked her lips and...

"C-o-o-ooo!"

"What the...?!" I was surprised. That's the last thing I expected to hear her say.

"C-o-o-ooo! C-o-o-ooo!" she said again, and then no trace remained of the sweet, vivid dream.

I got it...The bird was stalking me, and no, it didn't live in the drawing room. I'd selected Victoria's room because it was totally enclosed. Not even a mouse could get in here, not to mention a rather large bird. I'd realized some time ago that this was no ordinary pigeon, but now I was doubly sure of it. And the ceiling here was lower, but the bastard was now flying right beneath it. Just like before, here he was, taunting me with his screams.

I pretended that I hadn't noticed him, and started collecting pure energy from my source and concentrating it on my fingertips to generate a rather weak attack spell. As soon as the creature once again flew over me, I threw off the blanket and slammed green lightning right at it! That spell could stop a wild boar's heart, and this was a pigeon! But right before the spell hit him, the bird vanished. And then he reappeared in a far corner of the room.

"C-o-o-ooo?" The bird cocked his head and began to strut across the floor.

I didn't bother attacking again. I didn't want to lower myself. Instead, a plan was emerging in my head on how to trap the bird, but this required preparations. I intended to use a chain of spells I hadn't employed in a century or more, so I needed to refresh my memory. So, forgetting about sleep, I sat up on the sofa, made myself comfortable, closed my eyes and plunged into meditation.

At first the pigeon hid and was in no hurry to approach me. The he started loudly cooing, but I ignored him. Even when he started cooing right into my ear, I paid him no attention. I simply sat there concentrating my energy and weaving it into a complex structure within.

This went on for several hours, and gradually the pigeon began to lose its temper. He cooed, flapped his wings, and flew right past my face. He didn't dare shit on my head, at least, probably understanding I'd definitely have to kill him then. Finally, he totally lost it, and alighting atop my head, he pecked me right on the forehead.

It enraged me, of course, but in fact, this is exactly what I wanted. Opening my eyes, I smiled at the creature, but it immediately disappeared into thin air.

"Fly, fly!" I said, smiling. "I've already procured your mental-life cast..."

All I needed was one touch to acquire the cast. By pecking me on the forehead, the pigeon had given it to me. Now I'd have no problem tracking the bird. All I needed was to complete the tracking spell. Even if he flew a kilometer away from the castle, I could always feel where he was. It didn't matter where he hid himself. Nobody could escape this spell, not unless they were a healer, of course. Only we can change up our vital indicators at will.

I spent what remained of the night, and also most of the next morning casting the spell. It wasn't a complicated process, but it took some time. I had to decipher what I got from the cast, weave it into an energy construct, and then, well, none of this could be accomplished quickly. And what was especially annoying was being distracted by a phone call right in the middle of the process, but that's what happened. They were notifying me of the arrival of Georgy at the gate, along with two women. I told the guards to let them in and take them to the drawing room, and then headed there myself.

I'd already talked to the two new servants. And of course, Georgy had already explained the situation to them in detail. So I had no doubt that they'd be loyal, given how I'd saved their children. And I'd also told them about the consequences should they betray me. In short, they'd die a fast, though painful death. Most important, this death would be inevitable. Both women were impressed by this, and also believed me after seeing my abilities. And so I didn't foresee any problems with my new staff.

After I greeted them, I then passed the task of orienting them to the castle over to Victoria. She, of course, was amazed that I could find the two women in just one day. Well, didn't I tell her I'd do just that? So why be surprised? After this, I went back to generating my spell to handle the bird.

Ding!

"What the hell is this now?" I exclaimed, grabbing my phone. We'd received an email at the Family's address.

I felt like ignoring it and going back to my meditation, but then I noticed that the sender was Viscount Snegirev.

I had to see what the bastard was proposing. It was, in the end, quite predictable.

To Count Mikhail Bulatov:

I suggest we meet and discuss everything in a safe place. I give you my word that my guard will not attack your castle during our meeting.

Right. Wasn't that fishy? After all, he was the type. "I give you my word...*blah blah blah*." The Family email was akin to communicating in public. Imperial employees have free access to it and they record agreements. So that meant should he attack the castle while I was at this meeting, he'd have to compensate for all the damage down to the last kopeck. But he only mentioned *his* guard, saying nothing about the mercenaries. Uh-huh...

Well, yes, it would be interesting to see what this was about, but I didn't want to leave Victoria here without protection.

Although, why worry? We had plenty of weapons, and the guards were primed and ready to fight back. And we also had Chernomor back in action, and he was worth an entire army. Not to mention that Victoria herself was no helpless damsel. She had around fifty corpses in the basement, which is a considerable army in the hands of a necromancer. Most important of all, she possessed enough strength. And so off I went to meet Snegirev, my mind at rest. Before I left, I checked our sentries, and buffed them up a little by spending a tad bit of energy on them.

Then I summoned Timothy, and I took a seat in the SUV, along with two of our guardsmen. Yes, just in case.

It took us half an hour to get there, because the venue selected by the viscount for our meeting was located in the very center of the city. In fact, he seemed to be on the level as I saw not a single one of his guardsmen there. He sat at a table by a window, and when he saw me walk in, a smug smile appeared on his face.

"I'm glad you came, Count Bulatov," he did not extend his hand for a handshake. But that's understandable. Anyway, I wouldn't have deigned to shake it.

"Why did you convene this meeting?" I asked, sitting down opposite him. The waiters immediately began laying out the dishes, and I did not refuse partaking of what was offered. I'd get at least something from the meeting. I knew the viscount wasn't attempting to poison me, as I scanned every morsel before chewing it.

He grimaced slightly at my brash demeanor, but said nothing.

"Okay, let's get straight to the point," his said, his expression serious now. "How much money would it take from me to convince you to hand the Family over to me?"

"How much are you willing to pay?" I asked, my mind off of the delicacies before me now. This was interesting, indeed.

"A million rubles. That's a fabulous amount, is it not?" he said, baring his teeth in a semblance of a smile.

"Yes, that's a big fat wad of money," I agreed. "I can't even imagine what a million rubles all stacked up on this table would look like. Can you show me, at least approximately?"

"I don't have that kind of money with me, but a stack of that much money would look something like this," he said, indicating the height with his hands. Yes, it was a lot of money indeed.

"Let's make it two million," I said, and before he could speak I went on, "You take two million, roll it all up in one big wad, and shove it right up your ..."

"BULATOV!" he cut in, his tone menacing. Sheesh! Right when I was getting to the good part! "You're getting arrogant... But okay, I'll give you one more chance... I can offer you the position of serving me as my vassal. With full benefits, live and be happy!"

Well now, was he, perhaps, simply stalling for time? No, I didn't think so. But Snegirev clearly knew that I wasn't about to agree, and yet there he was, going on and on, making these ludicrous offers.

As if I could ever agree to any of his schemes, when he'd get Victoria and could do whatever he wanted with her. Worse still, I'd end up subordinated to him, and that would be the end of the Bulatovs. What Snegirev was suggesting was a way for me to form a new aristocratic Family. As I understood it, this was legally an option. That being said, there were no guarantees for me in any of this. Not that I needed any guarantees, as anyway I had multiple reasons for not agreeing to any proposal that emerged from Snegirev's mouth.

"Viscount," I interrupted his spiel.' "You look like an adult...Why do you spew this nonsense? You will never be a count! Just as you were born a viscount, so you will die as one... And the more you interfere with us, the faster this will happen," I added almost nonchalantly, having finished sampling another delectable dish.

"Well, what are you doing here then if you don't want to strike a deal?" Snegirev was taken aback.

"I just wanted to look at your face. Recently you've been really mucking up your attacks, and I was interested in seeing how you were taking it. Obviously none too well," I finishing, staring straight at him.

"Okay," he exhaled tiredly, "do you want me

to tell you something? Then I will, he said, taking a sip of his drink, and leaning back in his chair. "There are two guards with you now. Right? Yes, that's right," he answered his own question, and produced a mean smile. "And how many men do you have back at the castle? Ten? Oh, I'm sure I'm spot on with that guess! And you didn't think to have Victoria go somewhere safe, did you? Bullseye again, right? Gee, before now, I thought better of you, but you don't really care about the Family, do you? Maybe you despise it, even. Ha! Yes, to hell with Victoria!"

He kept on essentially interviewing himself while I carefully controlled my biophysical responses. You see, I knew Snegirev had an artifact that could read the reactions of whomever he was speaking with. It's a complex artifact, but it wasn't created to perform that function. However, whatever the case, the viscount was certain that he could see right through me. He asks something, then the artifact feeds him some data on whether I believed him or not. But the artifact was basing this data on my body's reactions. My heartbeat, my body's magical field, what hormones I was releasing, and so on.

But of course all this was under my control. So it wasn't at all difficult to deceive the artifact, and in so doing, deceive the viscount, as well.

"But, candidly, we couldn't find out anything about you. Who you are, from whence you came... It's like you dropped in on us from another planet," he chuckled. "However, all joking aside. I gave my word that my guards would not attack the castle, and I shall keep it. But nothing was said about *other* aristocrats..." And a jubilant smile spread across his face. "I would like to note that it was not *me* who attacked your castle, but one of my distant acquaintances."

"Oh, what a scoundrel! Whoever would have thought..." I said mockingly. "I didn't see that coming!"

"Make fun of me all you want," he took a slurp from his glass. "But as we speak a detachment of fifty fighters has marched on your castle. They easily did this with the help of a canopy," he said, continuing to slurp his drink.

A canopy, yes, this is a one-of-a-kind artifact. I read about it once; it's quite an expensive thing. And also quite dangerous. It can mask a small detachment, but there's a wicked payoff. Due to their exposure to a transcendental magical background, all these invisible people would be dying in terrible agony within a couple of days. Their channels will simply burn out from the inside, but apparently, the mercenaries under the deadly canopy weren't aware of this. However, the viscount himself knew, and so he'd sent the worst of the bunch into this battle. The strongest fighters among them were rank seven.

"It's clear that you and your artifacts provided the major contribution to your recent victories. But now here you sit, and thus, the castle is almost mine!"

"As far as I can recall, it almost *was* yours," I

said, smiling as I took another bite of cake. It was a tasty treat, I have to say. “So how did it go? Did you like it back then?”

“What would you do if I were to bring, say, a couple of thousand fighters there? Hmm...?” He also started eating some cake, and was silent for a couple of minutes. “I don’t understand,” he suddenly threw his fork aside. “Why don't you fly to the castle to save it? You’re just sitting here gorging yourself...”

“It’s a good cake,” I shrugged. “And what’s the hurry?”

Seeing my calmness, Snegirev began to grow noticeably nervous, and periodically flicked a glance at his phone. Now that I’d had my fill of the cake, I was enjoying the tea. I sat back, waiting for the phone call to come in.

“Ha!” he shouted, as the screen on his device lit up. “Let’s listen to the report!” he put it on speakerphone and picked up the call. “Hello! What's taking so long, idiots?”

“Um...” responded a deep voice at the other end. “Vika, how do you work this piece of shit device?”

“Chernomor, you’re already on the line. You can speak, and he’ll hear what you say!” That would be Victoria talking.

I watched how the dolt’s expression changed. Seriously, they were using one of his men’s phones.

“Right. So then, can you hear me, Viscount Snegirev? Even if you can’t, I don’t give a shit.

Listen up, anyway. Know that I've put a target on your back and if we see you around here, you're a dead man!" he snarled the last bit so fiercely that the viscount couldn't help but start.

And then, Chernomor hung up the phone. He probably crushed the phone in his fist right after that.

"That must've been a wrong number," I said. "Well, then, have a nice night! I guess I'll go now."

And then I got up, and headed for the door. I had no other business in the city, and back at home I had some unfinished matters to attend to.

"Here, have this!" I said as I passed by the waiter. It was a tip. I figured Snegirev wouldn't be leaving one.

"Thank you," he said, and bowed slightly as he accepted the gratuity.

I quickly walked to the car, plopped down in the back seat and closed my eyes, plunging into meditation.

The road flew by again unnoticed, and from afar I noticed a column of smoke rising above the castle. But when I got closer, I realized that it was not from the castle itself, but from the forest nearby. It was there that our patrol had spotted the enemy detachment, exactly one hundred meters from the wall. Why exactly one hundred? Well, it's simple.

The viscount's plan was based on his soldiers making their way into the castle under a cloak of invisibility, and then they'd attack our defenseless guards. But the Heartbeat chain of runes cannot be fooled by invisibility. And I'd put these runes on the bones of each of our sentries. All I had to do now was check the runes once a day, and when necessary feed more energy into them. Because of this chain of runes, my guards could all sense an approaching enemy within a range of one hundred meters.

And, in fact, they sensed the enemy when they were about that far from the castle. Subsequently, the coordinated fire of several heavy machine guns ended Snegirev's cunning plan to take the castle. The battle was over before Victoria and her zombies could even make their entrance. Now, all that remained was to watch as the guards collected all the trophies. The weapons weren't anything special, and not much was left of the clothes, nor did they carry any money on them. But the canopy artifact...that was worth a lot. I could sell it, or keep it for my own use.

Yes, it could slowly kill me and my people, but that was only if I were to activate it. Before I ever did that, I'd first remove any toxic energy from everyone's bodies, and that would prevent the otherwise inevitable consequences.

Now, I finally had a few hours of free time. It was not yet evening, and so I locked myself in my drawing room after ordering that nobody disturb me unless it was a matter of life and death. An example would be if, say, thousands of troops with aircraft and tanks descended on us. Nothing short of that. Leave me alone.

"Okay, it's curtains for you!" — I snarled as

soon as I activated an incredibly complex chain of spells. I'd factored in every little thing, even the size of the creature I was targeting. "This is it, you bastard..."

Rising from my chair, I closed my eyes and felt where my sworn enemy was hiding. Not even the viscount and all of his connections could vex me as much as this petty little fowl. But now I knew where he was. And the bastard didn't even bother to hide out in a deep hole.

"Sir?" the cleaning lady said in surprise when I burst into the tallest tower. She'd just started cleaning the tower, and everything was a mess. "I'll take care of it! There..."

Crack!

I was sprinting up the rotten stairs, and my foot crashed through one of them. Did that stop me? No. I was unstoppable! I'd fallen forward on the stairs, but I quickly scrambled to my feet and went on, ignoring everything around me.

The tower was in ruins, but I climbed. I reached the ceiling of the roof, but I knew there had to be an exit upward somewhere. It took me about ten minutes, but I found a hatch leading to an attic. I entered it as stealthily as possible.

"There you are..." I saw the bastard sprawled out on the floor in the corner.

The pigeon was on its back, its wings spread wide. A greenish flickering light surrounded them. His legs were twitching a little. He was in deep, lovely sleep right then.

Here comes my sweet revenge. I slowly

approached the sleeping bird, bent down, and...

"*C-O-O-O-OOO*, CHUMP!" I shouted, grabbing the pigeon by the throat.

Who knew a pigeon could look surprised?

CHAPTER 8

"MIKHAIL!" VICTORIA EXCLAIMED as soon as I walked into the drawing room

"What is it?" I looked inquiringly at her, but she just pointed at my shoulder.

"That...What is it?" The countess was jolted out of her meditation by the sight of me.

"You really don't know??" I was surprised this time. "It's a pigeon," I said, glancing at the bird perched on my shoulder. "Say hello to the lady, birdbrain."

"C-o-o-ooo!" the pigeon complied with my request, and even inclined its head at Victoria. *"Coo-Coo-Coo!"* We'd spent quite a while this morning rehearsing this moment, during which I'd flicked my finger at the little idiot's head over and over again — my way of slapping some sense into his tiny little brain.

"Wow..." the countess was astonished. "Does he...understand you? Or was that just a coincidence??"

I could only shrug, and sit down at the table. I'd encountered Makar on the way to the drawing room, as well, but he didn't deign to ask me why I had a bird perched on my shoulder. I asked him to bring me coffee in the drawing room, and now I sat at the table looking at the mail. It looked like something was in the works, and I had to see what it was all about. I was left to my own devices for only five or so minutes, though. It wasn't the pigeon that interrupted me this time. In fact, he'd flitted off my shoulder and onto the armrest of the chair by then. It was Victoria. She'd tried to go back to her meditation, but finally couldn't stand it.

"No, what gives?" she shook her head. "Where did that bird come from? What are you doing with it? What exactly is going on here?" Clearly she had far more questions in her head then answers. Although... I didn't see what the fuss was. Once I read something about sea pirates. Birds were absolutely normal pets for them. True, these were usually beautiful birds, such as parrots. This bird was just a pigeon, though, a common bird, normal in appearance, perhaps... but if you looked closely, you could see how the tips of his feathers were flickering.

"Well, his name is Kooky," I nodded at the bird relaxing on the arm of the chair. "He'll be living with us."

"What do you mean by that?" Victoria was even more surprised.

"He owes me, and now he's serving me -- that's how he's compensating me for damages. We've come to an agreement," I shrugged, and then went back to reading my email messages.

Victoria sputtered something or the other as if she was indignant. But that was fine. She'd get used to it. After all, this bird had truly confounded me with its endless nocturnal attacks. He seemed harmless, but I was still furious at Kooky the pigeon. All the more so as I now understood how intelligent the bird was. Moreover, he'd targeted me alone, ignoring the others in the castle, not even revealing himself to them.

It was quite devious, the way I'd managed to catch him. I made my way into the attic, grabbed the bird by the throat, and shouted into his face. *"C-o-o-ooo!!!"* Just like the bastard had been yelling at me. Moreover, when I had him in my hands, I poured a lot of energy into his strange, freaky body. This is what confused me. He had a truly strange body that was both material and magical. This is why, before, I could only hit his wings with my crossbow. Yes, this would momentarily paralyze him, but that was all.

The frightened bird opened his beak, and then morphed into something intangible. I don't even know what to call it. It was like Kooky was a ghost, but just for a little while. However, I could track him still thanks to my new spell. And so when he manifested again under an old sofa, I rushed right at him.

And he was trapped, as he couldn't take off whilst under the sofa. That being said, he scuttled along on his little legs pretty swiftly. He rushed from one mountain of rubbish to another, all the while cackling. Sometimes I could swear he was cursing at me. But then, wouldn't that make this an intelligent pigeon? But what would compel a smart creature to disturb the rest of a tired healer night after night? I'd long been wondering this. It took me an hour of chasing the scurrying bird to catch him, as whenever I got a grasp of his tail feathers, he would turn intangible and slip away. It drove me crazy. But each time I touched him, I poured a little energy into his body, and could therefore make changes to it. First, I paralyzed his wings, and then one of his legs. But even so, he continued to hop about on a single leg, hiding first under some junk lying around in the attic, and then jumping down the open hatch to the floor below.

I yelled at him and rushed down after him. I again managed to touch him. Kooky again disappeared and then reappeared not far away with two paralyzed legs.

I thought he was all mine by then, and that I could finally exact my revenge. But no! He pecked at the rotten stairs like a little jackhammer and squirmed through the hole he'd made as if he was a worm. A really fast worm, at that. And then he made it through the wall of a locked room in the tower.

I was forced to call in the guards. We blew our way into the room, blasting the windows out in the process, but victory was mine! The pigeon cowered in the far corner of the room staring malevolently at me. He was like a samurai who accepted his fate and was prepared to die. But then, I changed my mind. I no longer wanted to kill him. The bird struck me as willful and interesting, but most importantly, I'd won already. His fate was in my hands.

I realized that the bird truly was intelligent, so I started asking him why he was pestering me. After all, I wasn't the first to attack him, and I'd put up with his taunting me every night for quite awhile.

After asking all this, I was still left in the dark. All I got was that he'd lived in this castle long before I showed up, and he'd been happy with the status quo. And so he didn't like it when I burst onto the scene, so to speak. So that's all there was to it. What specifically he didn't like about me was still a mystery. Kooky couldn't say. Or else he simply wanted to keep it to himself. He had taken a disliking to me, though.

We could have ended our association right then, but it struck me as a good idea to demand reparations for damage done. And so I gave Kooky the choice: serve me, or die. If he chose the former, I could promise him he'd be well-fed and rarely bored. This would beat his former pastimes in which he hovered under the ceiling and shat on the head of counts, not that he wouldn't get the opportunity to engage in similar pursuits.

The pigeon took his time considering my proposition... But in the end, he nodded in agreement. So then I removed his paralysis and allowed him to climb onto my shoulder. He was quite comfortable sitting there, and looked downright regal as we made our way down the winding staircase of the tower.

"Sir!" exclaimed the new cleaning lady, who all this time was at the bottom of the stairs. In the time it took me to catch the pigeon, she'd washed the floor and put a lot of trash out into the corridor for removal. The guards helped her with the heaviest items, and now I found myself in a very clean, totally empty room. "I'm just about done here!"

Hmm... This tower reminded me of my own tower in my past life. True, my former tower was five times the height, and thirty meters wider.

"Oh!" exclaimed the cleaning lady then. "Made sure not to step in it!" she said, indicating the bird shit now all over.

"C-oo-oo!" shrugged the pigeon, as if to say "I didn't do it."

"You do understand that if even a drop falls on my back..."? But the pigeon looked aggressive, as if to say, "What d'ya think you're gonna do about it?" I changed his attitude pretty quickly, though. "I'll fix you up real well. You'll find yourself shitting once a week. Hope you like bloating up like a balloon. Do you read me loud and clear?"

"C-o-o-ooo!" and he saluted using his wing.

And then, assured that he wouldn't dare shit, I strolled into the drawing room, surprising Victoria, who'd been meditating. Once there, I turned my attention to Family matters.

"So how do you think you'll make use of the bird?" again the countess couldn't stop herself from asking. And indeed, how to meditate with a pigeon cooing right there?

"What ...?!" I turned away from my notes. "Ah, well, I haven't decided yet..." And that was true. I felt like Kooky would come in handy for something, but I didn't know what yet. "Kooky, fetch me..." Hmmm...It's not like the bird could serve me coffee. He'd spill it, or shit in the foamy milk or something. "Well, I don't know... bring me a pen."

Kooky rose, disgruntled, and threw me a look of contempt, but my eyes flashed green, and that inspired him to do as I asked. True, I didn't need another pen, and so then I told him to put it back where it was.

"There, you see? The bird is useful." I smiled, and again plunged into studying our financial situation.

Right now, we were in the red, meaning our expenses exceeded our funds. What can I say? Even if we were to buy bread, that would add to our dilemma, because we were earning nothing. We had to do something about that.

I spent the rest of the day studying our properties. I thought about how we could make use of them, and also calculated the lost profits from the factories taken from us. Why did I do this? I needed to decide which of our lost assets I wanted to recover first. I couldn't take it all back from everyone at once, nor did it make sense to take a piece of this and that.

Hmm...maybe I should write a book? Why not? Out of all of the literature I'd read here on the art of healing, only one book was of interest, and that one was, well, not entirely legal. This way, I could kill two birds with one stone. I'd teach the local mediocrities something about healing, and also earn a lot of royalties and such from their efforts. Ah, but there was only one problem. I had to keep my abilities under wraps, and so no book until the distant future. As for now...

I needed to think about how to bring in more people. We needed a lot of them, because we had to populate all of the villages surrounding the castle. As it was, they were nothing but dead weight, and did nothing for the Family's balance sheet. Of course, first we needed to secure these villages. Again, what it all came down to was that we were facing numerous enemies.

Thus, I pondered these matters until nightfall. Then, shortly before dinner, Victoria sent me off to attend to the first batch of disabled guardsmen. She also sent Kooky along with me. Didn't I tell her? Kooky was useful. I didn't tell the bird this, though. I simply gave him some seeds to thank him for his service thus far, and headed for our so-called infirmary. All we had here were beds, but now, the room looked a lot more comfortable, with clean white sheets, a sparkling floor, and so on.

The men needing medical aid knew what to expect, and were compliant with my treatment. This is because Chernomor had told them to shut up, lie still, and do what I told them. The old man obviously knew how to keep the men in line. These wounded soldiers all lying in their beds were so still that they looked like they weren't even breathing.

Victoria was also there, having decided to join us. Even now, it seemed she doubted my powers a little. This, despite how impressed she was by how I'd brought Chernomor back. Now, she wanted to see how I handled the vital energy of life. But I could also teach her how to better use her own Gift. Right now, just like many mages in battle conditions, she'd simply unleash her power in one big wave, and thus far all she could do with it was use it in simple spells. But with complex spells strength alone wasn't enough. Complexity required a far more subtle approach.

At the moment, though, I couldn't be distracted by the countess and her Gift. I was about to treat four wounded men at once. Two were missing limbs, and two were simply unconscious, and their internal organs were like soup, not to mention the state of their magical components.

"Right..." I murmured, after conducting a detailed diagnosis of the last patient. "If no one else had attempted to treat him, this would all be much easier. But they poked around quite a lot..."

"Is it beyond you?" asked Victoria, worried. "Is it that bad?"

"It's very bad, and that's fine!" I smiled. Victoria was at a loss, and I didn't enlighten her. "Everyone leave now! There's nothing for you to see here... And you," I nodded to a guardsman standing near us. "Do you have a knife? Preferably a surgical blade."

He blanched, but brought me what I asked for. The knife turned out to be not surgical at all, but quite high quality. So, after energizing it and removing harmful microorganisms, I kicked everyone out of the room and began the operation.

There are times when it's easier to do it all yourself. Take this guy — the local healers had treated his stomach wounds with dry vital energy. It had stopped the bleeding, but that was all. His intestines were still a mess, having healed themselves in haphazard fashion. This resulted in the formation of adhesions that entangled his internal organs as if they'd been put into a blender. I had to go in there manually to put them all back in place. After opening him up, I excised what needed taking out, not forgetting to monitor the patient's condition and pour vital energy into him when required. The operation itself didn't harm him at all, as the blood vessels touched by the knife immediately closed in spasms, and while the tissues I cut absorbed any drops of blood that escaped.

All of this took me around an hour and a half,

and in the end, he didn't even have any scars on his stomach, and I'd spent, at most, ten percent of my energy reserves. In contrast, his former healer spent around thirty times more energy on him, and the healing session had to be overseen by a surgeon. Really, since the healers here are so inept, and don't want to learn, why didn't people turn to regular doctors first? Better still, healers and the doctors should, in fact, work together.

The other three patients had, comparatively speaking, far simpler issues that needed addressing. I employed the knife just a couple of times more, but that was because I wanted to practice with it. What turned the tide for my patients, though, was my adjusting the pattern of energy circulation inside their bodies. Of course, I channeled in some of my own energy as needed. And two hours later, all four of the men were on the mend and in good shape.

"Well? Are you ready to serve me now? I smiled before leaving the room.

"Sir!" they all chorused almost in unison. "Until death! I swear! You're the head of the Family, right? The one everyone has been talking about?" It seems they hadn't yet been brought up to speed after all.

After they all swore their loyalty to me, they then asked me to help other wounded fighters. And so the entire next day, that's exactly what I did. Victoria finally believed in my strength, and this provided me with an opportunity to become a little stronger. I also practiced surgery. Yes, long ago I'd engaged in this practice, but now I was reaching new heights in terms of my skills with the knife. I didn't know what a book on surgery was doing in the Family library — I'd come across it by accident, but it was full of excellent information.

I spent the entire day referring to it and cutting into people. I didn't have to, really, but I just couldn't resist. If it was possible to spend less effort healing the wounded with the same effect, then why not try it?

Over the day, two dozen fighters were brought to our castle. And by the following morning, we now had some sixty soldiers in our guard, or, actually, even more. Subsequently, the courtyard was filled with cries of pain, as Chernomor began putting the men through his own version of boot camp. They gained new valuable combat skills, and I treated them as needed. In between treatments, I tried to figure out how to make use of the pigeon.

"Cooo?" Kooky tilted his head to the side as he saw me looking his way.

"Hmmm..." There must be something I could use this bird for. Again I peered into the pigeon's very soul, subjecting him to the most detailed diagnostics.

By then I'd succeeded in securing the feathered idiot's unquestioning obedience. Of course, I didn't take his word for it, and instead relied on an old trick. Now, any time I suspected him of treason, the runes I'd applied to his cervical vertebrae would alert me. And then, he'd either die swiftly without pain, or, conversely, slowly in great agony. I might also simply paralyze him, and be done with it. That's what I told the pigeon, anyway. In reality, I didn't yet have the strength to waste on doing this, but I could be very convincing -- after playing a little with the bird's nerves, I managed to convince him of my power over him. I didn't anticipate further problems from Kooky. And it was quite a surprise how intelligent he was, such that he should pick up on my not-so-subtle cues.

Just the same, I looked at him, and still didn't know how to make use of him. I did have a couple of thoughts about it, though. The fact that he could morph into a ghost wasn't the main thing. Of course, it was a big plus, that feature. For me, though, his main advantage lay in how receptive he was to magic. He had his own full-fledged source, with highly developed magical channels, and I could work with that. I could continue to apply runes to his bones. How else was I to communicate with him? The pigeon could serve as an excellent scout. He could go anywhere. I'd seen this that night I spent in Victoria's chambers. Really, this was a huge asset.

But the problem was how to communicate with him? I could create a chain of runes to establish a mental connection with Kooky, but that was just a temporary fix. In my world, that was used for when you were drunk or something, because it was far better to simply use the "Unity of Thought" spell. This allowed you to see, hear, and feel whatever your target saw, heard, and felt. For this, all you needed was a mental cast of their vitality, and that was it! You could then be a hundred kilometers apart, and yet know exactly what they were up to.

But with a bird, it was more complicated. I could inscribe runes on Kooky's bones right now, and draw the same chain of runes on my own bones. But then it would work both ways. I didn't want Kooky constantly spying on me. But on the other hand, maybe I could streamline and edit the transmission of signals a little...Hmmm...

"Come here, Kooky...come to me," I beckoned him over, but now he was playing his "I'm a dumb bird" trick. He cocked his head to the side and shat on the floor. Um, no bird, I'm not letting you play the fool. "Get over here, on the double! I'm going to upgrade you!"

He understood many words, but not all, and he was clearly interested in an upgrading, as he immediately hobbled towards me and climbed onto the table. And then I put him to sleep. The process of applying the runes was a painful one, so why waste resources on pain relief? And if, right in the middle of applying the runes, he decided to turn into a ghost, we can only guess what the results would be.

Kooky was unconscious for about an hour. That suited me just fine, and now...

"Get up, let's check the connection," I put the bird on his feet. For some time, Kooky shook his head. And then, uttering his signature *"Cooo!,"* he lifted off, fluttering in the air. "Do you know Morse code?" I asked, and in response, he shook his head. Hmm... In my world it was different from the code used here. And yes, it wasn't called Morse code, but in essence, it was the same. To send a message you tap-tap-tapped in intervals, or else used sound to do this.

Yes, I applied the connection runes to both myself and the bird, but I limited the range of functionality quite a bit. Again, I had no desire to feel what Kooky was feeling at any given time. Essentially, this chain of runes was created to basically share emotions and sensations with another person. Anything more would be difficult to transmit, such as images, and what would be the point? But I'd altered the runes a little, and now, by pouring some mana into the runes on my bones, I could transmit my voice to the pigeon. As could he to me. But what could he say besides *"C-o-o-ooo"*?

As a test, I sent him into the next room and taught him the basics of transmitting data through repeated sounds. One short *"Coo!"* meant "yes". And two short *"Coos!"* meant "no."

"Kooky, do you see Victoria?" I asked. Of course, I knew if he was responding correctly because I knew where people were by their heartbeats. Now, Victoria wasn't anywhere around. Kooky seemed to be flying around the armory, while the countess was in the dining room.

"Coo! Coo!" I heard it in my head.

Damn! I, the Grand Archmagister did not think things through here. Now the bastard could scream his cursed *"Co-o-oos!"* right inside my skull! As much as he wanted, and he didn't even need to be anywhere near me to do this. Um, yeah... I dug my own grave, so to speak. But so it was. If I must, I'll tweak the runes later.

As I experimented with the runes, I came up with several interesting combinations of magical signs that would improve the functioning of the entire chain. That would suffice for now. And eventually, little by little, I'll come up with a new chain that will completely suit me, because at this point, I was sure that the pigeon would come in handy.

"Find Victoria!" I mentally ordered Kooky, and, sensing my excitement, he flew all over the castle.

Right now, the countess was occupied with her workout, so the bird had to do a lot of flying. But in just ten or so minutes, Kooky's signal sounded in my head.

"C-o-o-ooo!" Kooky had completed his mission.

Okay, so that was done. So now the next step: How to get more detailed information from him? I'd have to teach him Morse code in full — no way around it. Without further ado, I summoned the bird back, and started refining the runes. This took a lot of energy, of course...I was already sweating. But all I managed to do was increase the communication range, which resulted in a greater energy drain inside the bird. I had no time to do more. My phone rang then, and though I cursed it, I was given some important information. One of the guards patrolling the far borders of our estate discovered some men out there. These were heartbeats somewhere in the forest, nothing more.

"Okay, retreat," I ordered him. I didn't see any point in risking anybody when I had a great scout right here.

I hung up the phone and stared at the pigeon.

"Cooo?" he seemed surprised, and cocked his head in that way of his. I, too, was surprised. This was because as I was talking on the phone, the pigeon had climbed onto the table, picked up a sugar cube with his beak, and dropped it into my cup of tea. And then he dipped his beak into the cup and started drinking it. But that was *my* cup of tea! And it was hot, too. How could Kooky drink it?

"Look here," I decided not to scold him for now. But later I'd make sure he understood that tea was sacred. Now, though, I simply showed him the map on my phone and pointed out where he should go. "Fly there and let me know when you've arrived."

"C-o-o-ooo!" He puffed out his chest and gave me a salute with his wing. Then he ran across the table like it was a runway, flapped his wings and disappeared into thin air.

All I had to do now was sit and wait. The guardsmen hadn't seen the enemy. He'd only felt the approach of five people. Moreover, he felt it at the very edge of his field of perception, a hundred meters away. That meant there could be a lot more of them there.

Rather than just waiting, I called Chernomor and told him to rouse the men, and also prepare machine-gun emplacements and the Svyatogors. These vehicles performed very well in the fight against infantry. I now had that costly canopy artifact that can cast invisibility over an entire area, but it would be folly to employ it. I decided I should sell it for a lot of money, which I needed more than I did the artifact itself.

Right away the castle came to life as men took up defensive positions and prepared to repel a potential attack. Just then, Kooky arrived at the destination.

"C-o-o-ooo!" I heard it in my head, and I poured more mana into the chain of communication runes.

"Do you see people there?" I mentally asked my feathered scout, and immediately he signaled "yes".

Hmmm... I needed to somehow adjust the volume of these messages, but that could wait. "A lot of people?" Again, "yes." But what did "a lot" mean to a pigeon? Okay, let's not worry about it. "Are these mercenaries?"

"Coo! Coo!" Kooky signaled "no".

I started asking a lot of questions, and the dove answered many of them with a *"Coo-Coo!"* These weren't mercenaries, nor were they the viscount's people, nor were they the viscount, who was someone Kooky knew by sight, nor was this some other Family's troops.

But then...What if...

"Are these offworlders?"

"C-o-o-ooo!"

A smile spread across my face. Looks like the money I needed had come right up to my doorstep — almost. All I had to do was reach out and snatch this unexpected bounty.

"Chernomor!" I shouted so loudly that I didn't even need a walkie-talkie. "Where's the Svyatogors? Let's go!"

I didn't even know how many offworld guests to expect. Along the way I set about interrogating the pigeon, which, by the way, wasn't very difficult. There were more than five of them, and less than ten. And that's all I needed to know, as I had with me twenty guardsmen and also three Svyatogors, as well as Chernomor and Victoria. I had no reason to take more, as that would leave the castle open to attack.

It didn't take us long to get there. Half of the roads were covered in huge snowdrifts, but this was no problem as we were in the Svyatogors. It beat leaping through the snowy landscape on foot.

This time I left the crossbow behind, opting instead to bring a sword I'd picked up at the Interface back in the port district. It wasn't as fine a blade as the one I got from the mercenaries, but the materials were from the world of the offworlders. Even in my old world we didn't have swords like this. Although they weren't strong blades, they were excellent energy conductors. It was all I needed. In fact, any stick would suffice, but this sword was far more convenient. It was superior to merely touching my target when it came to manipulating his body. That is, once I pierced my adversary's skin with this sword, it would take far less time and effort to do what I wanted to him.

As we made our way there, the offworlders succeeded in cutting through the forest to one of our villages. There were plenty of such settlements on our lands, but they were small, and to the chagrin of our offworld guests, they were also all deserted. Ah, well. How were they to know? Not that I cared. All I was interested in was their artifacts and weapons, which I hoped were fashioned from valuable resources.

* * *

Ten minutes later
Village of Merkino

“Commander...” the soldier said quietly, having already inspected a third house in the village. “No one here, either.”

“Damnation!” exclaimed the man dressed in a paltry breastplate and helmet. He’d had high hopes for this outing.

They managed to open the portal not far from his home. And so he’d quickly put together a detachment by dashing into the nearby tavern and recruiting some guys. They then headed straight through the portal. But they found themselves in a cold, deserted, inhospitable forest.

"To hell with it...Let's keep on looking," he ordered the handful of fighters. "And you!" he said to the two catchers. "Take whatever you can from the houses and carry it all to the portal."

"But there's nothing here..." the catchers mumbled. But, having provoked another outburst from the commander, they ran off to search some more. And soon they found something really valuable.

"C-o-o-o?" -- the bird was surprised when the door to the chicken coop swung open and two hungry men appeared on the threshold.

"Oh! A local bird! Let's take it with us!" shouted a catcher, pointing at the pigeon sitting in the chicken coop and pecking at some leftover chicken feed.

"Okay! Only...it looks familiar. I've seen that bird before..."

Without further ado, they shut the door to the coop behind them, and rushed to catch the stupid bird. The pigeon looked quizzically at them as they drew near, all the while pecking at the kernels of grain. And then, as the offworlders lunged at him, he suddenly vanished. Instead of catching the pigeon, the two men grabbed air, ending up planting themselves on the ground.

"C-o-o-ooo?" Now the pigeon was hovering below the ceiling above the catchers.

"You little shit..." one of them cursed,

jumping up to try to grab him, and failing.

The sounds of the flailing catchers emanated from the chicken coop for the next ten minutes, and finally the commander showed up to see what was going on.

"You idio..." he started saying, but then he saw two faces in the light of his flashlight. Both of the men were covered in something... "What's this? Did a Gvarnian stork shit on you?" The commander was referring to a gigantic bird that would often shit-bomb their urban citizenry.

"No!" responded one of the catchers. "It's...that...that...I can't think of what it is. I've seen that bird somewhere before, but I can't remember where!"

"C-o-o-ooo?" Now the pigeon manifested above the commander's head.

"Right you are. I've seen it before, too...Ugh! Yuck!" the commander grunted. This was due the pigeon's excellent aim. Moreover, the bird's timing was impeccable.

And Kooky drove the commander and his men into a frenzy. They were jumping around all over the village now, provoked by what seemed like the pigeon's taunts. The pigeon flitted from roof to roof dodging the snowballs and occasional crossbow bolts slung its way by the seven offworlders. Now and then one or two of them would try to clamber onto a roof after him.

"C-o-o-ooo!" With one last call, the pigeon flapped his wings, ascending skyward, and heading off into the distance. At this, the men gave

up. It was futile to go after the bird now.

"Okay, that was a waste of time," snarled the commander. "Get what you can and let's go home."

"Let's *not* go home," said someone new, and a stranger walked out from around the corner of the last house on the street. The dastardly bird was seated on his shoulder now, and was clearly gloating at the offworlders. A huge older man, and a girl dressed in a black dress followed the stranger, along with two dozen heavily armed soldiers.

"Damn!" said a catcher, slapping himself on the forehead "Now I remember where I've seen that bird! I saw it in..." but he didn't have time to finish. The crossbowman standing nearby raised his weapon, and shots rang out in response, shattering his protective artifact, allowing dozens of bullets to blast into him. The two sides came together in battle, then, although in no time the offworlders suffered a crushing defeat.

"Where was it he could he have seen you?" The stranger asked the pigeon on his shoulder, but the bird seemed to shrug.

"C-o-o-ooo!" And then he shook his wings.

* * *

The sortie, of course, was highly successful. The ride through the forests and fields was lovely, as was the stroll toward the village. We didn't drive right up to it, and instead parked a ways off so as to approach unnoticed on foot. The other fighters drove right up to the portal.

Did I feel like going through their portal now that we'd killed some seven of the offworlders? Yes, but this would be risky. There could be anything on the other side of the portal. For example, a clever trap from which even I may not return. I still lacked enough strength to take such a gamble.

In any event, we scored several artifacts. What was a shame is that I never found out where these offworlders had seen the pigeon before. So it goes. That crossbowman pointed his weapon at Victoria, and the guards had to take immediate action. They were just following protocol. They deserved nothing but praise for acting swiftly.

As no one else emerged from the portal, it soon closed up. And we returned to the castle. I asked Makar to brew me a giant mug of coffee, and then I locked myself up in my new study in the tower.

The cleaning lady had worked her magic, and the guards had put together simple but high-quality, comfortable furniture. Later on I'd procure something better, but for now what was there sufficed. And so, with Kooky now perched on the table, I sat down beside him in front of a big stack of documents on the Family's real estate in various cities. Yes, indeed, theoretically we had a lot of properties. I wanted to come to an understanding of which of them were still under our control, and if any might be sold, for example. Why shouldn't we offload useless assets? For the next hour I delved into this issue.

I soon needed more coffee, and sent Kooky to Makar. Of course, I could have just phoned him, but it was better still to employ a carrier pigeon in the digital age. I was, after all, an old-school Archmagister.

I sat back awaiting the arrival of the coffee when someone knocked at the door. The heartbeat did not actually belong to Makar, but just the same I bid whoever it was entry. It was Chernomor. He just stood there frowning at me for a minute. Then he sighed heavily and filled the office with his booming voice.

"Mikhail, we need to talk," he said.

"Let's wait," I said, motioning to the pile of papers. "In the morning I'll be all yours, but now..."

"No, now," he insisted. Did I mention that Chernomor was as stubborn as a flock of sheep? That's putting it lightly. He's worse than that. "Now!"

"In two hours?" I tried bargaining for time. After all, I could tell this was slated to be a serious conversation. At least, as far as Chernomor was concerned.

"Mikhail, who are you?" His first question surprised me. Fortunately, at that moment Makar came through the door with my royal mug of coffee.

It smelled good enough to fight over. I'd kill anyone who tried, actually. Right then, it was essential to my wellbeing.

Chernomor waited for Makar to leave, and then he slammed the door after him, almost crushing my pigeon! Just in time, Kooky turned immaterial, and then he reappeared on the table. The way he looked at Chernomor, I suspected someone was going to get shat on tonight.

"What do you mean, who am I? I'm the head of the Bulatov Family," I shrugged, although I knew what he was trying to get at.

"Don't trifle with me! I've been watching you! And I can only assume one thing, I'm sorry to say this," he went on. "But I know that you're an offworlder!"

CHAPTER 9

I LOOKED AT HIM. Yes, he seemed to be a grown man, and yet here he was, all bent out of shape because he thought I was from another world.

"Are you sure?" I smiled.

"Damn straight I am!" nodded Chernomor. "I've been studying you for some time now. You've slipped up numerous times..."

And he started going through various incidents when I allegedly "revealed myself." But was I even trying to hide who I was? What would be the point? Really, I fully understood how I must look from the outside. The way I'm so curious about things that are routine around here, for example.

"You do the impossible when it comes to healing, that which confounds scores of the most learned professionals!" boomed Chernomor. But of course he was right.

"Well what if I do? Your professionals are all imbeciles!" I responded hotly. And in my world, nobody would disagree with what was the obvious.

"There you go! You called them 'your professionals,'" he quoted me. "And your knowledge about magic is amazing, and also...the way you looked when they brought you that book on biology!"

"What do you mean?" I was surprised. "It was a good book. I read it from cover to cover — it was fascinating."

"That was a third-grade textbook!"

Well, he had me there. I wasn't making much headway in convincing him I was from this world. Not that I was really trying. Why should I? Chernomor was truly loyal to the Family. I'd told Victoria my story, and this old man guessed it all by himself. Of course, not totally, as right now he was under the assumption that I was from the world that interfaces with this one. He seemed to think that I'd simply learned the local language, and that was all I needed to move around unrecognized.

"Chernomor," I interrupted him. "You are right. I am indeed from another world, but not from the other world you think I'm from."

And then I told him exactly what I'd told the countess. Only, unlike Victoria, he didn't interrupt me, and simply silently listened to me. He nodded and now and then asked me to clarify something, but that was just fine. What mattered was that he didn't doubt me. The gist of his own assumptions had been spot on, and this pleased him.

"Hm..." Chernomor was thoughtful, and scratched his thick beard. "In short, I don't really care where you're from," he said, and pausing, he nodded to himself and went on. "The most important thing to me is that you regard this place as your home now. Only then will you do all in your power to bring the Family back to power," he concluded.

Hearing this, I was all the more convinced of his loyalty. He was the right pick for commander — I could trust him with anything. And although I hadn't allayed all of his suspicions, I was certain that we'd resolved this matter.

"Make sure that he doesn't turn into soup," Chernomor said, pointing at something on my table, and then he left.

"What ...?!" I asked, and looking at where he'd pointed I saw Kooky sitting right in my giant mug of coffee. He was actually drinking the brew — the foamed milk was all over his little face.

I had to flick my finger at him. But Kooky paid me no attention.

"*C-o-o-o!*" he purred contentedly. But that was *my* coffee! Yes, it had cooled off some, but the bird had no reason to bathe in it.

So I had to extract the bird myself, as if he was a tea bag.

"Have you lost what few brains you have in your tiny little skull?" I asked, setting him down, causing a small pool of coffee to form around him.

The situation devolved from there when he ruffled his feathers and shook himself like a wet dog, splattering coffee all over the table in the process.

"C-o-o-ooo!" And he pointed at the mug with his wing, as if inviting me to have a sip. Then, as if nothing was amiss, he strutted off to attend to his pigeon affairs.

* * *

Hideout for the mob
Somewhere in the port district

"Boss, we found him!" said a guy of about twenty years of age as he entered the dimly lit cramped room in which a fat, bald man was sprawled out in a cushy chair talking to a couple of bruisers.

"Go now!" waved the boss, and the two bruisers ambled out the door.

Looking at the kid, the boss then lit a fat cigar which immediately filled the room with thick, acrid smoke. The kid didn't even wince as the foul odor wafted over him.

"Well?" The boss looked at his minion. "Where is he? And who is the bastard?"

"Your car is now in the possession of some count..." said the minion, noting how the veins on the boss's forehead began to bulge.

This was far from the first time he'd delivered bad news to the boss, and so he knew to maintain a poker face. He was, in fact, the only one who delivered such reports. Any other messenger ended up leaving the office with a few broken bones. He, though, knew when to shut up and let the boss scream.

And that's what he was doing right now. First, the boss looked at the ceiling and then at the surrounding walls, clenching his fists until the knuckles cracked, and then he sat back and took a series of deep breaths, in and out.

"Yoga... I took up yoga and meditation, so now it's not as easy to piss me off," the boss told him for some reason. "Now my mind is clear of anger and confusion," he said, repeating the words of his coach, some gray-haired Asian who arrived on one of the ships. "When you think about it, most likely someone sold my car to this count."

"That's not it. He didn't even switch out the plates..." the minion began, but didn't finish what he was saying.

"F*ck the f*cking yoga!" yelled the boss, jumping up and slamming a fist on the table, breaking it into two. "Aaaarrgh!" he yelled, and threw his chair against the wall.

He then went at the few other items that passed for furniture there. Not even the cabinets escaped his wrath. Only the lamp extending from the ceiling survived, but only because the boss was short.

The minion stood like a statue, waiting for the boss to calm down. And the rage subsided once there was nothing left within reach. Finally, the boss again was able to breathe in and out, in and out.

“In short, f*ck the yoga,” he said again. “It doesn't work.” He turned his gaze onto the minion, and went on, “So who is this count? Is the Family a strong one?”

“Bulatov. There are two members in the Family. And a whole lot of guardsmen,” he went on, showing the boss a report with several photographs.

The boss quickly looked through the documents, stopping at a photo of the countess.

“Hmm... Gather the guys, have them pay these Bulatovs a visit,” a smile appeared on his face. “But bring this wench to me as compensation. As for the count, make him suffer.”

“But... This is Viscount Snegirev’s zone of interests...” the guy saw how the veins on the boss’s forehead began to swell again, and fell silent just in time.

“I don’t give a shit about the viscount and those who stand over him. That car is *my* ride! I expect to see it in my courtyard, cleaned and polished!” growled the bald man. “Enough! Go now!”

The minion immediately left to convey the boss’s orders, leaving the boss to prop up his broken chair, in which he then sat looking thoughtfully at the photographs.

* * *

“C-o-o-ooo! C-o-o-ooo! C-o-o-ooo!”

“I’ll replace your wings with arms. Want

that?" I awoke to the sounds of my living alarm clock. And then I turned it off. I simply brushed the bird off of the side table by the couch I slept on. "Urrrgh!" I hated waking up like this.

But then I realized why Kooky was raising such a fuss. It turned out that my phone was ringing. It wasn't a familiar number, but oh well, I was already awake. So I picked up the call.

"Hello," I heard the voice of an elderly woman. "Mikhail, I called to tell you that the mob boss knows who stole it from him," the voice issued rapidly from the phone.

"Did you understand any of that?" I covered the mouthpiece, and turned to Kooky. But he just spread his wings. "And you are who, exactly? And how did you get my number?" I returned to the call.

"It doesn't matter," answered the old woman, now I was sure of it. "But he's sending his men out right now."

Hmm...I still wasn't totally awake, and to hear this kind of gibberish already, well... I had to charge up my brain with a jolt of energy to get it to function properly. I stole something from someone...Was she talking about offworlders? What she herself an offworlder? No, it had to be something else...

What else did I steal? Was it that towel I took from my room at the tavern? But as I recall I'd paid for it...

"Ah! I got it! Are you talking about a car?"

"Yes!" affirmed the old lady.

"Well then, thank you. I'll take note of this, then," and after I spoke, I heard a series of short beeps. "What on earth was that?" I asked the pigeon, and he again spread his wings, indicating he sure didn't know.

Well, okay. I wasn't at all worried about some gangsters. They could try whatever they wanted. If they did, I'd simply end up with whatever they had of value on them.

After conveying the message to Chernomor about the possible arrival of guests, I began checking the family email. And yet another message surprised me then. I was so surprised, that right away I got dressed and went downstairs to see Victoria, who was already in the dining room tantalizing me with the aroma of coffee.

"Make sure there aren't any feathers in your cup," I warned her. "Trust me, someone here likes to take coffee baths," and I glanced at the feathered asshole. Meanwhile, he looked nonchalant, as if all he ever did was peck at chickenfeed and such. Immaterial chickenfeed for an immaterial bird.

I'd come to see Victoria for a reason. True, what I said made her choke on what she was eating, and after she was done coughing, I delivered the details.

"We've been invited to a reception in honor of something," I showed her the letter. "It's an invite from the Baulov Family. I don't see any reason not to accept it," I shrugged. These functions were where aristocrats did their networking. While we were rich in enemies, we were poor in allies.

Yes, I knew that we weren't likely to find too many of the latter at this ball. But clearly it would be worth it to check out who was there. Perhaps we'd see Snegirev at this event. If so, I could compel him to challenge me to a duel, in which case I'd dispatch with one of our biggest pains in the tuchus. Of course, I wasn't foolish enough to count on that kind of luck."

"I can't go!" Victoria said. But seeing how taken aback I was at hearing this, she only sighed sadly and turned away. "I have nothing to wear."

"What, really?" I was surprised, but said nothing. I could have pointed out that she wasn't naked as far as I could tell. But these were aristocrats, and clothes were really important to them.

So, I paused in thought, and then I opened up a cabinet and extracted a thousand rubles.

"Here, this should be enough..." I handed it all to her. "Can you order something?"

"Hmm..." the countess pulled open a drawer in the side table, and found a few more bills there. "Actually, I could use some shoes too. Not to mention an evening bag," she said, flashing a smile.

"Woman, do you want to clean me out?"

"Kooky," I turned to my pigeon. "I'm giving you your first combat mission." Hearing this, the bird puffed out his chest. And he looked downright fierce. "If she keeps on robbing me, you have carte blanche to peck her on the forehead."

"C-o-o-ooo!" responded the bird, saluting me with his wing, and glaring at the countess.

"But I'm not kidding. I really do need an evening bag," she responded. "The one I have now, well, everyone has seen it already."

"C-o-o-ooo!" Kooky responded, beginning to strut towards the countess.

She, though, just shrugged, and activated her "Aura of Death." In so doing, she covered both the bird and me in necrotics. At this, Kooky lost his martial aspect. And instead of marching on Victoria, he marched on a small bowl of seeds in the corner of the table. Before long, he made the seeds disappear.

"Cooo?" He cocked his head then, imitating a truly stupid bird, even by pigeon standards.

"Okay, Victoria," I smiled, looking at my cunning, fearless colleague. "Take what funds you need for this. But don't spend more than you need. You yourself know full well our Family's financial straits."

She said nothing in response. But she smiled, and then called Makar, and off they went to do their shopping. It was too risky for her to actually go to a store, so instead they elected to turn to the Internet.

Meanwhile, I kept myself busy. While Victoria was busily planning what she'd wear, I checked out who this Family was, studied their possible connections, and was finally convinced that they were not among our enemies. The Baulovs had moved to Arkhangelsk not long ago, and I think that's why they invited us. After all, for whatever reason, the local aristocrats shunned the Bulatovs.

I was, frankly, disgusted by the locals who didn't welcome us. How to respect sheer cowardice? And that is what was behind their unneighborly relations with us. There was a powerful patron behind Viscount Snegirev, and he was set on destroying my Family. Apparently everyone feared him.

After that, I immersed myself in business matters, and then some meditation, and also with fostering communications with Kooky. To this end, I was teaching him Morse code, which he not only picked up on, but began to study on his own. This world's version of Morse code was quite different from what we used at the academy in my former world.

Kooky really was intelligent, and easy to train, and despite his nasty character, I found I was growing rather fond of him.

Yes, I'd entertained thoughts of punishing him in the past, but, then again, why should I? All those nights he'd deprived me of sleep, and the dirty tricks, like bathing in my coffee...well, this was all harmless fun in the end. Kooky knew better than to cross the line, and that's what mattered. Even when it came to that coffee episode. At the time I was talking to Chernomor, and it had grown cold. I wouldn't have finished drinking it.

Anyway, before I knew it, it was evening.

Timothy drove up in the SUV that was now being sought out by the gang from the port district, and we sat in the back to go to the reception.

I stared at Victoria. She'd selected an evening dress that truly suited her. Yes, again it was black, and she looked great in the colors of the night, perhaps because she's a necromancer. Whatever your power, it generally emanates from you.

That being said, I didn't myself feel compelled to always wear green. Not at all, in fact. Not in this world, nor in my past world. My attire in my past life was never an issue. No matter what I wore, I was still the great Archmagister Mikhail, and I was always recognized by any living creature, even if I was in the most remote corner of the planet. In this world, it was more complicated.

Victoria noticed how I was looking at her, and for some reason she blushed. She lowered her eyes, and all the way there she stole glances at me. I was contemplating how she'd spent our investment of thousands of rubles. She'd selected a dress with rather a severe cut and which revealed very little of her flesh. I wondered why — perhaps she was embarrassed by her scars? Perhaps I should offer to remove them? This would take me a couple of minutes at most, and a minuscule expenditure of energy. It would be a simple matter. All I'd need to do is "motivate" her body to reject the scar tissue, and replace it with fresh, healthy skin.

Actually, the way scar tissue forms is quite interesting. I'd recently studied this. Scar tissue is exactly the same as skin tissue, but with one difference. The arrangement of the collagenous fibers is completely different, which is why scars look the way they do. Roughly speaking, scar tissue grows more rapidly than the more complex tissue that makes up the skin. And that's why, in the event of an injury, the body quickly forms the scars s to protect the wound from germs and such.

As I pondered this, we arrived at the event. Time to focus on matters at hand. Timothy pulled up at the entrance to the mansion, and Makar jumped out to open the door for Victoria.

We then we went inside, and right away I noticed that there were far fewer guests here than at that ball, where I'd first met Victoria. But there was one familiar face, that being Count Cherepanov, if memory serves. He was standing there holding his ubiquitous glass of wine, but as soon as he saw me, he broke into a smile.

"Oh! Count Bulatov, in person!" he exclaimed, raising his glass in greeting. He immediately came up to Victoria and me and kissed the lady's hand. Then he extended his hand for a handshake. "Mikhail," he came closer and spoke much more quietly. "Please enlighten me if you will...What is this reception in honor of? No one will tell me..."

"As far as I understand from the invitation letter, it is in honor of the Baulov Family's recent move to this region," I told him, and he slapped his forehead with his palm.

"And I keep walking around looking for whose birthday it is today. Phew, you just saved me," he laughed, and that was the end of the wine in his glass. Having lost interest in us, he immediately wandered off looking for a refill.

Seeing him, I decided I might as well relax a little. The countess and I made our way to the table with appetizers, and, intercepting a waiter, we also picked up some glasses of wine.

I noticed a strange dish on the table. A large tray on which all kinds of greens and vegetables were beautifully laid out, and in the center of all this splendor was a stuffed bird, as if sitting in a nest. At least that's what it seemed like at first glance.

"What are you doing here?" I whispered to Kooky, who sat with his eyes closed pretending to be a stuffed fowl, or something.

He opened one eye, and nodded slightly towards a bowl of what looked like garlicky croutons.

"C-o-o-ooo!" he 'murmured" conspiratorially and closed his eye again. I immediately looked around to make sure that no one saw us, and when I turned back to the "nest," Kooky was gone.

But then I saw his beak peeking out from above a closed dish near the croutons.

"Fly under the table," I whispered to the pigeon, as he ducked back under the cover of the dish, causing the lid to clatter as it fell back into place, attracting some notice. As soon as everyone turned away, I scooped up a few croutons and tossed them under the table. Soon, I heard Kooky down there cooing in contentment as he pecked at the treats.

Except for my interactions with Kooky, the evening passed quite sedately. Victoria and I stayed side by side, quietly chatting about various topics. She told me about how carefree her childhood had been, and I shared with her some episodes from my past life. But nothing too deep. After all, you never knew who might be listening.

I noticed many interested glances, mostly directed at the countess. She paid no attention to them.

We danced a little and talked with the head of the Baulov Family. Baron Baulov, it turns out, somehow knew that we were the black sheep of the neighborhood. But he'd invited us anyway, probably out of politeness.

His family was involved in transportation services, and recently, they'd also expanded into moving freight by ship. In fact, that's why they'd relocated to the Arkhangelsk region. Clearly the Baulovs were quite wealthy, although not particularly influential.

I managed to overhear several conversations. Why else would I be here? I knew how to channel my hearing such that from one end of the room, I could listen in to conversations at the other end. I found it unpleasant to hear the contemptuous mutterings of some of the locals about our hosts. Some were even openly snarky, saying he was a fool to invite the Bulatovs to their reception. I, of course, noted who spoke thusly. They were now added to my lengthy black list.

Over the course of the evening the only event of interest was the duel. I'm beginning to understand why aristocrats love them so much, because bloodshed is the only thing that can brighten up such otherwise boring evenings.

And I took part in it as one of the seconds. One of the guests, the youngest son of some local influential count, decided to show everybody who was boss here. At least, that's what appeared to be the impetus for his rudeness.

"I don't need your apology. You, Count, look like a snickering, drunken pig. You should go back where you came from and stay out of our business," said a plump guy who looked like he was around twenty years old. And it's not like Cherepanov did anything except accidentally bump into the upstart, and right after doing so, he'd apologized.

Cherepanov wasn't at all offended by the kid, and instead, he smiled, as if in anticipation. Even though he reeked of booze, and he could barely stand on his feet, he calmly turned to the young guy, looked him up and down, and put his unfinished glass on the table.

"Well, I assume you won't refuse a snickering, drunken pig's challenge to a duel?" He smiled as he launched a ball of energy into the face of the kid. "To the death, of course."

The plump upstart was expecting this, so in no time Baron Baulov set up the venue for the event. His servants fenced off a wide circular area, and all the guests gathered around in anticipation of the showdown.

Right away, Cherepanov sought me out to ask me to serve as his second. Of course, this involved few responsibilities. All I'd have to do was observe the duel, making sure it was a fair fight. Oh, and I also had to announce the start of the duel, which I did with plenty of swagger.

As soon as I did so, Count Cherepanov's demeanor changed radically. Before, he had a drunken smile on his face, and was teetering on his feet. But once the duel commenced, he was dead serious, with not a trace of alcohol in him. What this meant, though, was that all of the booze in his system had migrated to his bladder, so Cherepanov had to quickly wrap up this fight.

He didn't employ his Gift to the full extent; he simply covered himself with a powerful cloak of ice, and he extended his blade by half a meter right when he thrust it into his opponent. Not expecting this, Cherepanov's adversary was dealt a serious blow right away. And then, Cherepanov's icy blade rapidly sliced through his opponent's throat so swiftly that some of the onlookers failed to see it.

But had he hesitated even a second, his adversary might have acted. As it was, Cherepanov's opponent didn't even have time to throw up his shield, and, as he possessed an "Earth Attribute," had he done so, he might have been invincible. Fortunately, Cherepanov knew how to deal with little punks like that.

"I do beg your pardon!" the count exclaimed, interrupting the hush that had fallen over the onlookers. "But I simply must dash to the loo now!" And then he was gone in a flash.

The servants swiftly cleaned up the aftermath of the fight, and then they presented me with the captured sword. I have to say that it wasn't the costliest blade, although it was still rather high quality. It was unadorned, but fashioned from offworld materials. He had nothing else of value on him, and I couldn't help but wonder if he'd been sent here specifically for the purpose of engaging Cherepanov in a duel. Most likely this was the case.

"I don't understand," Cherepanov said, as soon as he was back, "this is the third duel that's come my way out of the blue. What have I done to provoke such a negative reception from the locals here?" he asked as a bottle of wine materialized in his hand. He had to do something about the alcohol he'd just expelled.

"I can relate to that," I said with an ironic smile, and he burst out laughing and thumped me on the shoulder.

"They're just jealous," he laughed. "Your countess is a real beauty, while I, well, I can drink as much as I want! Not everyone is so fortunate."

We chatted for a while longer, and Cherepanov urged me to take the trophy blade, but I refused. I already had Snegirev's sword, so what did I need it for?

And nothing else of note took place that night, although we had to leave early. Chernomor called and reported some movement a kilometer from the castle. One of our sentries sensed heartbeats, and quite a few of them, to boot.

On the way back to the castle I sent Kooky out to do some reconnaissance. He subsequently reported that the armed detachment descending on us was of a considerable size. As Kooky now knew some Morse code, I was provided with some details.

I knew the detachment was comprised of seventy men. As they were neither mercenaries nor soldiers from some Family or the other, I had to assume these were from that port district gang. So that old lady who'd called me this morning was on the level. This horde of men were out to take my car, and yet I'd discounted what she'd said. Not that I was worried about a force of seventy mafiosi types. And as they were in need of a car, I might as well show them our entire fleet.

"Chernomor," I dialed the old man's number, and he immediately answered. "Remember how I talked about that artifact... Yes, the one that creates a cloak of invisibility. We still have it, right?"

* * *

Somewhere near the Bulatov castle
Deep night

"Seryozha! Hey, Seryozha? You hear that?" Igor poked his comrade in the shoulder. They were slogging through the snowy forest, mostly in silence.

"What?!" huffed Seryozha in a tired voice.

"Is that you pissin' in your pants?" snickered Igor, and laughed "Relax. It's always scary the first time."

"I'm not scared," responded Seryozha. But in fact, he did feel jittery. He'd only recently joined the gang, and this was his first assignment.

The boss said that all they had to do was bust into the castle, throw their weight around, and kill anyone who put up a fight. But they had to make sure not to kill the countess, who was supposedly easy on the eyes.

They could do whatever they wanted to the count, though. But the snippets of conversation from the others made him nervous. They were talking about what they wanted to do to the count, and who would get first crack at the countess once the boss was done with her.

And they were all so sure that this was going to be like a walk in the park. Everybody was so nonchalant, it was like they were on their way to the local watering hole.

I guess he was the only one who was feeling spooked. He didn't like the way the others were talking; he didn't like the thought of torturing or raping people. He thought he'd just be working security at the gang's casino, but here he was plowing through these woods. Not that the casino would've been easy pickings, but he had to do something to feed his two kids.

"Let's tie the count to the roof of the car and

drop it off at the boss' home," guffawed somebody.

This cracked all of the others up.

"Yeah, but first let's cut off his balls, ha!"

"You're too much, Igor!"

"Me, I want to ride back on the countess! Yeah!"

Hearing this, Seryozha knew for sure. He knew he wanted no part of this, even if he now had to look for work elsewhere. If he couldn't find something better, he'd send his kids off to an orphanage and take work on the first ship that would have him, or...

Thinking thusly, he gradually fell behind the others. He was haunted by the feeling that someone was watching them, and yet again he spotted a strange-looking pigeon. The bird was always perched on some branch looking at them, and then after they'd pass under it, the bird would reappear on the next high branch they passed under.

"Seryozha! Don't lag behind, we're almost there!" yelled one of the others, the one who'd invited Seryozha to join the gang. "Look, you can see the castle!"

The seventy thugs on the march weren't even trying to be stealthy as they marched toward the imposing edifice. Rising above the trees, it looked mysterious, and even a little scary. None of the men were put off by the fact that not a light was to be seen through any of the windows.

"What? Have they taken to their heels and run off? Dammit! How are we supposed to find the boss's car?" said the commander of the operation. But the voice that responded to his query was unfamiliar.

"No worries. You have a whole fleet from which to choose a vehicle for your boss!" Who was that? The voice came from as if out of nowhere, and everybody in the horde of gangsters fell silent.

"Whazzat!?! What are you? Show yourself!" The commander sounded frightened. And with good reason, as there didn't seem to be anybody out there. But then...

As if out of thin air, six armored cars appeared all at once. And then, they all flicked on their huge headlights and headed their way, the machine guns mounted on the roofs trained right on the invaders.

"You... you mothers!! Do you know who we work for?" growled one of the gang. His bravery was surpassed only by his stupidity. The others were simply frozen in place.

Seryozha was by then some twenty meters behind the others. By now he was sure this was all a bad idea. Thus, he burrowed into a snow bank behind a tree and covered his head with his hands. Just in time, because then the air was filled with the roar of six heavy machine guns firing in unison, mingled with the screams of sixty-nine invaders.

* * *

"Oh! And who might you be? What's your name?" I walked up to the only survivor. Before I could stop them, my men had killed all the others. But this lucky guy had managed to escape by burrowing into a snow bank behind a tree. Now all that was left of this tree was a stump.

"S-s-seryhozha...," he said in a trembling voice. "P-p-please d-don't kill me."

Really, why should I? I didn't want to slaughter them all. As it was, they were thieves out to rob me, and they'd been summarily executed. This one was lucky that he'd stayed behind the others.

"I'll let you live if you answer all of my questions. Agreed?" I decided to give him a chance, and I also took the opportunity to cast a monitoring spell on his body.

Simply put, I now had this guy in the palm of my hand. I could discern changes in his heartbeat, and also his breathing, and more. I could, in short, tell if he were to lie to me. Snegirev tried to apply such a spell on me, but he'd used an artifact. Of course, I easily manipulated his attempts to deceive me, but this guy's weak Gift would not enable him to override my monitoring spell.

I could tell that this was no killer, and it was a mystery what he was doing with this horde of thugs.

"I'll tell you everything I know!" he said. "But

I haven't been in this gang for long."

Well, that meant he might not know all that much, but at least he seemed to have no desire to lie to me. It turns out this guy had already decided that he wanted no part of this action, and I saw no reason to kill him, especially since, anyway, he'd decided to bail, and ditch the gang.

"Okay, you're free to go!" I said, waving my hand. "Don't return to your boss. He won't give you a second chance."

At first, Seryozha didn't believe me, but then he turned and headed for the forest.

"Sir!" he said, stopping for a second and turning back. "There are several buses not from here, about a kilometer off. We hid them in the forest..."

"Not anymore. I've got my men driving them to the castle," I laughed. "Go now, before I change my mind." And hearing this, Seryozha disappeared into a thicket of trees. I tracked him a little, and once he made it onto the road, I called Kooky back to me. My sneaky little scout.

I'd interrogated Seryozha about what the boss wanted. Apparently, he didn't just want his car back. He also was out to harm my Family. Worst of all, they were supposed to bring Victoria to him. I could not fail to punish the boss for this. Thus, I picked up their commander's phone, gathered together a detachment of my men, and headed to the city to pay the big boss a visit.

* * *

An hour later
Somewhere in the port district, the gang's hideout

"Hm..." the bald boss looked at the screen of his phone. "Kristoff is calling, so shut up!" he growled at the bruisers gathered around his desk. The men did as told, and the boss answered the call.

But what he heard was some stranger's voice rather than that of his commander, Kristoff. What gives?

"Hello, you bastards!" said the cheerful man at the other end of the line. "I'm calling to make you an offer! Let us resolve our issues peacefully, what say?"

"Who the hell are you?" asked the boss, barely restraining his anger.

"Your men are dead. All of them," said the stranger. "I can forget about your attempt to attack me, but only if you promise to never again move against me..."

"What!?" growled the boss, feeling a tidal wave of wrath rising inside him. "Are you insane, scumbag?"

"Oh, I'm disappointed in you," said the voice. "My offer is most generous, so why do you scoff at it?"

The tell-tale veins on the boss's forehead were throbbing now, and his face flushed a vivid purple. How dare anybody, much less the scumbag on the other end of the line, talk to him like that. Not anyone, not even the duke, their patron, was allowed to disrespect the boss.

"Why you...you! I'm going to grind you into powder," he croaked into the phone. "Do you really think those guys mean anything to me? F*ck'em!...Yeah, sure, you may have big brass balls, I won't argue. But that's even better! Because I'm going to castrate you and shove them down your throat!" he was screaming by then like a wounded hippopotamus.

"Oh, did I wound your pride?" laughed the stranger, and just then some greenish, sticky matter landed on the boss's shiny bald pate.

At first, the boss didn't know what it was, and so he ran his hand over his head, smearing the bird shit all over. He and everyone else looked up to sound of *"c-o-oo"* and saw a bird clinging to the dangling lamp hanging from the ceiling. He seemed to be mocking them, and then he flapped his wings and disappeared into thin air.

* * *

"Good job!" I gave Kooky his just dues for excelling at his latest mission. In fact, it wasn't my idea to crap on the boss's head — Kooky had shown real initiative there. What was especially helpful, though, was how he'd managed to disable the cameras.

As the bald boss man retched and threw whatever was at hand at the wall, I was approaching his house. Not much had changed since my last visit. Only the two Doberman dogs on guard here had been replaced by human Dobermans, er, guards.

Or, rather, they were real combat types. But yeah, all it took to make the one suffering from chronic gastritis pass out was a shot of energy to his stomach. As for the other one with the old skull injury, I gifted him with convulsions. None of this cost me much, and I didn't have to waste crossbow bolts.

And thanks to the bird shit all over the security camera, I had no problem penetrating the walls surrounding the mansion and making my way to the garage. The security there had been beefed up, too, by two armed guards, who were a little stronger. Their Gifts were rather weak, although one of them was closer to average on the Gifted scale — I would place him at the eighth rank. But they'd been unable to raise the alarm. This time, though, I'd had to use my crossbow.

And now here I was, standing beside the gang leader's brand-new car. He'd apparently come to terms with the loss of his former vehicle, and this time he'd gone all out by purchasing a much larger, far more luxurious SUV. I, who knew very little about such matters, could tell just by looking at it how sophisticated and powerful this beast of a machine was. But since I'd killed the guards, I guess I'd have to get behind the wheel and drive the thing. Which would not matter at all, except that I'd yet to learn how to operate these marvels of engineering.

"Timothy! I need your help!" I said after calling my driver. I didn't have much time, and the mansion guards were no doubt on their way. I had to learn how to drive on the fly, over the phone.

"What's going on?" asked Timothy.

"Here I am sitting behind the wheel, and I don't know which pedal to press to make it go," I said. Yes, before calling Timothy, I'd taken a look at all of the buttons and pedals and levers and such. But none of this was intuitive to me.

"Um..." he thought. "What kind of car is this?"

"The big kind! And it's black! That's all I know," I admitted. "It has a steering wheel."

"That's good," said Timothy. "How many pedals? And did you start the car?"

Damn. This was getting complicated. Okay then. I told Timothy as much as I could and then, a couple of minutes later, there was a growl and purring sound from under the hood. And then I did everything according to his instructions, and... off I went. The car went exactly where it needed to go. It turned out to be easy to steer, but out of habit, I still hit the flowerbed in front of the house. I also damaged the fence. And then I accidentally rammed a parked car. Fortunately, it was night outside, and there were almost no pedestrians on the street... Almost none...

Well, okay, if I end up hurting anybody, I'll just heal them.

"I thought that one pedal was for backing up, and the other was for moving forward," I admitted to my driver, and he laughed.

"You should see all the pedals on a plane," he said.

"Oh, then I have to hijack a plane next! I like this," I smiled as I took out a road sign. I wondered why they didn't place the driver's seat in the middle?

"Better not, count!" Timothy said, sounding alarmed. "You should start with a bike. And then move up to a car..."

"Damn!" That was me

"What is it?"

"No worries," I said, looking at what was left of the bus stop. "Timothy, I think you'd better take over here. Can you find me? Just follow the trail of destruction, and I'm at the end of it..."

CHAPTER 10

AH, YES, WHAT CAN I SAY? It's a good start to the day when you wake up to the smell of coffee wafting from the kitchen. Quite nice, that, especially considering that we had all of three servants in the castle. I can only imagine what it's going to be like once I had a full staff! Speaking of, I'd have to task Georgy with finding more servants, but it could wait a bit.

Once I was fully awake, I summoned Kooky the pigeon back. I'd had him tracking the gang leader with the mission of eavesdropping on him. And as I was devouring my breakfast with gusto, including the compote, my feathered scout reported to me in the kitchen. Both Victoria and Chernomor were also enjoying their breakfasts, so Kooky refrained from investigating the pot of soup on the stove. I could tell he wanted to, though.

However, he was afraid of Victoria, not to mention Chernomor. But the countess's Aura of Death kept Kooky in check. That being said, back when I asked her to do something about the bird long ago she only laughed about my dire situation.

"Coo-coo-coo-coo..." my faithful feathered scout began delivering his report in Morse code about what he had seen and heard in the gang leader's hideout. I had yet to become totally fluent in the local Morse code, but I got the gist of what he was communicating.

Yes, I realized I could use the chain of runes to enable the pigeon to deliver messages all night long, but this would cost me enormous amounts of energy. And why would I need live action reports like that? Instead, I spent my energy on enhancing Kooky's ability to hide, and also on helping him retain what he heard so that he could later provide me with the highlights.

"Am I... hearing this right?" asked Chernomor, looking up from his plate. "Is the bird communicating in Morse code?" And he listened carefully to the pigeon, clearly surprised. "Yes, that's right. Apparently this gang leader is now ready to do whatever it takes to put you in your grave. And ... and he's sent assassins after you! Hmmm...when I think about the idiots that he sent last time..." he mused, scratching his bushy beard. "The ones stacked in the basement now, waiting to serve Victoria."

Really, having Chernomor translate Kooky's communiqués was quite convenient. The commander was far better than me at comprehending Morse code. Of course, Timothy, who'd helped me a great deal when it came to teaching Kooky the code, was also fluent in it. Although Morse code hadn't been used in aviation for quite awhile, my driver still knew it like the back of his hand.

"Coo-coo-coo-coooo-coo-coo," Kooky finished his report and plopped onto his butt, his legs splayed. The bird was exhausted. He even used his wing to as if wipe the sweat from his forehead.

And then, he suddenly grabbed a piece of freshly baked bread from the table, and jumping onto the floor, began pecking at it.

"Haruumph..." I coughed to attract the notice of the bird. And once Kooky looked up at me, I motioned to the table. My scout shouldn't have to eat off the floor.

Kooky reluctantly flitted onto the table with his chunk of bread, and began pecking at it from there. That made me wonder what it was he should be eating. I'd have to conduct a diagnosis on him targeting what was best for him. Perhaps he was a natural carnivore?

"Cooo?" He looked at me with disgust, and I knew right then that no, he was vegetarian.

Indeed, what Kooky had to report intrigued me. He'd had a lot to say, and I was glad Chernomor could relate it to me. Kooky had not only eavesdropped on the boss, he'd also flown around the hideout, and listened in on the boss's minions. It seemed that these guys weren't about to leave me alone, and that they were gearing up for a real war.

And so, right after breakfast, I called Georgy. As I recall, he'd put together a lot of information about this gang, but had only provided me with the essentials. That's all I needed back then.

This time, we talked on the phone for over an hour. What I learned was that the gang controlled half of the port district. The other half belonged to another, equally interesting gang. As it turned out, the leader of the second gang had also taken an interest in me. Whatever. Every drunkard staggering about the port district could be out for me for all I cared. What drew my notice was the big boss who'd more than once targeted my castle. He was firmly on my radar now.

Of course, he controlled a lot of properties primarily in the port district, but also a few in the industrial zone. This included, for example, a huge warehouse chock full of a range of merchandise. The merchandise was in the form of payouts from ships under the gang's protection once they entered the port.

Georgy also told me how it was this boss could act with such impunity. It seems his patron was an influential duke who covers up the gang's shady dealings for a small cut of his profits. But really, how small? The duke regularly pocketed half of the earnings generated by the casinos and brothels and other avenues of income from the gang's enterprises, and in return, he ensured that any cases opened by the police "disappear."

In fact, this gang boss once destroyed an aristocratic Family. The duke who was the head of the Family tried to put a stop to the way the gang was forcing regular business and people in his district to pay tribute. The duke would push the authorities to do something about it. He paid for his efforts with his life. The gang showed up at his estate, mowed down the guards, and also everybody else. This included the duke's wife and servants. The only reason his children survived was that they happened to be at school at the time of the attack. But just the same, the gang threatened them until they abandoned their claims to the Family's name and holdings.

"...and that's how the boss showed them that he was not to be trifled with. And that's how it went down," Georgy said, concluding the sordid tale.

"Well, once I have my way with him," I said, "it will be no trifling matter."

"I have no problem believing you," said Georgy. "Well, I've shared with you everything I managed to dig up about them. But I might be able to tell you something about what they're planning right now after I make a few calls."

"I'm already up on their latest plans," I smiled. "A little bird told me," I said, looking at the pigeon. "So that'll be all for now," I said, and was about to hang up when I remembered something else. "Oh, and don't forget to keep looking for new servants for this place... Right now we need carpenters and mechanics most of all. But you know all this."

"I'm on it!" he said, adding, "You can count on me!" And with that, we both hung up.

I was taken aback by one takeaway from our conversation. It was that a pathetic goon from the port district was richer than me by legions, if not more. The boss was rolling in money, and had properties galore, to boot. It was time to correct this situation.

From what I'd heard from Kooky and Georgy, they were finally taking me seriously. So they were making real plans, strategizing about how to get their hands on me so as to inflict pain and suffering on me, and how to go about depriving me of my Family and my property. In light of this, I saw no reason not to seize the initiative and act first.

Thanks to my scouts, I was aware of the existence of this warehouse. Georgy had only heard about it, but Kooky had seen it with his own eyes. He'd observed several containers packed full of valuables being offloaded there. How do I know the containers held items of value? It had to be so, because these gangs required handsome tributes in the form of goods. Moreover, they'd transported the containers there on trucks. Although my fleet of vehicles was a nice size now, I could always use more trucks.

And so I spent the entire day preparing for our foray. I meditated, and with Kooky's help I studied the terrain, and took note of where the guards were stationed. Surprisingly, there wasn't much security around the warehouse. After all, who in their right mind would steal from the mob boss himself? The guards were more for show, and not particularly interested in their duties.

For example, Kooky had no problem penetrating a room in which two security guards were laconically eating sunflower seeds as they monitored footage from surveillance cameras. Right away, Kooky went at their sunflower seeds, causing quite a stir. The two men frantically tried to catch the impudent bird, who easily flew all over the place, crashing hard into the monitors. And then, Kooky grabbed the bag of seeds, and simply vanished.

As darkness began to fall, I finalized my preparations. I took with me two dozen of our men, and headed for the industrial zone. Victoria and Chernomor stayed back at the castle, from where they would be assisting this foray. In fact, I wasn't using our men to fight, which was, actually, their usual function. I planned on handling the warehouse guards on my own. I did, however, need men to load the trucks and do the driving.

As the two security men tried to restore the surveillance equipment taken out by Kooky, I set about taking out the guards stationed at the warehouse, one by one. I did this as stealthily as possible, taking advantage of how nonchalant they were about their duties.

The two guards stationed at a side entrance, for example, were in an animated discussion about not much at all. Despite Kooky's report, I was still surprised at how easy it was to get close to them.

Kooky alighted on the head of one of them, and as his colleague guffawed at the sight, I emerged from the shadows and placed my hand on his shoulder. All it took was a small burst of energy to put the weakly Gifted guard out of action. A couple of seconds later, I neutralized the second guard, as well.

Thus it was that I disabled all six guards without firing a shot or making a sound. However, I did have to do a lot of walking in the process. The warehouse was actually the size of a hangar for planes, and inside it was lined with industrial shelving. Most of the shelves were full of merchandise, and there was even machinery there to procure items from the higher shelves. There were also quite a few hefty metal containers usually used in shipping, and these were stacked on top of each other outside the warehouse itself. I even saw a small parking lot for loaders and other machinery. At each of these facilities, two guards had been stationed. When the only ones left for me to contend with were the duo stationed in the security booth, I looked at the bird and thought maybe I could employ him as a mode of transportation. What with all the seeds he'd consumed, he was one fat bird.

Maybe I should think about performing genetic mutations on Kooky back at the castle? If, for example, I could enlarge him enough, I could ride through the air on him, as if he were a flying horse. But no, he might suddenly activate his ghostly form when I was high above the ground.

Also, he already eats a lot. Could I really afford to feed a gigantic version of my feathered scout?

Anyway, all that remained doing was to show the guys the loot, and have them start loading it all into the trucks. We spent all night at it, and managed to load up what seemed to be the high-value items. Once dawn neared, though, we had to stop, as we saw groups of workers trudging to their jobs. We didn't need any witnesses, so time to call it a day.

"Sir, where should we..." said the guardsman who was sitting behind the wheel — yes, I'd tried to drive the truck, but as there were more than two pedals, I was confused, so he'd be driving the rest of the way. Now, he asked "Where do you want us to unload this stuff?"

Good question. I looked at the column of some twenty trucks lined up at the castle. Hmmm...We really didn't have anywhere to put it all. What was truly a shame is that the Bulatov warehouse wasn't all that far from the boss's warehouse. It was located just one kilometer away, but some duke had taken it from us half a year ago. However, this was not the time to take it back, and so not only did I have nowhere to unload this merchandize, I didn't even know where to park the trucks. And so we ended up parking all the trucks here and there around the castle, which, technically, wasn't even protected by castle walls.

Victoria came up with a solution. At first she was astonished to see all the trucks chock full of whatever, but then she told me about a nearby village. It wasn't likely to be attacked in the near future, as it was situated too far from the road, and therefore not easy to access. In the past, they used it to house all kinds of agricultural equipment — tractors and industrial tillers and such. Before it could be stolen or destroyed, she'd sold everything. So now, the two large warehouses there could be used for all of the brand-new trucks. Finally, I could see what it was that the mob boss felt was worth storing in his warehouse.

"Tell me, Valery," I asked, as he dropped off one big box. "Who needs so many door knobs and hinges and such?"

"What do you mean?" he asked, and also looked inside, surprised to see that the container was filled with boxes of fittings for home construction and such. They weren't even the best quality — just regular door knobs and hardware for domestic construction. "I must've misread the packing slip. I thought what was in this crate was loaded with ingots that'd be easy to sell," he said, scratching the back of his head.

Okay, well, as it was, we had hundreds of identical door knob. I didn't even know where to put them.

In the next container, we found hundreds of towels. I'm talking about a delightful selection of colorful towels of all shapes and sizes. All of this we'd also sell, except for what we could use in the castle.

One after the other we opened up the trucks and the containers, and I found myself plunging deeper and deeper into my musings. All of this stuff needed to be sold, and the range of items, well, it was impressive. Right now, I not only had a lifetime supply of door knobs, I had enough of them to ensure that half of the apartments in Arkhangelsk had them. I also had tons of erasers, a couple of tons of chewing gum, and several hundred simple wooden chairs. Stuff. Lots of stuff. However, now and then I came across something interesting. For example, the pallet loaded with brick we'd retrieved right from the center of the warehouse. I personally pointed it out, as the packing slip indicated it was just that, brick. But this clearly wasn't ordinary brick, rather it was something offworldly. I checked the selling price of this brick on the Internet, and saw that it was approximately equal to twenty tons of plates, cups and bowls. Which is also something we managed to steal.

"C-o-o-ooo," sounded in my head, and I found the pigeon only by tracing his heartbeat. *"Coo-coo-coo-cooo,"* he uttered, clearly communicating something to me. I didn't understand half of it, but from what I caught, the pigeon thought that he'd died and was now in pigeon heaven.

I so understood why. How often does a bird come across tons of premium birdseed? Having found it in a container, Kooky had no intention of ever emerging.

"This must be why he insisted I take this particular container," said one of my men. "I was going to grab the one next to it."

"What was in that one?"

"I don't know, but on the box was a picture of a cell phone. You instructed us to listen to the pigeon, though...Right?"

"That's right..." I clenched my teeth and my fists. But if I thought about it, it all made sense. Kooky selected what he deemed the most valuable cargo. "What else did he indicate?"

"Over there," a guard took me to a nearby container. I pried open the outer boards, and opened a massive iron door to a case inside.

"Grass? What kind of idiot ships dried grass across the ocean?" I asked, bewildered.

"Sir!" said a guardsman.. "Let's put this...this container someplace special, okay? This isn't ordinary herb...it's...well, magical..." He was trying to tell me something.

At first I didn't get it, but then, oh yeah, I understood. We had a similar herb in my world. But it was legal there...Here, though, for possessing this herb we could land in prison. So I told the men to take this container out to the forest, and...

No, don't burn it. That would get half the region stoned. What would happen should, say, the wolves inhale any of it? Worse still, what about bears? No, better not create problems for ourselves. But it did seem like a nice gesture to unload several tons of dried "weed" near the gang's hideout. Moreover, we could cast it about outside, so that it would take them awhile to gather it up.

In general, only time will tell how profitable

our foray to the warehouse ends up being. I immediately tasked Victoria with researching where and how to sell all that we'd scored after our men inventoried it all, and even roped Georgy into helping out. In fact, he knew best where and what could be sold in the shortest possible time. I didn't care if he ending up selling it for half of what it was worth. I did not want these mountains of consumer goods to simply gather dust. Better to get them off our hands and be done with it. And this included the trucks, of course.

As for the bricks, we'd keep them. They were of use to us. I'd have them installed in the castle walls, and I'd apply runes to them which would function much better than if I were to draw them on ordinary brick.

I could use them to create a system of smart traps, or build a shield against gunfire and explosives. At the very least, I could create energy accumulators from them, after which inside the castle, well, it would be easier to restore one's reserves. Yes, so much to think about regarding the bricks, but to do anything with them we needed a mason.

By the time I returned to my castle and went to bed, the day was in full swing. I told Kooky to wake me up should there be an emergency, and then, my night's labors done, I crawled under the blankets and was out like a light.

Bzzzz...

I heard a strange sound at the edge of my consciousness. I paid it no mind, though, as I was in the midst of vivid dreams. I knew that should anything happen, Kooky would rouse me.

But then, I heard the sound yet again, and I had to peel my eyes open.

Hmmm... The bird didn't wake me up. Instead, I saw Kooky's little pigeon head sticking out from under the blanket on the pillow next to me. His beak was open and he was enjoying no less vivid dreams than my own.

"Hey, birdbrain," I said, giving him a tiny shove, and he seemed to mutter as he turned his back to me. This, after adjusting the blanket with his beak. "Right. I can depend on you. Totally and completely..." I muttered as I climbed out of bed.

The noise I'd heard came from my phone. I'd turned off the ringtone when I was at the mob boss's warehouse, but I'd left "vibration" on. That's what woke me up rather than the feathered bum.

As usual, this was an unfamiliar number, but by now I wasn't surprised.

"Hello?' I croaked into the phone, and heard in response an incredibly cheerful voice.

"Count Bulatov! Did I wake you up, or what? No wonder you love to sleep so much!" Who was this? "It's me, of course!" Ah, yes, indeed it was. "Count Cherepanov, remember?"

Sure! Of course I did. But there was one thing I didn't understand. Where did everybody get my personal phone number?

"Yes, good morning count!" I croaked. "How's doings?"

"Oh, just fine!" he exclaimed. "But I'm bored!

Would you care to pay me a visit? They brought me some exemplary wine. I need an excuse to open it. And it would facilitate our getting to know each other!"

I sought out a hidden agenda behind his invitation, but couldn't find one. Time for me to give up being paranoid, because, though eternally inebriated, Cherepanov was a solid guy. And it wasn't hard to believe him when he said he lacked a circle of friends here. Or perhaps he simply lacked anyone around with whom to share a fine bottle of wine. Moreover, it would be great to meet up with him again. Primarily because he'd invited me to his mansion. Why not join him, chat awhile, relieve his boredom? But not right now.

"Sure, how about a little later?" I responded. "Right now I've got the mob out to get me, not to mention Snegirev."

"Oh! I hear you! The vino can wait! I'll look forward to seeing you in a couple of days, once you've wound up your affairs. Agreed?" he asked.

"Sounds good," I said, and with that, we both hung up.

But that was the end of my sleep, because just then, I saw I'd missed a couple of calls from Georgy, and I also suddenly received an incoming message from him. It seems he'd found more servants for me.

Four in total, all with injuries of varying severity. Only one was ready for action right now, while the others needed some healing and recuperation time lasting a day, or even two.

Which suited me fine. One was a carpenter, and the other was a mechanic. The former had simply sawed off his fingers, but the latter was, it seemed, on the verge of death. Well, actually, he probably had another two weeks or so, but he wouldn't enjoy them, not at all. He'd trashed his liver, having overly-imbibed all his life. Well, once I was done healing him, he'll never drink again.

I went to see him first. He was spending his last days at home. This was a small apartment near the port. Before, he used to work for a car repair shop right by his apartment building, but then they canned him due to his drinking. Georgy said that this guy not only had golden hands, he knew his stuff. I'm not sure what he meant by "golden hands," but, okay.

The mechanic's apartment was rather sparsely furnished. He had a thin rug on the floor on which he lay, and that was it. Ascetic, to say the least. Anything else he'd had in terms of furnishings had been sold for booze.

"Let's dispense with business matters right away," I said instead of greeting him. "Once you agree to serve my Family and I heal you, then your drinking days are done. One sip might not kill you, but at the very least it will cause excruciating pain," I leaned towards him, and saw the fear in his eyes. That's right. This was no ordinary mask. It hinted at the approach of death itself.

"I... agree... Sir... Please, I swear! Never again!" he muttered. Of course not ever again! He'd be physically unable to, even.

I had some misgivings, but Georgy told me that this guy was highly qualified, so I decided to give him one last chance.

I spent nothing at all on this. In fact, there was no need for treatment. All I did was improve the circulation of energy, as well as his blood flow, and compel any normal liver cells to begin dividing, and then, the body would gradually get rid of the damaged tissue. That's all it took. No need for a liver transplant. Sadly, this trick only works for the ungifted. For stronger people, anything I could do would be far more complicated.

Next, I gave the man five rubles, and told him to buy himself some clean work clothes and show up at the castle the next day. We could use his services right away. As for the tools of the trade, he could work that out with Georgy.

After that, we moved on, traversing around the port district. I went around to the other prospective servants and told them what to expect should they agree to serve me. All of them said they'd work for free, if need be. Being invalids, it's not like they had much in the way of other prospects. And on top of employment, I was offering them miraculous cures.

But before I could get to the last two, my cursed phone started ringing. It was Chernomor. Apparently a column of Snegirev's forces was heading towards the castle. And apparently he himself was with them. Well, that would be serious. I had to get back, or else my men would have a hard time dealing with them.

Georgy executed a U-turn right then and there, and put the pedal to the metal, tearing back to the castle. We as if flew back, and I was tossed about in the back of his yellow cab like a sack of potatoes, and came close to activating my Diamond Armor a couple of times — I thought he'd surely crash. I'd be fine. I knew how to self-heal. But what made Georgy think he was immortal? Did he think I'd be there for him? Was that it?

And then the car shook and we heard a huge crashing sound. It was a booming sound, as if a thunderstorm had begun. Or something else massive and powerful.

"B-z-z-z!"

That would be my phone, and then the radio in the car turned on.

"Attention!" The sound issued out of the speakers. The alert sounded along the entire street, and all of the cars on the road suddenly stopped. "This is not a drill!" said a voice that descended as if from high above.

Meanwhile, my phone screen lit up. A message arrived in the Family's email account which I just had to read. Literally. I could not close the email message as it expanded to fill up the entire screen.

"All residents of Arkhangelsk, please proceed to the emergency shelters!" sounded the strangely bored voice from the speakers. Georgy's face drained of color, but he didn't slow down until I urged him to do so. As it was, I was having a hard time reading the message.

Hmm... They write that I, as an aristocrat, was obliged to join in repelling the attack. However, I could refuse with good reason. Interesting. What would be "good reason"? If, say, my beloved cat were to die, would that suffice? Or how about if my grandmother was ill? I wouldn't have to help repel the attack?

Whatever, I clicked on the "Accept," button, indicating that I'd join the fight, along with my guard. A map then opened up on my phone with a marker indicating the area to which I was to proceed.

"I repeat!" said the announcer. "Danger code red! Please depart the cordoned off perimeter and seek shelter!"

"How often does this happen here?" I asked Georgy with a smile. My driver was white-knuckling the steering wheel as he awaited further instructions.

"N-n-never..." he stuttered. "We've had Interfaces, but never code red... Red — that's bad..."

"Alright!" I interrupted him. My sensor of spatial anomalies, indeed, indicated the opening of a huge, powerful portal. It was big enough to allow a cruiser through, although that wasn't likely as it didn't open out to the sea

But that wasn't all. There were also numerous smaller portals opening all around the city and I told Georgy to head for one of them. I had both my mask and my cloak with me, and these days I didn't even go to the restroom without my sword. So why was it I agreed to aid in the defense of the city so swiftly?

It's elementary.

"Hello, Snegirev?" I called the viscount.

I heard his disgruntled voice at the other end. He was no doubt considering what to do — accept his civic duty, or make up an excuse.

"If you're still heading toward my castle, I suggest you gather your idiot forces together, turn around, and go back to where you came from," I said with a smirk. All because Kooky was now circling right above Snegirev's considerable detachment. He was conducting surveillance, eavesdropping, and shitting all over the place. But of course. There was I reason I fed him so well.

Snegirev was seeing red now. And he looked red, as well — his face was apoplectic and he was sputtering, unable to speak. All this because his attack was a bust.

You see, because I'd accepted the call of the Emperor himself, I was now officially under his protection until such a time as the major Interface portal was closed. And should anybody attack my estate while I was off battling the offworlders, then they'd have to contend with the Imperial guard, who would ensure that not a trace remained of the Snegirev Family. An offense such as taking advantage of me whilst I was defending the homeland would be seen as high treason, and subject to swift and severe punishment.

Snegirev didn't have anything to say. He cut

off the call, but I had the pleasure of hearing my feathered scout's report. Apparently, Snegirev destroyed his phone, and then began screaming at the heavens above. In response, my scout lobbed more of his special shit bombs at him. What a shame he missed the viscount's mouth. And then, the viscount turned his guard around and headed for the city.

Theoretically I should also have my guards head here to help close the giant portal, but I had other plans for them. Having finished my communications with the viscount, I immediately called Chernomor and ordered him to begin preparing to defend the castle. I'd be a fool not to, given Snegirev's treasonous nature. He'd assume that my men would be tired out after defending the city, and so he'll likely strike as soon as the portals on the outskirts close. We'll have prepared a big surprise for him, though!

"Sir!" Georgy called after me once I donned my mask and got out of the car. "What should I do? Can I help you?" Good for him — he'd found some courage. But he'd just be in my way.

"Clear out of here, get away, as far as you can, and wait for me to call," I said, smiling under my mask. "And also start thinking about where to sell the artifacts I'll be collecting."

CHAPTER 11

GEORGY TOOK OFF WITH A SCREECH as he powered the yellow cab down the road, leaving me standing on the street. All around me people were fleeing in panic. One after another, cars coursed down the road. Civilians were moving one way while powerful, heavy armored trucks packed with soldiers loaded down with hefty big guns headed the other way.

According to the messages, the offworlders had taken over several city blocks at once. That being said, it seemed to me that they were swiftly expanding their territory. Small portals kept on popping up in various locales. It seemed to me that it was only a matter of time before this entire district was overtaken by the offworlders, and then they could well move on to the neighboring one.

I saw one portal not far from me. It was in the

courtyard of an apartment complex, and a fairly large detachment of offworld fighters emerged from it. I counted some twenty of them, and before too long, after them would come the catchers. They were going to have a feast in light of all of the defenseless civilians all over the place ready to be scooped up. People were rushing about helter-skelter, hardly looking at where they were going. It was no surprise that some of them were running right into the clutches of the invaders

Suddenly, an extended burst of gunfire sounded, taking a number of the offworlders out of the picture, although some were only wounded. But the armored truck that delivered the blow to the offworlders was then showered with magic projectiles and caught fire. I rushed to the rescue, arriving as the offworlders were attempting to bash in the windows of the armored truck with their swords.

I could sense survivors in there, one of whom was seriously wounded while the others were ready to fight back. Although the machine gun mounted atop the truck was destroyed, the soldier who'd been manning it managed to duck down the hatch into the truck and close it behind him. The offworlders were doing their best to get to him now, and I doubted that he'd be able to last much longer.

I felt my energy spreading throughout my body. My muscles were aching with the overload as I rushed toward the armored truck. My sword was imbued with vital energy and I thrust it into the back of the nearest offworld fighter, easily penetrating his armor plates and neutralizing his protective artifact. The tip of my sword entered between the ribs, ending in his armpit. His heart stopped then, and I moved on to the next enemy combatant, who'd pried open the edge of the armored vehicle's narrow windshield. Just as he was about to shoot a fiery stream from an artifact ring into the truck, I swung my sword and cut off his hand.

I needed to pick that hand up before I left.

At first, the offworlder didn't realize what had happened. But his magical defenses were useless against my blade, which was imbued with vitality. He was unable to parry my next move, and my blade passed through his throat. But the results were bloodless, as the wound immediately healed, along with his damaged airways, due to the properties of my sword.

As a result, he started suffocating. Meanwhile, someone shot an icy ball at me. But I'd been anticipating this kind of thing, and had amplified the strength in my legs and simply jumped to the side. The offworlders had included a number of warrior mages on their team this time. All wore light armor, and could employ rather weak attack spells, and fight with swords, as well. But they also had more artifacts with them! Thus, although they were more dangerous, I favored encounters with such adversaries.

Sadly, I wasn't able to finish the job with the icy ball lobber. Just then the door of the armored truck opened and a gun barrel poked out from it. A burst of gunfire ensued, demolishing the warrior mage's defenses. And then, bullets riddled his body.

"Shield wall!" I heard an offworlder shout, and all of the warriors swarming the armored truck jumped off and gathered together in a big huddle facing outward.

Aha, that must be their commander. As he looked just like all the others, I didn't realize this until he issued that order. But now, looking closer at him, I saw that the coat of arms on his cloak was different from everyone else's. He had more stars and stripes on it. Well, they, too, must have ranks and titles — I'd have to investigate this when time permitted.

The offworld warriors all lined up in a row then holding their shields aloft over their head, and a second later a transparent dome manifested above them. A hail of bullets showed down upon the dome, only to ricochet right off of it. It seemed to be impenetrable. As the soldiers ran out of ammo, the detachment under the dome of shields began to slowly advance.

Watching all this, I prepared my next move, which began with a powerful weakening spell. Well, how powerful, really? It wasn't close to full strength, but I could still confound the enemy. At least I assumed they didn't expect it when I suddenly busted through one of the shields creating the dome. My green eminence flashed, and from each of the mages under their shields, thin threads of vitality extended toward me.

The spell I'd just cast is called "Life Link." Now, for a couple of seconds at least, it was like I was touching them, and could do what I wanted to influence their bodies. However, I couldn't reach the commander. Apparently he was quite a strong warrior, and Gifted, to boot, so I could do nothing in the little time I had. As for the others, it cost me a lot of energy, but I amplified their hearing to unimaginable levels.

Why, you ask? Well, what if one of them was wearing an artifact against magical attacks? This wasn't, technically, an attack. Indeed, I was improving their ability to hear. A lot.

And then, inhaling as much air as possible, I screamed as loudly as I could. I was impressed at the results. Nobody expected anything like this, and they all fell to the ground, clutching their ears. Everyone except the commander. He came at me with his sword, but in vain. I sped up to meet him and hit him with multiple strikes at once. I gave it my all, and could feel my muscles tearing and my tendons snapping from the strain, not to mention the stress on my ligaments. As for my bones, well, the load on them was tremendous.

The offworld commander was also fast and strong, but it wasn't enough to save him. However, he wasn't foolish enough to rely on his protective artifacts alone, as he realized that I could get around them, and so we ended up facing off with our swords.

With every clang, our swords sparked, and I

kept on pushing him back as he slowly retreated toward the portal. The commander had been the center of the protective dome, but it soon collapsed, allowing our fighters to make short work of the offworlders still huddling on the ground in agony. Next, our guys moved toward me and the offworld commander, but I ordered them to stay put, because I didn't want to have to heal them once all this was over.

And then, I managed to inflict a minor wound on the commander. It was just a small slash, but that was enough. The blood clot that ensued slowly floated toward his heart, and from there to his lungs. Once it settled in there, it started growing.

What was the malady created by this called in this world? No, why bother trying to remember. Thromboembolism of something pertaining to the lungs. All these names for such matters just served to confuse me. In any event, the commander's neck was now the color of an eggplant, and he looked terrified. Dropping his sword, he clutched his throat and struggled to breathe. And yet, he wasn't giving up. He reached into his bag and fished something out that reeked of mana. I didn't like that at all. Stop right there, offworlder!

I leaped forward, and plunged my sword downward into the space above his collarbone, penetrating a slew of vital organs. Just like that, the commander's lifeless body fell to the ground. I bent over him and picked up the artifact he'd planned on unleashing, and stashed it in my pocket.

By now, I found myself right by the portal. It was sparkling with all of the colors of the rainbow, and beyond it, I could see the outlines of a medieval city and also some silhouettes. I could see that world in clarity only if I were to pass through this sparkling haze.

And then, the portal started flashing. Again, and again... Only now were the catcher beginning to emerge from it. They were smiling, and looking at me with anticipation, as if I was their first victim. Could they be more insolent? They seemed to feel right at home with nothing to fear. But finally, the first few noticed the reception we'd given their warriors.

But I didn't have time to wipe the smiles off their faces. I heard the roar of an engine at my back, and saw shock and fear replace the smug expressions of the offworlders.

"Sir! Get down!" shouted a soldier. I didn't need to be told twice. I threw myself onto the ground as something huge and powerful rumbled past me. I felt a hot wave of air wash over my back, but didn't look up. Then, the sounds died down, and I could finally get up and survey the field of battle. Actually, this was more like a massacre. Generally speaking, catchers aren't equipped to defend themselves. But our soldiers had called for backup whilst in the midst of battle, and naturally help had come.

What had slowly rolled into the courtyard was

like a huge tank that crushed whatever was in its path, even parked cars. Aiming its twin cannons right at the catchers, the massive machine of death had fired a short burst of explosive shells. Thus, just like that the catchers were obliterated, gone, with only their charred remains splattered all over the place. I, too, did not escape totally unscathed. Several fragments pierced my clothing and flesh, but by the time a couple of soldiers ran up to me to see if I was okay, any wounds I'd suffered were already healed.

"Sir! Are you hurt? How are you?" asked one in a rush as he tried to look me over. "Medics! Come here! It's urgent!"

"Calm down," I stopped him. "I'm fine! No need for medics," I said. I didn't want them to see how swiftly I'd healed. "I used an artifact. No worries!"

"Phew..." the fighter shook his head. "Okay, well, anyway we're short on medical staff. No healers, even...Yeah, we've lost a lot of our men."

Wish he hadn't added that last bit, because it spoiled my mood. Yes, I know I'm as cynical as it gets — it's downright mandatory for a healer, in fact, be he a healer, an Archmagister or a student. If you've done what it takes to cultivate and grow in your practice, that means you've seen a lot of death and suffering. And no, you can't take it all to heart, because you'd end up burning out on the job.

This was a major, monumental Interface, but for some time now I've known something of this sort was inevitable. And this wasn't yet the worst of it, and by the time the people of this world realized it, it could well be too late. That being said, considering their impressively advanced technology, they had a real shot at victory. Like that stunning caterpillar-like tank — what was it worth? Which, by the way, left as soon as it was done incinerating the offworlders.

Now, though, the entire city was a treasure trove of artifacts. I'd already scored several charged protective artifacts, one offensive one, and another in my pocket that was still a mystery to me. I suspected it was a medical artifact. I'd study it first, and most likely sell it.

I could gather up enough of the offworlders' artifacts today to restore the castle, and I could hire guards, along with an army of servants, maybe buy more military equipment, or even some planes or helicopters. Although, once I priced one of them, and even a simple helicopter was crazy expensive, and why?

But I'd really like to get my hands on some artifacts, and also repel attacks from offworlders, all the while growing stronger. Sadly, I had my principles, and I did not want to deviate from them.

"C-o-o-ooo!" my scout notified me that he had arrived, and had surveyed the terrain en route to me.

He immediately set about delivering a report. I'd improved my abilities with Morse code a little, although some of the information flew past right by me.

I'd summoned Kooky for a reason. There were so many beating hearts around here, I really did need him to provide me intelligence. Theoretically, I could easily distinguish foreigners from earthlings, but the chaos and confusion were so great now, I could also get confused. Why not have my bird survey the area from above?

Our fighters wasted no time leaving the courtyard now, off to the next cluster of offworlders. They stationed two machine gunners at the portal, though, just in case more offworlders were to exit. This, by the way, rarely happened, but it was better to play it safe.

Off to the side, I saw a wounded soldier who was about to be evacuated. I quickly approached him and placed my hands on him. I didn't bother with the external wounds, but I used my powers to imbue his damaged organs with strength. It wasn't a miracle cure, as he needed time to mend, but at least he was no longer in pain. As I was busy treating him, Kooky returned from his surveillance mission and now he reported his findings.

It was as expected. From the massive portal that launched this event, an entire army had emerged, and now a vicious battled was in full force. Our soldiers were using tanks, aircraft, and heavy weapons to steadfastly repel the attacks of mages and numerous troops. Also aiding our forces were the strongly Gifted, including aristocrats, and also their personal guardsmen. But the enemy forces were overwhelming in terms of their numbers. They'd already captured three city blocks and kidnapped everyone there, marching them through the portal. There were also small spatial rifts that allowed the enemy to carry out lightning attacks in which they captured even more people.

I sensed a burst of energy, and then I saw a huge fireball streak across the street and crash into an apartment building. It exploded, and a column of flame shot up into the air, sending tons of crushed stone flying, until only the foundation of the building remained. Shards of brick and mortar continued falling over a radius spanning hundreds of meters, inflicting injuries on the fleeing civilians and the soldiers manning the defense. I managed to take cover behind a neighboring building, although the resulting fires managed to do a little damage. Phew... the bastards almost destroyed my mask.

Well, what fun, right? And I again wished I could join the fray, score some artifacts and weapons in a fair fight, but yes, my principles...No way could I discard them.

The pigeon told me that there was a field camp not far away, in between the burnt house and the one I was at right now. The red crosses on the tents indicated their function. In this world, red crosses were posted to signal where to find medical assistance.

“Ehh...” I sighed sadly, as I sensed the opening of another portal nearby. Thirty offworlders sprang out of the portal, to no one’s surprise. These included some clearly powerful mages wielding costly artifacts.

But no, I ran in the opposite direction. Our forces were heading right to the new portal, so they'd manage without me. It was such a pity that I'll be missing out on the artifacts, but...I had to adhere to my principles, and I am a healer. And so I headed for the field camp, and had Kooky carry on with his surveillance.

He flew above me, and reported on how the battle was going. In some locales, our forces were regrouping to more fortified positions, and elsewhere the guardsmen of a particularly strong Family were able bust through a formation of offworlders and inflict enough damage on them to force them to beat a retreat

All around me, it was like a minor earthquake, and magic missiles occasionally few over my head. As I made my way to the field camp, I witnessed a fight with a powerful offworld mage. He hurled balls of sparkling flame at the aristocrats fighting him. Meanwhile, the aristocrats fired back at him with all of the magic at their disposal.

Concentrated darkness, electrical discharges that looked like lightning bolts, chunks of concrete ripped out of the streets, clods of earth — they sent all this in a continuous stream at the enemy mage, but he fought back, and seemed to be relishing the battle. With a wave of his hand, he sent his magic this way and that. He was also helped by a large detachment of offworld warriors, and even catchers. They were all drawing closer to some of our gunners, and it looked like they were all about to engage in hand-to-hand combat. I was about to help out, but just then I heard a loud, extended whistling sound, and then several missiles hit the place where the mage had been standing.

His body was then consumed in the resulting bonfire. Soon, all that remained of him was a pile of ash. Aaack! All of the lovely artifacts he'd had on hand were also in that pile of ash. I was choking with angst over the barbaric disregard displayed by our defenders towards the precious artifacts.

Ah, well. There was nothing to be done about it.

Right after the explosion, a couple of combat helicopters flew over our heads. These were Imperial combat choppers, both of which displayed the Empire's majestic coat of arms on their sides. They fired a few more missiles, and headed off.

But then, all of a sudden, several icy spikes pierced one of departing choppers. Each icy missile was two meters long, and they penetrated the chopper through the bottom, exiting through the roof right where the pilot was seated. There was no defense against a magical attack of such power. The surviving chopper responded with a barrage of fire targeting the source of the icy spikes. As the chopper's attack was unanswered, I could only assume that the mage's icy spikes were great for attacks, but did nothing for his defense.

I continued on to the camp, and was there in a couple of more minutes. I discarded my mask on the way there, so as to avoid attracting unwanted attention. The camp had a lot going on. Though only fifteen or so minutes had passed since the start of battle, it was overflowing with the wounded and dead, with more coming in.

"Lay him down over there! Faster!" I found the man in charge here right away. Attired in a uniform, he snarled at his subordinates, and issued orders to all and sundry. "Do it on the double!" he said to a fighter he'd grabbed by the collar. "There's another tent there! You're responsible for unloading the equipment," he said.

His orders flowed from his mouth like a torrent, as his men rushed about all over the place. I was impressed by how competent he was, his gruff demeanor and curses notwithstanding. His orders were clear and to the point.

"What do you want?" he asked me after he was done dealing with a new influx of wounded from a truck with a red cross insignia. I'd been standing there for some five minutes trying to figure out where to go.

"Count Mikhail Bulatov," I introduced myself. "I'm here to help."

"Great! Colonel Chibirev!" he responded. "How many men do you have with you? Any engineers or technology to contribute? Heavy weapons?" The colonel pulled out a tablet from his pocket and opened a map up of the area, with several points marked on it. All of the data changed in real time. “Can you get over to any of these areas? Your choice!”

“Um...” I said, “I’m here on my own as I just happened to be in the city.”

“Hm...” the colonel frowned. “So... What is your Gift? Tell me so I can send you where you’re most needed.”

“Healer,” I shrugged, the colonel smiled and said “Great! We have plenty of fighters, but not enough healers... Over there is the tent with the severely wounded, and that tent is where the less severe cases can be found. They can still breathe freely. Choose either one! We have only three healers for the entire camp,” he waved his hand to illustrate this. “Now please, forgive me! I must attend to other matters.”

And he turned away to go back to snarling at his subordinates. Alright then. I knew where I was most needed, and headed for the tent with the severely wounded.

Looking around, I was impressed by the abundance of equipment. I wondered where it all came from. In the space of a half an hour or so, it was like they'd opened a clinic. I entered the inconspicuous-looking tent, and saw evenly spaced rows of beds with shattered, battered men in them. The medical personnel included four nurses, two doctors dressed in white coats, and a trio of healers.

These were local healers, as evidenced by the stupidity radiating from them, and the lack of intelligence in their eyes. They reminded me of baboons. I jest, of course. Both in my former world and this one, the art of healing required a wealth of knowledge. And the only reason the local healers here were so weak is that they didn't know anything about the basic postulates of controlling external energy. Nobody taught them about it, and for whatever reason, the primary institutes of healing neglected the benefits of fashioning healers into mages.

Two healers who looked to be elderly men were working on a guardsman for an aristocratic Family. They'd stabilized his condition, and were trying now to reduce the blood loss.

"Good afternoon, colleagues!" I walked up to them and put my hand on the patient's forehead and carried out a quick diagnosis. "Gentlemen, I don't recommend pouring energy into him now, as there's a risk of incurring thrombosis..." I forgot what they called it here. Hmm... yes, that's what it was! "...thrombosis of the bronchial cavity."

"Mesentery, actually," the old man shook his head. "Why are you bothering us? You're not even certified...," he grumbled "Run off to the other tent with the less severely wounded...Don't interfere with our work!" he said, waving dismissively.

Right, be that way...Okay, I resisted the impulse to gift him with diarrhea. Why waste the energy when people's lives depended on me? But I remembered the old man's face. His colleague also supported the old man's diagnosis, so he'd get it, too, the next time we met. The upshot was that these two were old friends, it seemed, so I'd best not even work with them.

So I didn't respond to their provocations. Anyway, the guardsman's life wasn't in danger, as I simply blocked the flow of energy to his intestines. The pompous old doctors wouldn't even notice it.

"They drove me away too..." the third healer said quietly. He was a young guy, around twenty years old.

He was in the process of pouring his meager reserves of energy into some poor fellow whose arm was torn off. I immediately joined him, because his patient was losing blood, and was approaching critical levels.

"Wait, you're feeding him the wrong energy," I interrupted his treatment. What's remarkable is that the guy immediately stopped and looked at me in bewilderment. "Hmmm..." I put my hands on the patient and made a quick diagnosis. In addition to the missing limb, he had a ruptured spleen and a couple of bruises to his internal organs. These needed treating first. But if I was to cure all of this at once, I'd end up facing a lot of questions.

"We need to replenish the blood right away," I said, placing my hands on the patient's chest. His skin was already pale and his breathing was ragged. "And oxygen... How to give him more oxygen..." I began to think out loud. No, I could, of course, strengthen his lungs, but that, too, would look strange. That kind of magic often produces visual effects, such as a green mist emerging from the patient's mouth. I didn't even know if they were capable of producing magic of that caliber here.

It turned out that they could, but in their own fashion. The still perplexed young doctor gave me a strange look, and a second later a tube was sticking out of the unconscious man's mouth. Then the guy attached a long hose to it, pressed a couple of buttons on a device, and... Indeed, it helped! I immediately felt how the patient's blood began to fill with oxygen, and it was all I needed to proceed with my treatment. If only we could increase its volume...

While I was busy restoring the broken magical channels, my assistant dealt with this problem. He poured some liquid into the patient's circulatory system, and I was surprised to note how quickly his condition began to change.

I did my thing, too. I sealed the torn vessels so that blood would stop flowing out of them, and that's all it took for them to start growing together. All in all, the young healer was a big help in the end. What a pleasant surprise. He didn't even use his Gift; rather, he relied on his knowledge of anatomy and local methods.

Now that we'd done what we could for our first patient, we moved on to the second. The young healer and I were a team now. What I liked was that right away he helped me, and this was without question, although I could see from his face that he did not understand why I chose to pour energy into one channel rather than another. You see, he was used to the clumsy approaches he'd been taught at the academy. I understood this from what he told me as we worked. Yes, even though we were up to our ears in blood and guts, we could still talk to each other.

His name was Roman, and he'd graduated from the Academy of Healers just half a year ago. He happened to live nearby, and that's why he'd ended up here at this camp. He worked in the hospital as a junior healer and was at the same time learning what he could from the professors. The idiots. I mean his professors. From what Roman told me, I gathered that he was also doing studies on his own on surgical methods of treatment that didn't require him to use his Gift.

This impressed me, the fact that he was drawn to new knowledge. Most healers here eschewed medicine as practiced outside their craft. They were of a mind that healers should rely solely on their Gift.

"Come here, help me," I called him over as soon as another wounded man was brought into our tent. By now, the tent was already full, but fortunately, another tent was set up for more of the severely wounded. And Roman and I migrated over to it. This way, we could avoid interfering with the "real healers." That's what the two old idiots called themselves.

Roman ran up to our new patient and froze, preparing to activate his Gift.

"First, I'll close the central and paravertebral channels to reverse the flow of the peripheral energy concentrated in his system, and in the meantime you need to saturate the longitudinal circulators, and at the same time open the base membrane... Twenty percent, I think, will suffice," I said, ready for him to do his part.

But he just stood there dumbfounded. I could tell from his expression that his brain was working hard, although I didn't see any steam issuing out of his ears.

"I'm sorry, what did you say?" he uttered after a few seconds.

"What's unclear?" I asked. I felt like I'd put everything out there in plain language.

"Nothing is clear, to be honest," he said with a shrug. "They don't teach ancient ancestral practices at the academy," he lowered his head guiltily. "I don't even know what the patient's condition is."

"What do you mean, you don't know? Who but you will carry out diagnostics, hmmm?" I fully understand that this meant that the local healers didn't even know how to perform the basics, such as diagnostics. "In short, this poor guy was hit by an enemy with a rare Gift, and so now, his body is as if fighting with itself."

In fact, the patient looked like he was in seriously bad shape. I couldn't even tell if he'd been poisoned, or if the attack had employed elements in the patient's body, as both methods could produce this effect. But right now, although this man lying before us didn't have a single visible wound on his body, he was close to breathing his last. He was starting to swell up, and his breathing was slowing, and let's not even talk about his blood pressure.

"So he's experiencing anaphylactic shock. I can do something about that," Roman beamed, and then, for whatever reason, he pierced the patient's vein and began to pour some kind of liquid into it.

I didn't even have time to intervene. But right before my eyes, most of the patient's issues were as if resolved. I, of course, wasn't idle in the meanwhile, and did what I could to enhance the healing process with my magic. And in just a few minutes, the man on the verge of death opened his eyes and sat up in bed.

"F*ck me..." he murmured. "Oh, sorry," he noticed us. "What happened to me?"

But we ignored him. By then we'd moved on to the next patient. They were many in number, and all were close to death, so we couldn't allow ourselves to be distracted.

Outside we kept hearing the roar of blasts, and Kooky would fly in to report what was going on. Indeed, at one point, I almost felt like running out there brandishing my sword. The offworlders made it to the fence around the camp and were preparing to bust into our scene. But the security guards here weren't pushovers. A dozen soldiers with strong Gifts showed the offworlders who was boss in this fair land, and I wasn't needed. However, that attack on the camp led to even more new patients.

"Healer! Over here!" I heard a loud cry, and

five hefty guardsmen carried some boy into our tent. I rushed over to his bed and...

Trouble.

"Sir! Save him! This is the youngest son of Duke Maltsevsky! Please, do your best!" the senior guardsman flew up to me. I saw that he was in a real panic. Apparently, he was supposed to spare nothing to protect this kid, but he'd failed to cope with this gravest of responsibilities.

"The duke's son..." and yes, this was trouble. Unless I used my full abilities, this fourteen-year-old kid was going to die.

What had happened was that a magic projectile had flown straight into his face, and even though his protective artifact took part of the damage, one of his eyes had been replaced by a gaping hole revealing blackened, cracked skull bones. This was in addition to the damage to his body. The resulting explosion from the projectile had done a number on him. He had a slew of broken bones, but his brain...thankfully, his brain was intact.

I wasn't sure, though, why he was still alive. Although... A magical aura emanated from his chest, and after digging a little, I found the small artifact. It was supporting the barely glimmering life in this boy.

An artifact...Not a bad idea.

"Well, since this is the son of the duke himself..." I said and nodded. "I advise everyone to turn away," I addressed the doctors and guards gathered in the tent.

And I began rummaging around in my pockets. I did have an artifact to heal serious wounds, but I wasn't really going to use it. But in my pocket, oh joy! I found a pretzel! It's a simple, rather large pretzel that I use to reward Kooky when he deserved a treat. Kooky loved pretzels. Yes he did.

I pulled the pretzel out of my pocket, making sure everybody noticed, but also ensuring they couldn't see what it was, then I carefully positioned it on the kid's chest with my hand over it, and a brilliant flash of green light suddenly illuminated the tent. The magic pouring out of my hand sparkled for several seconds. I concentrated my energy with all my might and directed it to healing the critical wounds. The internal organs were damaged, many blood vessels were affected, and, most importantly, I targeted the magical channels. Some of them had been scorched by the powerful magical explosion, while others were damaged by this young man himself. I ended up discharging a massive amount of energy, and I worked hard on the patient.

Thankfully, judging from my feathered scout's latest report, the flow of wounded would soon dry up. Our forces had pushed the offworlders back to the giant portal and now the end of the battle was only a matter of time.

After a few seconds, my source was completely depleted, and I stopped treatment. But now the boy looked totally different. Before, he looked like his head had been boiled for soup stock, but now, he had unblemished skin growing over the bone, and his eye was completely restored. As for his hair, that would grow back in time. I wasn't about to waste my Gift on cosmetic matters.

"I'm done. You can take over from here!" I said, and went over to a chair in the corner of the tent. It happened to be empty, which suited me just then. "You," I pointed to the nurse, "bring me tea."

Patients continued to arrive, but the chaos that had reigned was over. So I left the work of the infirmary to Roman, and only occasionally got up to heal the wounds of the especially seriously ill. And yes, I was as stealthy as possible. While I left cosmetic wounds untouched to the naked eye, I eliminated dangerous internal damage. Let them then think that they were lucky.

The duke's guards were full of gratitude, but I simply kicked them out of the tent, and their charge, as well. He'd almost immediately come to his senses, and now looked around, not understanding what had happened.

Thus it was that time flew by. Towards evening, the flow of otherworldly troops dried up completely, and all that remained was to finish off individual detachments. But, said Kooky, regular Imperial troops had arrived. These guys didn't fool around, and they fired on the offworlders without holding back, and they also unleashed all the magical means at their disposal, as well. I even felt a little sorry for the poor offworlders. But, really, they'd been terrible guests, so they got what they deserved.

"Cooo?" And I saw a feathered head emerge from behind the chair in which I had been resting for about twenty minutes. "What ...?!" I turned to him. "Okay, here you go, you deserve it," I fished the "magic" pretzel out of my pocket. I'd stashed it there on the sly when nobody was looking. Of course, it was now covered in blood. I guess you might call it "Duke's Son Sauce." A real delicacy! I tossed it behind the chair, and I soon heard Kooky doing his "cooing" thing as he pecked at it.

I leaned back and closed my eyes. My source was totally drained, and so now, before heading back to the castle, I might as well sit still for a little while. Fortunately, the main portal had collapsed by now, and I didn't expect any more patients.

* * *

Meanwhile, somewhere on a deserted road

It was incumbent on Viscount Snegirev as an aristocrat to take part in repelling the attack of the offworlders. And he did just that, although only on paper. He dispatched two dozen guardsmen to the city, but they were tasked primarily with protecting his properties there. And he had most of his men take their time heading for the city. By the time they reached the outskirts of Arkhangelsk, the Imperial Army had already pushed the offworlders back to their main portal.

And so Snegirev had his column halt their march, and then he began thinking about his next moves.

"What bad timing..." he thought, shaking his head. Indeed, his attack on the Bulatov castle had been thought out to the smallest detail. He'd assembled the strongest fighters he could to swiftly overpower the enemy's forces, and he himself was going to handle the newly minted Count Bulatov.

The entire rout, though, relied on the element of surprise. They counted on catching the Bulatovs totally off guard. But by now, his targets had plenty of time to put together a defense, including all sorts of nasty tricks. He could picture them mining the forest and roads, and even worse. And thus, he'd be a fool to carry on with his attack on the castle today. He decided, instead, to radically alter his plans.

He made a couple of calls to his men in charge of intelligence, and found out exactly where Mikhail Bulatov was. His locale wasn't difficult to discern, since, as a healer, he of course spent the siege in the field camp, treating the wounded. Until the threat from the offworlders was dealt with, though, he was untouchable, because hostilities between Families were prohibited during national emergencies.

It would be a different matter once Count Bulatov was heading back to his castle.

Snegirev snickered, and then he ordered more of his forces to head back to their barracks.

"And you," he said, emerging from his car to

instruct his finest, most loyal guardsmen. “Stealth is of the essence. Intercept the count, kidnap him and bring him to me right away. Do you understand?”

“Let me get this straight, viscount,” responded one of the fighters. “How much force can we use?”

“Just don't kill him. Otherwise, do whatever you want. I need him alive, though. Or, at least, breathing,” the viscount chuckled. “He won’t be expecting this.”

“Will that be all, Sir?”

The viscount waved his hand, indicating that yes, it was, and then he headed back to his estate with his main forces.

There were several roads to the Bulatov castle from the field camp. But they all converged at one particular intersection. And while it was against the law to block roads, there was nothing to stop anyone from simply singling out one car and pulling someone out from inside it.

It’s not that it was entirely legal, but no one would know what happened. As they say, ‘no body, no crime.’ And as Count Bulatov’s entire guard was no doubt throwing itself into defending his castle, well, the count himself would be traveling all by his lonesome.

Snegirev smiled contentedly for the first time in a while, and set off. He felt like rubbing his hands in glee thinking of his brilliant plan. Now, at last, he’d be snuffing out the only obstacle in his path to procuring the count’s title. He couldn't wait for Count Bulatov to step into his trap. And this time, he wouldn't be emerging from it alive.

* * *

Tap-tap!

Someone was pecking at my forehead, and I tried to grab the scoundrel by the throat. But Kooky flew upward, and then a second later, a young man who looked to be around twenty-five years old approached me. He was clearly an aristocrat. Walking into the close to empty tent, he motioned everybody else out.

Hmm... Looks like I relaxed enough to fall asleep. And while I was out, all of the patients were taken elsewhere. Now, they were packing away all of the equipment. Hmmm...Kooky probably woke me up on purpose as this young aristocrat was making his way over to me.

"Mikhail Bulatov?" asked the young man, and I nodded in response. "Nice to meet you. I am the Duke Maltsevsky's heir apparent, Kirill Maltsevsky!" said the young man proudly. "On behalf of my father, I offer our gratitude for saving my wayward brother."

"What makes him wayward? Despite his young age, he decided to risk his life to defend the people of this city. He deserves nothing but praise," I shrugged. "He'll grow up to be a man of distinction."

"He should have waited for the Imperial Army's main forces." the young man began to argue, but then caught himself and moved on. “But that's not important now,” he said, shaking his head. “Our men told me what it cost you to bring him back. And our Family owes you his life. Our father, the duke, will compensate you in full.”

What was he talking about? Ah! I’d made it look like I’d used up an expensive artifact to cure the lad. Of course, it was a pretzel, now fully consumed by Kooky. Looked like I was going to score some major points from that pretzel.

In response to Kirill, I nodded, slowly stood up, and slowly headed for the exit. The battle was now over, and all of the offworlders had been disbanded by our Imperial Armed Forces. So now it was time I headed home.

“I did what I had to do,” I nodded to Kirill. “He also performed his duty. So we’re even. You owe me nothing,” I said, and left the tent. I was surprised to see that the field camp had been totally dismantled. So, did they leave this tent up to let me sleep?

Maltsevsky followed me out, and we headed towards the exit from what had been the camp. True, the road was blocked by troops, which meant that I couldn't call Georgy to come get me.

“Damn...” I cursed quietly. “Where is the nearest unblocked road?”

“Why do you ask?” asked Kirill.

“Well, I need a taxi. I want to go home, you know,” I smiled, surprising the young heir apparent.

“A taxi?” he asked. “I can’t let my brother’s

savior take a taxi. You must allow me to take you home. It is the least my Family can do for you right now."

I thought about refusing, but... why? He was clearly into doing this, after all. And so I nodded my assent, and we both headed for one of the cars in his entourage.

We settled into the back seat, and the powerful car set off. As we approached the various roadblocks along the way, they were immediately opened for us, and soon we were flying through the deserted streets of the city, and heading for the castle.

But halfway there, we came to a sudden stop. There was a big truck right in the middle of an intersection. Our driver had to slam on the brakes to avoid hitting it, and Kirill and I were both thrown forward, almost hitting the back of the front seats.

"What the hell..." he shouted, but then he realized what was happening.

Our car was blocked from behind, and now armed men were pouring out of the truck. I immediately recognized who this was by their uniforms. These were Snegirev's men, no doubt about it. Yes, they were out to get me.

"My god, how stupid..." I said, shaking my head and laughing. By now, the men were rapping on our door, although not for long.

Because Kirill himself opened it and stepped out. Snegirev's armed thugs tried to point their weapons at him, but with a single blow, he killed three of them at once.

"I am Kirill Gerasimovich, the heir apparent to the Family of Duke Maltsevsky!" he growled, and in a flash his body was sheathed in magical armor, and his hands looked like molten liquid steel. Wow, that was a rare Gift! Interesting to see it in action. "Do you really think you can overpower me?"

"Oh noooo...!" the armed thugs all gasped in unison, but it was too late.

We had in our entourage five cars altogether — the heir apparent's security force. And now they all surrounded our would-be attackers. In no time at all, Snegirev's men were face down in the mud, and then Kirill's men disarmed them; then they were handcuffed and packed into the trunks of the cars.

As for me, I sat enjoying the show. Once it was over, Kirill sat down next to me again, and as if nothing had happened, we proceeded on our way.

* * *

Two hours later
Viscount Snegirev's office study

"Yes, your Excellency! Of course, your Excellency! It's just a misunderstanding! A silly little mistake! I'll make it right!"

The viscount broke out in a sweat as soon as the duke's call came in. And once the duke started speaking, his sweat glands began to work at full capacity.

"How can you make it right, viscount?" asked the duke calmly. "You sent a bunch of scum to kill my son, who is, at present, my heir? And your timing happened to be when?! YOU DID THIS WHEN MY YOUNGEST SON HAPPENED TO BE SERIOUSLY WOUNDED?!" The duke raised his voice, and the viscount was beginning to feel alarmed.

He knew this was all a misunderstanding, but it certainly looked as if the viscount was out to kill the last heir.

"No, no, let me explain! I didn't order my men to kill anybody! This is all an unfortunate misunderstanding!" Now white as chalk, the viscount was practically squealing.

"So then, you were trying to take him prisoner? To what end?!" the duke was, again, deadly calm.

"Duke Maltsevsky, I swear! It was all a mistake. I am now at war with the Bulatov Family, and for unknown reasons he ended up in your heir's car!"

"Understood. We'll get to the bottom of this!" suddenly the duke wanted to cut the conversation short, but Snegirev couldn't stop talking.

"Forgive me, Gerasim Markovich, but...What about my guards? Might I pay ransom for them?" In response, he heard the duke sigh heavily, and then a series of short beeps.

Snegirev continued sitting at his desk in his sweat-soaked clothing. Gradually, his chalk white skin changed to a burgundy hue and, screaming in fury, he threw his phone at the wall, shattering it into a thousand small pieces.

CHAPTER 12

"WHY DID YOU DO all this digging?" I asked Chernomor, who'd been in full charge of planning the strategy for defending the castle.

I wasn't even able to drive up to the entrance. The Duke was surprised that the long access road up to the castle had been dug up, and was now a ditch. Only a tank could make it through. And that would only be by approaching circuitously, through the forest. I, too, was surprised. Of course, Chernomor didn't dig up the main road, just our access road through the grounds of the castle. Had he damaged the main roads, well, I'd have no way of avoiding an unpleasant conversation with the Empire's authorities.

I exited Kirill's car, and hoofed it to the castle. Along the way, I saw camouflaged fortifications in the forest, and our men hiding among the snowdrifts. I even saw an armored car buried in the ground -- the only thing above ground was the machine gun.

"What do you mean, a ditch? We dug a trench! And we'll do more digging, too!" said Chernomor with a wave of his hand. "You told me yourself that the viscount was headed this way with his army."

"Yes, he was, but that was then, this is now," I said. "He has other matters to deal with, so you can stand down for now."

Hearing this, Chernomor nodded, but Victoria, in contrast, who'd also been working on preparations for the defense, shook her head.

"Mikhail, you don't know Snegirev like I do," she said. "Just because you don't expect him to attack doesn't mean he won't. And when you say you're sure he won't, then I'm all the more sure he will."

"Really? I shrugged. "Well, in any case, I'm played out. I'm depleted, no energy left at all. Right now, I'm useless, and need to replenish my source. If, of course, hostilities break out, we'll have to come up with something."

Perhaps I could "borrow" someone else's energy, but I'd need a lot of it. Yes, that would be a little hard on me, but later I could deal with the consequences. When it was a matter of life and death, you had to do whatever it took.

I told Victoria and Chernomor to carry on, and went off to rest up. Before plunging into a much-needed meditative sleep, I ate a hearty meal.

How nice it was to have our own personal chef in the castle now. Of course, she was nervous in light of the looming hostilities. Besides the ditch outside, the guards had covered the windows with sandbags, and more.

Now in my tower study I made myself comfortable, put the phone on "do not disturb," and then...

"C-o-o-ooo!" Kooky, of course. He materialized out of thin air. I'd summoned him, actually. I didn't want to spend already scarce energy on any more remote communication.

"I'm going to bed now, so you're on reconnaissance duty. Keep an eye on Snegirev and his people, patrol the area, see whatever else of interest is out there. Immediately report anything unusual to Chernomor." There. That was done. Time to immerse myself in meditation. Everything began sounding muffled, and my consciousness began to plunge into darkness.

Suddenly, at the edge of my mind, I heard my feathered friend flying about in a frenzy. He was flapping his wings and cooing up a storm as he flitted about the room. Anymore, though, I just didn't care. Yes, I got it, he had his troubles, and I had mine, so deal with it, bird!

Tap-tap!

Er, was that my imagination, or was he pecking on my forehead? That way he had of waking me up was beginning to really irritate me. I suddenly jumped out of bed, planning to grab him by the throat and...

"Who the hell are you?" I asked, surprised at what I saw. This wasn't Kooky, but some other pigeon.

"Cooo...," purred the stranger, cocking his head.

My rage immediately subsided to be replaced by bewilderment. What happened to Kooky, and who was this stupid bird? What was going on here?

By now, having slept six hours, I was doing much better; energy again filled my source. Good thing, because at least I was fit for battle. But why was this pigeon pecking me on the forehead?

"Go on, fly away now," I waved at the bird, who was now sitting on my alarm clock. The bird just sat there, though, so I picked him up and set him on the floor. "Just sit there and don't even move."

"C-o-o-ooo!" shrugged the bird, looking at me cockeyed.

That's good. At least the bird understood me.

I left my tower room then to see if I could find at least one other human. I wandered all over the castle, checked the drawing room and the kitchen, and saw not a living soul. Did they attack us, and had I missed everything? To my relief, I sensed three beating hearts in Chernomor's office, and headed right over there.

There I saw Chernomor with one of our guardsmen, and Kooky. Kooky was vigorously tapping out a message on the table, as Chernomor translated the Morse code into human speech and dictated it to the soldier.

"A ship came to the port... A big one... Found an attic in it full of white pigeons... Nothing like..." Chernomor said monotonously. "Oh! Write it down! Some kind of activity was spotted not far from the village of Negorovka — machinery, vehicles... Kooky, what kind of equipment did you see?"

"Cooo-Coo-Coooo," responded Kooky, looking at Chernomor as if he was an idiot.

"You're saying...pigeons don't know about that kind of thing? What's this nonsense all about? Did you see any tanks? Or were they just trucks?" Chernomor was frustrated now. "Was it like this, or like that...?" Chernomor drew some images.

"Cooo-coo-cooo," Kooky spread his wings.

"I see! The pipe was this long?" Chernomor was animated now. Kooky nodded, yes it was that long. "So then, there are two tanks stationed five kilometers to the north!"

I stood there watching them as the interrogation went on. Kooky actually had a lot to say. Moreover, here he is providing intelligence about real-time events going on kilometers around us. Lots of what he shared was of no interest at all. But Chernomor put up with it, because among the stories about how a squirrel hid a nut in a hollow, or how the owls around here were completely insane, some really useful information slipped through.

For example, from what the bird said, it looked like Snegirev was probably preparing to attack us yet again. The mercenaries had seized three of our villages. And the viscount's guardsmen were stationing themselves in strategic positions, and also conducting reconnaissance. Yes, they were planning an attack.

That bird... he found a way to keep an eye on things. I'd told him to carry out reconnaissance and security, but being the lazy sort, he'd delegated some of the duties. He'd called in other pigeons to do some of the surveillance work. Was the way he did this natural, or some kind of spell? I didn't know, but he had a way to connect with other pigeons. And his feathered friends could now communicate to him everything going on out there while he sat on the table sipping other people's tea.

I wondered how many feathered scouts he had working for him. Was it hundreds, or even thousands? Maybe we could train them to attack the enemy en masse with shit-bombs? But then again, from what we'd learned thus far, there were probably no more than two of them.

"By the way, Victoria was looking for you," said Chernomor, and the bird coooed indignantly. Chernomor had interrupted his report on the transgressions of the local foxes. "Okay, got it! What else...?" he again turned toward Kooky, who seemed to have far more to say.

Okay, Victoria wanted to see me. Off I go. Only where was she? Well, at least my energy levels were replenished. I activated the chain of runes and quickly discerned that the countess was in the courtyard behind the castle. Rather than going there, I simply called her. Yes, that would suffice.

It seems that I'd received a package. The courier could only deliver it to a representative of the Bulatov Family, and so that was Victoria. It was a rather large wooden box with a letter attached to it. The countess didn't touch it, and now it was at the castle gates with two guards watching over it. Hearing this, I could only praise the countess. Good for her! No need to mess around with mysterious packages. Especially one sent by a duke who was not a personal acquaintance of Victoria's.

"You can go now," I said, dismissing the guards, and I set about examining the box. I also felt it, so as to check for any magic contained therein. And yes, there was! This box contained an artifact. But what kind? Might it explode as soon as I opened the box?

No, it wasn't that kind of energy...The artifact was like some kind of sponge, ready to absorb energy in its pure form, and then...I didn't know what, for sure. I needed to study it in more detail, but didn't have the time.

"Are you going to open it?" asked Victoria impatiently. She was looking at the box from a safe distance away.

"Well..." I scratched the back of my head. "Take a couple more steps back.

You never know. I can heal my own dear self, but the countess already had enough scars. Speaking of, I wondered if she was ever going to ask me to do something about them?

I decided to read the letter before I opened the box. It was nice handwriting, rather ornate, and the paper didn't seem to be poisoned. Duke Maltsevsky himself expressed his gratitude to me. Several bills, twenty thousand rubles, also spilled out of the envelope. The duke also said that he understood how expensive the healing artifact I'd used must have been, and therefore decided to repay me not with money, but with another, no less valuable artifact, which was in the box.

So... thousands of rubles don't suffice? Well, who's complaining? I could use the money, especially now.

"And he also says here," I turned to Victoria and pointed at the letter, "that we can contact him at any time should the need arise."

"He's just being polite." she said, shaking her head. "I'm never going to contact him. I'm not in any hurry to be his vassal. It's not worth it."

She had a point. I could, in fact, ask the duke for help, but then I'd have to return the favor, in spades. Just as he'd given me this artifact as payback for the one he thought I'd used. Okay then. Let's see what's in the box.

It wasn't hard to open it. It opened itself as soon as I moved my hand over it, and there was the gift from Duke Maltsevsky himself. And yes, I have to say, I'd never made better use of a pretzel.

"Oh..." Victoria said, peeking at it from behind me. And curiosity trumped safety as she went up to the box.

"Well then," I said, scratching my nose.

We both stood stock still as we looked at the artifact.

It was a crossbow. Just what the doctor ordered, especially for me. It was made entirely from offworld materials, but the design was incredibly complex.

"Oh, here are the instructions," I said, picking up a sheet of paper at the bottom of the box. "I'd best study them before using this thing."

"You're definitely not from around here," laughed Victoria.

"What do you mean?"

"Nothing," she waved her hand. "Read them, then."

I wondered what that was about. Apparently some local joke. Or was there something about reading instructions? I'd be a fool to try to use this thing without reading the instructions.

This wasn't just any crossbow. Apparently, it was a multi-charged crossbow, with bolts that were fed into it from a magazine, sort of like a ten-shot machine gun. I could then swap the magazine out and keep on firing.

There were two magazines included with the crossbow, which was good. And also a healthy supply of bolts, which were also made from offworld materials. The perfect weapon, especially for me.

But the most important feature of this amazing weapon, which had to be worth at least a hundred thousand, was that I could supply clean energy to it. Not everyone could do this, which is why this feature wasn't mentioned in the instructions. But I'd taken a close look at the artifact. I could pour my own energy into each shot, and depending on how much I used, the power would vary.

"Can I try it out?" asked Victoria as she reached for it, but I grabbed her wrist.

"No! This is a complicated artifact! We need to test it at a safe site first. Otherwise it might explode or something," I was adamant. And then, picking it up, I turned and headed for my tower study. I brought the bolts with me, as well as the two magazines.

Really, I'd get right down to it. What a great thing, this crossbow! As I made my way down the corridor I tried pouring energy into it, and the runes carved on the crossbow flickered in response.

I rushed into my tower study, put the weapon on the table and then...

"Cooo?"

"What the hell are you doing here?" I was surprised seeing the pigeon on the floor. It was the ordinary one, the dolt. Although, I guess I'd told him to stay here until further notice. And he'd obeyed my instructions, although I'd issued them an hour and a half ago. "You can fly away now..." I said, pointing to the door, but as he fluttered off, I shouted after him. "Oh, and go call your boss!"

"C-o-o-ooo!" The pigeon sounded put off by that.

"Okay, maybe he's not your boss. What is he to you then? Your sweetie?"

"Coo-coo-coooo!" The upset bird almost attacked me.

"Okay, sorry! Go see Kooky! No more fooling around, or else..." my eyes flashed green, and the pigeon immediately backed off.

As soon as the pigeon was gone, I began experimenting with the crossbow. First, I looked it over inside and out yet again. I studied both its magical components and its mechanics. Its mechanism really was subtle, yet complex, but thanks to the instructions, it wasn't too difficult. Ten minutes later I'd loaded it, and was ready for battle.

What really made this convenient is that I always had access to the bolts. The difference from revolver cartridges was that since theses bolts were kept outside in the barrel, I could imbue them with energy whenever I wanted by simply touching them. Indeed, this crossbow was as if made just for someone like me.

The sight was also quite nice, and not unlike the kind used on sniper rifles. Easy to use, and accurate. What confounded me now was finding a suitable target, and finally I decided to sacrifice an oak cabinet. Anyway it was ugly, and I'd been thinking of throwing it out.

The first bolt went all the way through the thick cabinet wall. I charged the second one with energy, and it whistled as it passed through the wood, leaving behind it a clean hole. But that was all I could do before my feathered friend made an appearance. He reported that we could expect an attack by five in the morning, but no sooner. At least, that's what the viscount had said to his guardsmen over their two-way radios. Of course, Chernomor had already called to report the same thing to me, so I was hearing old news from the bird.

"Okay then, Kooky," I said, setting the crossbow down on the table next to the disgruntled bird, and taking a seat, looking tellingly at the bird. "Come to me, birdie-birdie-birdie," I said coaxingly.

But in vain. Now, the bird seemed to want nothing to do with me, and was even backing away. But I knew what to do. I paralyzed his wings and feet before he could hide behind the wardrobe. And then I began operating on him. I wouldn't even need anesthesia if I was to simply tie him down on the table, which I did after spreading his wings out on either side. But I wasn't that cruel, so I put him into a deep, dark sleep. The operation took about two hours. I had to strain my memory, and expend a lot of effort, as well.

Chimerology is, to put it mildly, not a standard specialty for healers. Among us are, frankly, some disturbed personalities, and that's who was drawn to this field. They'd come up with some amazing, horrific monsters by mutating ordinary animals multiple times. I myself wasn't that skilled at it, though, and also didn't want to use up too much energy. But somehow I managed.

I improved the density of some of Kooky's muscle groups, and also his skeletal structure. That of birds, of course, differs from our own. His bones were hollow so as to enable him to fly.

But Kooky was strong, so he'd do fine. Especially because I'd fortified his abilities enough to compensate for my changes. Then, I turned my attention to his beak. Now, Kooky could peck a hole through an iron door.

No, I wasn't out to make Kooky into a deadly aggressive assault pigeon. He would still serve me as a scout who had license to shit with impunity on our enemies. My reason for enhancing Kooky was something else entirely. He had a new function now, in addition to his former responsibilities.

"Cooo?" Kooky expressed his surprise as he came to his senses.

"Arise now and go! To work, obviously," I spoke ceremoniously to my newly enhanced scout. Judging by his look, he didn't yet realize what I'd done. "You are now much stronger. I worked on your muscles, bones, even your beak. You even have sharp little teeth," I said, shuddering at a memory that surfaced.

A chimerologist I knew once had some fun with my brother's favorite bird. The parrot was always in my brother's chambers, a bright sight to behold. And then he manipulated the bird so that it grew teeth. They were snowy white, and looked like human teeth. It was nightmarish, I must say...

"*Ur...*" the pigeon waved its wings, jumped on

the spot, and even assumed a boxing pose. Yes, looked like he approved of the upgrade.

"And now, your first new duty," I picked up the crossbow and fired. The bolt went halfway into the oak cabinet door, and I pointed at it. "Retrieve it!"

"C-o-o-ooo?" At first Kooky was confused, but then he got it.

But he refused to do it. So after we bickered a bit, I promised him I'd do something to enhance his legs next time, and he agreed to do my bidding. It turned out to be anything but easy to extract the bolt from the oak door. Although I'd made him much stronger, I wasn't sure he was up to the task. But after a couple of dicey minutes, the bolt was again lying on the table.

We spent more time training and experimenting. I worked on this and that group of muscles to facilitate Kooky's ability to extract the bolts, and we were both finally satisfied with the results.

By now, it was dark outside, and I didn't see any point in further delays.

Snegirev would be attacking at dawn. That's when most sentries started to nod off, and so an ideal time for an attack. But I wasn't going to sit back and wait for him to make his move. I had my own plans, after all.

I went to see Chernomor, and we agreed on a strategy. All this time, Kooky flew back and forth with his reports on the deployment of enemy troops, and the routes they were planning on taking. This was crucially valuable info, because it allowed us to lead Snegirev's own intelligence network by the nose. Several times they encroached on our territory as they sought to scout out where we'd set up ambushes or traps. But our guys always managed to hide before they were spotted.

So by now the viscount was confident that all our forces were concentrated at the castle. But of course! It's not like we'd dug our trenches because we wanted to plant potatoes there someday.

To enable my plans, I needed transportation, though. First, Chernomor suggested I take a snowmobile, but then he recalled the last time I tried driving a vehicle, and so he suggested I take a horse. Yes, I knew how to ride one of those! The ones in my former world were, of course, slightly different, primarily in size. They were rather skinny and small here, and I felt like I'd overload the beast when I first mounted it. But Chernomor assured me the horse could take it.

"Well, buddy? Are you going to obey my commands?" I said upon seeing him, and stroking his neck.

"Neeeiiiigh!" responded the horse, and I knew then that I couldn't really converse with him. I saw not a wit of intelligence in his eyes, nor in his face. And yes, he was drooling, to boot. Okay, yeah, as long as he didn't drip saliva on me.

Anyway, I climbed onto the saddle and rode this, my trusty steed, into the forest. The beast handled the snowdrifts well, so I swiftly arrived at my destination. And then...

"I'm sorry, but I have to paralyze you. I don't think you understand me..." I told the horse and injecting a little energy, I forced him to pretend to be dead. I could just tie him to a tree, but I'd be in a hurry once I left, and it would take time to untie him.

Then, I headed for the first village. I'd left the horse not too far away, and could only hope he wasn't hit by a stray bullet. And then, as soon as I detected heartbeats, I fired to kill. I used ten bolts in all, and they all found their targets, after which I rushed back to my horse.

As I made my way back, Kooky retrieved the bolts and delivered two or three at a time to me before going back for more. I would then load them back into the magazine, and imbue them with my power. And by the time I made it to the next village, my weapon was again ready for action. Moreover, I also had two full reserves of bolts.

Things were more complicated at this next stop. There were a lot of men patrolling the street, while the mercenaries were holed up in the barn. I didn't yet know how to bust through log walls, so I had to get closer. Most of the men inside were sleeping. And I understood from previous experience that they were stationed here as backup, and didn't expect an enemy attack.

I fired my first two bolts while on the move, taking out the men guarding the barn. Then I drew near the door. I could now tell there were forty people sleeping inside, so I quietly opened the door. I saw no reason to kill everyone in here. My intention was not to commit mass murder. All I wanted was to create enough of a commotion to make the mercenaries think that an entire army was attacking them. But I just couldn't resist the temptation. So, ten minutes later, I climbed onto my faithful steed and spurred him on. Behind me a roaring flame rose in the air, engulfing the big barn in which the mercenaries slept.

Yes, it was my barn. My village, and I'd do what I wanted with it. Okay, maybe it was harsh of me to burn them all alive like that, but then again, they were armed thugs encroaching on my territory. Anybody sent after them should know that they, too, would be met with just deserts.

By the time I reached the third village, the soldiers were on the alert. They knew by then what had become of the other two villages, as all three settlements were located not far from each other.

But no matter. They might be ready for me, but I, in return, was ready for them! And so this time I didn't even bother dismounting. I simply ordered the horse to stop, and...

I fired all of my bolts off in a matter of seconds, and they all went straight to their targets. As it was incredibly dark out, they couldn't see me, but I could see them, and in no time, several heartbeats stopped, and the rest were seriously injured.

My pigeon no longer needed to be told what to do, and I, well, I played my Knight's Move!

"Ready?" I patted the horse's neck.

"Neeeiiiigh!" he responded joyfully No, he wasn't ready...Clearly he didn't understand me. But he didn't need to understand, so, spurring him on with my magic, I headed straight into the deepest thicket in the forest.

* * *

A few minutes later
Mercenary infirmary

"It's made from offworld materials," concluded the field medic as he studied the bolt he'd pulled out of the wounded man. "And it's imbued with...healing power! What kind of sick bastard imbues weapons with healing power?" He looked at the commanders gathered around the surgical table. The surviving commanders and most of the officers were killed outright by these crossbow bolts.

"So, what's with him?" the commander asked, indicating the wounded man. The bolt hit him in the thigh without hitting any major vessels, so no one was particularly worried about his life. He'd come himself to the infirmary and asked for help.

"What do you mean?" The medic looked at the wounded man in surprise, "Oh, he..." and his expression changed as he looked at the readings on the instrument panel. "He's dead now..."

"What do you mean he's dead? That wound didn't kill him!" exclaimed the commander, and he, too, began examining the soldier. But he was now pale and his lifeless eyes were fixed at the ceiling.

"Right then. You bring me all of the other crossbow bolts," the medic said to the mercenaries, who were all frozen in horror. "All of them!"

They all jumped to it then, rushing outside to do his bidding. But ten minutes later they returned with surprised faces.

"Sorry, but there aren't any more bolts..." the first one threw up his hands. "There are holes in the corpses, but the bolts have disappeared."

"How can that be? Are you saying that someone, right under your nose, pulled them out of the corpses and took them away?" he was almost yelling. He very much wanted to study what kind of spell had been used on the bolts. "Okay. Everyone clear out of here!" He waved to the fighters and turned back to his desk. He needed to study the artifact right away, and even the corpse frozen on the surgical table didn't bother him. Yes, they needed to conduct an autopsy to find out why he'd suddenly died like that, but...it could wait.

Everyone filed out, and he was soon all alone in the makeshift surgical room. Actually, almost all alone.

"C-o-o-ooo!" a pigeon alighted on his desk just then. And next, the bird stalked over to him, and pecked him in the hand. In surprise, the medic dropped the crossbow bolt onto the table *"C-o-o-ooo!"* The pigeon swiftly picked it up and few off.

"What the hell is going on here?" The medic scratched his head in bewilderment, once he recovered from the shock.

* * *

Meanwhile....
Snegirev's estate

"Sir! The mercenaries are under attack!" The voice of the guard commander sounded from the viscount's phone. "I have a report on the losses..."

"Which village?" Snegirev interrupted him, a crooked smile spreading across his face. He didn't really care how many had died. He'd already paid for their lives. But he disliked having to change his plans.

"All of them!" reported the commander. "Almost at the same time..."

The viscount then bombarded his commander with questions and listened to the responses. And what he heard made the viscount ever the more happy.

From what he'd learned, the commander was sure that almost all of the Bulatov forces were busy attacking the mercenaries.

"I would never have thought that you were such an idiot," the viscount said quietly, hanging up the phone. "Stupid, stupid, stupid! But what a lucky bastard...," he shook his head, remembering recent events and his own downfall. To him, it all appeared to be Bulatov's dumb luck rather than his own actions that led to the most unfortunate circumstances with the duke and his son.

Snegirev sat in thought for a couple of minutes, and then, picking up his phone, he called his commander.

"Listen up! I want you to take all your forces and proceed as planned. Understood?"

"Understood! Permission to act?" responded the commander, sounding pleased. Indeed, the viscount had promised in advance a handsome reward for each kill he made that day, so he was ready and willing to move forward with the plan. And what he'd get were he to capture the countess, well, that was a fabulous sum.

"Do it!" Snegirev nodded to himself, and leaned back in his chair with a smug grin. All that remained now was to await the results. And this time, the lucky punk pretending to be a healer had no way out.

* * *

An hour later
Somewhere in the forest

"Mikhail, I understand everything!" Chernomor growled into the two-way radio, "But...how? We'd have to retreat! Meaning, you'll decide? We need you here!"

The hulking commander growled, not understanding what he was hearing. And this was because Mikhail was spewing nonsense. At least, that's what it seemed like to the seasoned warrior. He wanted the count to participate in the defense with them. But for whatever reason, he'd disappeared even before the battle began. And then the enemy started advancing against them, much earlier than five in the morning, when they were expected. But at least the guards were ready, and the intelligence was functioning well. And thus, they were able to greet the viscount's forces with all of the "cordiality" at Chernomor's disposal.

Real carnage soon followed. The enemy was marching straight to the castle, trusting their own intelligence, and was wholly unprepared for the abundance of traps and ambushes. Then, led by Chernomor's excellent command, the Bulatov guardsmen swooped down on them like a swarm of giant locusts and then swiftly retreated into the deepest recesses of the forest. However, they couldn't repeat that trick, and so soon a rather more routine battle ensued. Chernomor and his men occupied the trenches, and were now firing all their weaponry at enemy forces that seemed to be many times superior.

And after hours of battling, his men had used up all of the artifacts left by Mikhail, and also all of their ammunition.

"Mikhail!" Chernomor boomed into the two-way radio again.

"I'm listening. What's wrong?" responded the count, sounding disgruntled. "Hold on as long as you can, that's all! Why are you distracting me?"

"What do you mean, distracting? This is the

decisive battle!" Chernomor growled, looking at Victoria. "The countess is here with me, and if they break through the defenses..."

"They won't break through. And if you stop distracting me, they will retreat in... hmm... two minutes. Can you hold out that long?" And then the connection abruptly ended, and all attempts to contact the count were unsuccessful.

"Tell me, what's his plan? What's he up to now?" asked Chernomor, turning to Victoria.

The countess was doing all she could, but she'd spent all of our energy on the last batch of zombies, and was depleted now.

"Just trust him..." she shook her head. "I'm already tired of trying to figure Mikhail out, so...Hmmm...what happened to the enemies?" she peered out from the trench they were in and began to look around. "Two minutes haven't passed yet, have they?"

"He said 'about two minutes,'" snorted the old warrior and, plopping onto the ground, he closed his eyes, clearly spent. "But, damn it! What did he do?"

Victoria plopped down next to him, and shrugged. By now she fully believed in Mikhail, and stopped second guessing him. Meaning, if he told them the enemy would retreat, then they'd be doing just that. And yes, they had turned back, and the countess, unable to resist it, simply fell asleep from fatigue and magical exhaustion.

* * *

The Knight's Move means... I recently learned that in this world, they, too had a game like our chess. But here, the knight either moves up or down one square vertically and over two squares horizontally OR up or down two squares vertically and over one square horizontally. Meaning the knights here were tricky devils.

And I could see why they depicted their knights as horses in this world. It's because the horses here were as dumb and unpredictable as it gets. Or else I just lucked out with the one I was on. Because on my way to my final destination, he managed to break a leg not just once, but twice. Once, we crashed headlong into a tree and at such speed that I, too, suffered some fractures. But what really offended me was that, try as I might, I couldn't activate any mental activity in this animal. I tried and tried, pouring energy into his brain, accelerating his blood circulation. But no, it was all in vain. All the horse could do was whinny and neigh.

Anyway, we rode around thirty or forty kilometers. We reached the estate, my destination, but I didn't attack it from astride the horse. Instead, I "parked" him in the forest, and also cast a couple of spells to imbue his skin with some energy. Now, should any wild beast come across the paralyzed horse, they'd steer clear of this steed. He'd stink most unpleasantly, and no, he'd be bad for their diet.

I fired a couple of shots and headed towards my target. My goal was Snegirev's so-called summer residence. And I have to say, he'd poured a lot of money into it. It was located on a huge, elegantly landscaped territory, with all sorts of paths, and ponds, and even a lake, and right in the midst of this fairyland was a large, luxurious wooden mansion. I had to admit, this structure looked to be as big as my castle.

First I took out the guards patrolling the grounds. There were at least five more people in the house, and four people were huddling in the outbuilding at the edge of the main house. I wasn't going to shoot them just like that. If they were simply servants, I saw no reason to take their lives. And, in fact, that's what they were. The outbuilding was the servants' quarters, and the four souls inside were fast asleep. I silently slipped inside, and placing my hand on each one's forehead, I ensured that they would sleep far longer in great peace. Tomorrow, they would awaken fully rested and refreshed, and only then would they see what had transpired.

There were five other guardsmen that I made short work of. My bolts were extra special, because the spell I'd cast on them was such that the victims were unable to scream, even. The bolt caused them to experience a sharp flash of pain, and then lose consciousness, even if they possessed a weak Gift. None of them possessed even an average Gift, so it was easy to shoot them, one after the other, like ducks in a pond.

"Who are you?" I opened the door and almost collided head-on with a big fellow. I didn't expect him. I hadn't detected his heartbeat.

And as much as I'd like to know why this was, it was not my fate. Without even thinking about it, I fired off a bolt, and he fell onto his back with no sign of life. Maybe I should have Victoria come get him and interrogate him? Although she might not be able to, being a rather weak necromancer.

Well, really, who cared how he managed to hide his heartbeat? I didn't feel any artifacts nearby, so let this mystery remain a secret.

I was quite stealthy making my way into the building, and yet I was spotted. Kooky alerted me to the danger, just in time. Thanks to my bird, I ducked into a corridor and shot the guard coming after me. I had to use my sword on the last one of them, who got close enough to me to make it awkward to use the crossbow.

But, the unforeseen notwithstanding, in a matter of minutes I'd cleared out the viscount's summer retreat. After quickly checking all the rooms, I found Snegirev's office, and making myself comfortable in his chair, I called Snegirev to boast about my accomplishments.

Psh-sh-sh

That would be my two-way radio interrupting me.

"Why now" I complained, picking it up.

It seems that our forces had reached the limit. Now they had to retreat to the castle where they'd be shot by a cannon or something, or else they had to somehow hold on there in the forest.

But worst of all was that our forces were out of ammo. Really, we certainly had something or the other to fire at them in our warehouse, but how to get it to them in time?

However, this fight would soon be over. According to Kooky, the situation wasn't as bad as Chernomor thought. Yes, our forces were battered, but then again, so were the viscount's. But due to our clever tactics involving lots of ambushes and surprise attacks, the enemy had suffered heavy losses. Plus, his intelligence had clearly failed Snegirev, and I'm afraid to even imagine how he was "rejoicing" now, realizing how we'd deceived him.

At that very moment, Kooky was flying over the battlefield, providing me with reliable information about the status of our forces and those of the enemy, and I could see the battle dragging on for another fifteen minutes, no more.

I didn't spend much time talking to Chernomor and I didn't bother telling him about what I was up to. What for? Let it be a surprise. So after cutting the connection, I picked up my phone and took an amusing photo --- what do they call here? A "selfie," it seems...yes, not that it mattered. The main thing was that I took the photograph in the viscount's personal office against the backdrop of his portrait hanging on the wall. I then sent the photograph to Snegirev's Family email, and waited.

True, I didn't have to wait long. Seconds later I received a call.

"Well, hello there!" I smiled. "How're things?"

"You...you," the viscount sputtered. "You..." he couldn't find the words to fully describe how he felt.

"True...true! With my allies, I have captured your residence," I grinned. "So then, bye-bye! I have so much to do...There are so many trophies here, my eyes are all agog!" And then I hung up.

In fact, I really did have a lot to do. I lied a little about the allies. My only ally now was hovering in the sky above the viscount's troops, constantly reporting on their movements. But Snegirev didn't need to know that I was alone. Now, he had no option but to send some of his forces here, so I didn't have much time. And there were so very many items of value here.

Just as I expected, the viscount's men attacking the castle pulled back and headed out. According to Kooky, Snegirev himself, and also some of his forces that hadn't been involved in the attack were heading to the summer residence. But it would take them half an hour or more to get here. And in that amount of time, I could do, oh, so much!

* * *

An hour later
Summer residence of Viscount Snegirev

"Damn! Damn! The dog! The filthy cur! Scum!" If

only the viscount had some hair on his head, he'd be ripping it out now. Actually he did have a few strands, but they ringed the back of his head.

Now, surrounded by his bodyguards, he was cussing out all of the Bulatovs. All because his favorite residence, which he'd only recently built and spent a small fortune landscaping, was no more. It had been turned into a monstrous bonfire.

But what upset him the most was not that he'd lost his luxurious summer home. He was more worried about the powerful blow to his reputation, because it was here, in this residence, where he always received his overlord, Count Kurchatov.

"I'll make him pay..." Snegirev hissed. "I'll destroy him, grind him into pieces..." he clenched his fists until his bones crunched, and took a step forward and ...

Thwuck!

The arrow burst out of the darkness, and suddenly there was a thump. It stopped a few centimeters from the viscount's forehead and seemed to levitate for a couple of seconds before falling limply onto the snow. His bodyguards jumped into action, and in a flash they knocked the viscount onto the ground and several of the elite forces threw themselves on top of him to shield him from attack. The rest instantly dispersed in a circle, their weapons pulled, ready to fire. Several minutes passed, and then they dragged Snegirev into his armored car and they sped off, having failed to locate the shooter. The viscount, still sweating and shaking, looked in awe at his protective artifact. It was now covered in cracks, which meant that it was spent. All he could do with it now was throw it away.

But he didn't even think of doing this. After all, the other, far more powerful artifacts simply missed the crossbow bolt, having failed to recognize it as a threat. This was a cheap one, a gem, but it had saved his life.

Now, the viscount was seriously worried about his personal safety. Finally, he fully realized how dangerous the new count was, and he was at a loss at what to do about it. But as soon as he calmed down a little, Snegirev, with shaking, dirty hands, pulled the phone out of his pocket and dialed a very special number.

“Hello, Sir, Count Kurchatov... I’m not trying to be impertinent, but I simply have to ask you for the Combat Suit... Yes, as soon as possible, preferably right now...” he was silent for a couple of seconds, listening to the count curse, but in the end, he received consent from his master. “Yes, I’ll send you the location right now. Thank you, sir!”

Then, he quickly typed in the approximate coordinates for where he wanted the Combat Suit and its operator dropped off, and only then did the trembling in his hands begin to subside.

“Let’s see how much you like this...” he smiled grimly, looking out the small armored window of his car.

END OF BOOK TWO

Want to be the first to know about our latest LitRPG, sci fi and fantasy titles from your favorite authors?

Subscribe to our **New Releases** newsletter: http://eepurl.com/b7niIL

Thank you for reading *The Healer's Way!*
If you like what you've read, check out other sci-fi, fantasy and LitRPG novels published by Magic Dome Books:

NEW RELEASES!

Crossroads of Oblivion
a portal progression fantasy adventure series
by Dem Mikhailov

Gakko Academy
a portal progression fantasy adventure series
by Evgeny Alexeev

War Eternal
a military space adventure LitRPG series
by Yuri Vinokuroff

The Hunter's Code
a LitRPG series by Yuri Vinokuroff & Oleg Sapphire

I Will Be Emperor
a space adventure progression fantasy series
by Yuri Vinokuroff & Oleg Sapphire

An Ideal World for a Sociopath
a LitRPG series by Oleg Sapphire

The Healer's Way
a LitRPG series by Oleg Sapphire & Alexey Kovtunov

A Shelter in Spacetime
a LitRPG series by Dmitry Dornichev

Kill or Die
a LitRPG series by Alex Toxic

Living Ice
a portal progression alternative history series
by Dmitry Sheleg

Reality Benders
a LitRPG series by Michael Atamanov

The Dark Herbalist
a LitRPG series by Michael Atamanov

Perimeter Defense
a LitRPG series by Michael Atamanov

League of Losers
a LitRPG series by Michael Atamanov

Chaos' Game
a LitRPG series by Alexey Svadkovsky

The Way of the Shaman
a LitRPG series by Vasily Mahanenko

The Alchemist
a LitRPG series by Vasily Mahanenko

Dark Paladin
a LitRPG series by Vasily Mahanenko

Galactogon
a LitRPG series by Vasily Mahanenko

Invasion
a LitRPG series by Vasily Mahanenko

World of the Changed
a LitRPG series by Vasily Mahanenko

The Bear Clan
a LitRPG series by Vasily Mahanenko

Starting Point
a LitRPG series by Vasily Mahanenko

The Bard from Barliona
a LitRPG series
by Eugenia Dmitrieva and Vasily Mahanenko

Condemned
(Lord Valevsky: Last of The Line)
a Progression Fantasy series
by Vasily Mahanenko

Loner
a LitRPG series by Alex Kosh

A Buccaneer's Due
a LitRPG series by Igor Knox

A Student Wants to Live
a LitRPG series by Boris Romanovsky

The Goldenblood Heir
a LitRPG series by Boris Romanovsky

Level Up
a LitRPG series by Dan Sugralinov

Level Up: The Knockout
a LitRPG series by Dan Sugralinov and Max Lagno

Adam Online
a LitRPG Series by Max Lagno

World 99
a LitRPG series by Dan Sugralinov

Disgardium
a LitRPG series by Dan Sugralinov

Nullform
a RealRPG Series by Dem Mikhailov

Clan Dominance: The Sleepless Ones
a LitRPG series by Dem Mikhailov

Heroes of the Final Frontier
a LitRPG series by Dem Mikhailov

The Crow Cycle
a LitRPG series by Dem Mikhailov

Interworld Network
a LitRPG series by Dmitry Bilik

Rogue Merchant
a LitRPG series by Roman Prokofiev

Project Stellar
a LitRPG series by Roman Prokofiev

In the System
a LitRPG series by Petr Zhgulyov

The Crow Cycle
a LitRPG series by Dem Mikhailov

Unfrozen
a LitRPG series by Anton Tekshin

The Neuro
a LitRPG series by Andrei Livadny

Phantom Server
a LitRPG series by Andrei Livadny

Respawn Trials
a LitRPG series by Andrei Livadny

The Expansion (The History of the Galaxy)
a Space Exploration Saga by A. Livadny

The Range
a LitRPG series by Yuri Ulengov

Point Apocalypse
a near-future action thriller by Alex Bobl

Moskau
a dystopian thriller by G. Zotov

El Diablo
a supernatural thriller by G.Zotov

Mirror World
a LitRPG series by Alexey Osadchuk

Underdog
a LitRPG series by Alexey Osadchuk

Last Life
a Progression Fantasy series by Alexey Osadchuk

Alpha Rome
a LitRPG series by Ros Per

An NPC's Path
a LitRPG series by Pavel Kornev

Fantasia
a LitRPG series by Simon Vale

The Sublime Electricity
a steampunk series by Pavel Kornev

Small Unit Tactics
a LitRPG series by Alexander Romanov

Black Centurion
a LitRPG standalone by Alexander Romanov

Rorkh
A LitRPG Series by Vova Bo

Thunder Rumbles Twice
A Wuxia Series by V. Kriptonov & M. Bachurova

Citadel World
a sci fi series by Kir Lukovkin

You're in Game!
LitRPG Stories from Our Bestselling Authors

You're in Game-2!
More LitRPG stories set in your favorite worlds

The Fairy Code
a Romantic Fantasy series by Kaitlyn Weiss

***The Charmed* Fjords**
a Romantic Fantasy series by Marina Surzhevskaya

More books and series are coming out soon!

In order to have new books of the series translated faster, we need your help and support! Please consider leaving a review or spread the word by recommending *The Healer's Way* to your friends and posting the link on social media. The more people buy the book, the sooner we'll be able to make new translations available.

Thank you!

Till next time!

Made in United States
Troutdale, OR
10/08/2024

23552072R00206